# The MMRPG Apocalypse 3

# The MMRPG Apocalypse 3

## Jeremy Chambless

Published by Level Up in the United Kingdom in 2025

Cover illustration by

ISBN: 978-1-83919-687-4

www.levelup.pub

Also by Jeremy Chambless:
*The RPG Apocalypse*
*The RPG Apocalypse 2*
*The RPG Apocalypse 3*

# Chapter 1: A New Type of Class: Neither Offensive nor Defensive

The month after our arrival at the walled community we planned to use as our base passed quickly and almost without incident. The residents of Warm Spring did a wonderful job at keeping wandering packs of ghouls and zombies from entering and disturbing our group. This allowed us to stay in the housing complex and relax, with no one wanting to go out to seek levels or loot.

I used the month to recover to my peak condition and to discuss with the others the next step our party would take. This was the first interval since the apocalypse that there had been any moment of reprieve from the constant struggle of day-to-day existence. The True Believers had made no re-appearance, and there were no daunting announcements made by the 'Game' masters.

The current peace would not last for long, though. Everyone knew it, but no one wanted to be the one to speak that aloud. Every day was a day closer to another announcement, or some Earth-shattering event that would have us on our last legs.

Richard constantly urged Mark to reach level 10 so he could receive a class, and with that new abilities and a better strength to protect himself. That was pushed off for nearly three weeks until Mark couldn't take the nagging anymore. It helped that Glenn agreed to level up along with him.

The monsters in the area of the complex were not very strong, only levels eleven to thirteen. With the assistance of Jessica and my undead squad, quick work was made of the older men's EXP requirements and the two of them were pushed to level 10 in a single day.

Gathering the Class Changing Stones they needed could have been a different story, but fortunately there were plenty in our inventories from previous encounters.

Neither Mark and Glenn had even learned a skill, and because of that, myself and Jessica were curious to see what options the game world would provide them. There was a level of intelligence to the system: you would not receive melee class options if your only ability used a bow or was a spell, for example.

Glenn was the least hesitant of the two, and immediately after reaching level ten used the Class Changing Stone. His face showed confusion for a brief moment before his eyes fixed in concentration. "There aren't any battle-class options."

Slightly confused, I asked, "Do you mean your options are supports?"

"Not in that way," he started to clarify. "These sound like... 'life' support classes." He emphasized the word life, and yet I still didn't quite understand what he meant. "I know what I'll pick because this is the only one that suits me." He spoke resolutely.

Once you used the Class Change Stone, there was no further access to your character sheet until your class was selected. This was to ensure you couldn't tailor your class options specifically by going back and forth between the menu, trying to find out what miscellaneous event or stat might influence the outcome. From Glenn's face, I could see that he was spending some moments contemplating his new abilities. There were four of us present—myself, Jessica,

Mark and Glenn—and Mark was just as keen as I was to find out what Glenn meant.

"What are you then?" Mark asked in a tone that was almost angry. Because it was his turn next to select a class, Mark was probably frustrated not to get more information from Glenn.

"I'm an Apocalypse Architect," Glenn said at last, presumably having finished contemplating his abilities. "It's a class that has nothing to do with fighting in either attack or defense or support. I can create special structures that have various special effects and uses." Before anyone could ask for an explanation, he moved to a wall and pushed his hand against it. There was a deep blue glow that resonated from his hand and outward before flashing several times.

The originally bleak wall suddenly had a rather inconspicuous blue sheen to it. "What did you just do to it?" Jessica asked.

"I've given it a special kind of reinforcement," Glenn said, "it should be able to withstand attacks better now."

With a skeptical expression on her face, Jessica couldn't help but draw her bow and nock an arrow. It shot out with incredible force before impacting the wall with a thunderous bang. The blue sheen flashed like a barrier and some of its luster disappeared, but the wall had not exploded into a mess.

The meaning behind Glenn's 'life' emphasis became clear to me.

"It takes quite a bit of MP though," Glenn added.

Jessica nocked another arrow and shot it at an unenforced building just fifteen feet away. The wall suddenly had a crater in it two feet wide and several inches deep. It was easy enough to see the strength of the reinforced wall was several, or even dozens of times, more resilient than ordinary bricks and mortar.

"It's not just that, though," Glenn said, "I can reinforce objects, but I can also fully construct structures out of this energy—it just requires my strength be enough and for me to have the proper materials. I can also imbue certain effects into the things I create, the stronger I get, the more resistance they will have."

This must have been one of the classes the announcement mentioned. It wasn't useful in battle, but clearly displayed incredible prowess in creating a safe structure or fort to live in. Who knew how dangerous the world would become in the coming years and months? Classes like these might be a requirement to survive. This system was cruel—but it was not without hope.

The concrete structures of the human world would not hold up to the ever-increasing power of players and monsters. I felt pleased with Glenn's choice, "We can continue to level you up so that you'll be able to show the maximum capabilities possible," I said.

It wasn't an issue to keep leveling like this, even if it considerably slowed down. With an EXP potion and some hard grinding, getting Glenn to level twenty could be accomplished. Not only that, when venturing through Dungeons he could construct temporary structures to protect us from enemies and the elements. He would earn his spot in the party and the EXP that came along with it in time.

"Do you still have the Spawn Protection Stone?" Glenn suddenly asked me. He must have heard us mention it on multiple occasions.

"I do," I said wondering why he asked.

"It's one of the special items used to augment my abilities. Using it will give the special properties of the stone to the structure, but also enhance its effects several times."

I didn't hesitate to remove the magic stone from my inventory and offer it to Glenn. "Take it," I said. If he could construct a home using it as a medium, we wouldn't have to worry about anything spawning upon us.

He shook his head, "It wouldn't be smart to use it just yet. Let me familiarize myself a bit more with the abilities and also grow in strength. The stronger I am when I use it, the better enhanced effects it will have. Just don't use it or it will be a waste."

I nodded and put the stone back into my inventory.

Throughout this exchange, Mark had been looking more and more thoughtful. "I'm torn between using a Class Stone now, without a skill, or learning a skill to tailor the stone specifically to a class type that I want to become."

That was one of the ways to game the system. If you had the help of someone powerful enough to bring you to level 10 like Mark did, you could learn a skill at that point and pick an ability that would push you towards a certain fighting archetype—ranged, melee, or support essentially.

"I think…I'll wait a bit to choose my class," Mark said suddenly. "I'm not sure if I would prefer to fight or have a logistical class like Glenn." No one urged him to make a choice now. After all, class selection determined your future in this post-apocalyptic world.

We took our time walking back to the three-story building we now called home. There were enough rooms for all of us and some extra. Monsters didn't spawn inside, but they did spawn immediately outside the structure regularly. It wasn't a problem for us, but for lower-level members like Mark or Glenn, it meant they could never leave their rooms without some form of escort.

Glenn talked the entire way back, mostly listing the names of special consumable items he could use to improve materials. It was fascinating to hear what their effects brought when used to augment structures. Items with curious names like Void Stone, Shadow Dust, and Boxed Starlight. There was no information available for what these were, or where to get them.

The most surprising and mind-boggling one mentioned was that he could change the material so as to allow it to teleport us to another location. Glenn referred to it as a warp gate. Unfortunately, we didn't have any of the items he mentioned that were needed for the creation of this augmentation, not a single one. They were most likely rare consumables only found from rare mobs or perhaps in dungeons.

I slowly grew accustomed to my new lifestyle. Breakfast lunch and dinner were structured around intervals of slaying monsters outside, mobs which were pitifully weak. The EXP wasn't great for us higher levels, but Glenn and Mark slowly grew strong enough to dispatch them on their own.

At least I had a safe bed to sleep in and a roof over my head. The bare necessities had been met, and I started to question if a life like this would be so bad. My hunger levels had gone down a lot, so I only needed to kill one enemy every two days to satiate my pangs.

Unfortunately, good things never lasted. Merely six weeks after first arriving, the world experienced catastrophic changes. There was no announcement and no warning. The ground began to rumble incessantly.

The sky roared and shook as if gods fought over the horizon. Hollow booms came every few minutes as if bombs had been dropped. It was thunder in my eardrums, and the quaking came shortly after.

It wasn't just quaking though; the trembling was so intense even crawling off the floor proved difficult. The stable ground I once knew provided as much foothold as a ship in rough seas. Our home was no longer a home.

We fled from our little reprieve as though from hell when it became clear the buildings could no longer stay standing. Even the sound of concrete smashing and rebar whining as the weight of the structures could not hold themselves up anymore was drowned out by the constant bellows of a furious earth.

"Is the world ripping in half?" Maria yelled. Her hands were above her head, doing her best to block the falling pine branches and debris. "For Christ's sake!" She swatted another foot-long branch away before it knocked her on the head.

We raced through a grove that cut directly through a park. Pine trees towered above us, their leaves swaying and rocking as if two-hundred miles per hour winds ravaged them. "A little more!" Jessica shouted, "there is a small clearing barely a mile away, right next to the lake, there would be nothing looming over our heads there."

We were fortunate such a situation was happening mid-day for us. A lack of light would have made this deadly, even to us. A wall of concrete or even towering trees falling upon you would be enough to end your life in an instant.

I was certain no current scale could measure quakes on this level. It felt as if I ran along a trampoline that constantly shifted up and down beneath my feet. Every step could have been fatal; at least none of the monsters and enemies we knew to be in the area were roaming and adding to our difficulties.

Whether the monsters were around or not didn't matter—we ran for the clearing regardless of if that might pull a train. I was struggling to keep the small debris from landing in my hair, or worse of all my eyes.

A sprint that should have taken fifteen seconds took minutes. Someone hit the ground with every other step, and someone raced to help them up each time. No one voiced a complaint; only constant encouragement. "Just a bit more!" Alan grabbed Richard around the ribs and hoisted him off the ground.

My ability to walk must have looked like that of a toddler taking their first steps. Everyone took a tumble into the grass when we finally made it out of the trees. Some of our urgency disappeared, as no one who fell bothered to get back up. We crawled along the ground until we were close enough to the lake.

"If the world opens up and swallows me, so be it!" Anna said defiantly. She was face down on the grass, and even then it shook so hard I thought she might prove prophetic. No one laughed, and even Maria began eyeing the ground suspiciously.

I stabilized myself and stared at the lake in front of me. The water shook too, as if it was ready to begin boiling at any moment. The incessant shaking broke the surface tension, water droplets sprayed a light mist over the bank, and occasionally onto us.

"What is happening?" Glenn yelled through the roaring. Only now could we catch our breath and talk about it.

"Your guess is as good as any," Lucas shouted back, "seems like an earthquake, though."

"Thank you captain obvious." Maria couldn't help herself.

"Earthquakes are a result of tectonic plates shifting," Mark started to talk as if we were in science class.

"English please," Alan cut him off before Mark could continue his lecture.

I could see that Thomas was almost laughing but he caught himself, "It means the land is moving, and likely smashing into other vast areas." The light heartedness of his tone let me know we would be okay through this too.

"Some world restructuring then?" I thought aloud. Restructuring was putting it lightly…because the shaking didn't stop.

# Chapter 2: A Reorganized World Without Shelter

The world rumbled and shook for two whole days before the earthquakes stopped.

I could not sleep at all on the first night, but by the second, I wasn't able to keep my eyes open. Most of us had thrown up multiple times, and I had a splitting headache that wouldn't go away.

I had been scrambled through and through, and when the quaking ceased, the steady ground almost felt abnormal. This first time standing up after the shuddering ended, I fell back down again, as did Lucas and Maria. Our legs were shot and our balance was temporarily ruined. We sat for over an hour after it was over, waiting with dread for an announcement that never came.

Eventually I worked up the courage to walk around. What I saw wasn't unexpected: the entire community was devastated. Not a single building remained standing, it was one hunk of rubble that provided no more shelter.

The monsters that were missing hadn't respawned yet, and that led our discussion to the theory that we were in for a big restructuring. Lucas started to refer to the event as an expansion. Even Thomas caught himself calling it a patch.

It wasn't just our home that had been wrecked, but as far as the eye could see, all remnants of human civilization had been destroyed. The towering city in the distance was now just debris that stacked up to two stories high. Anyone who was still alive there would have found it hard to escape.

The world that had recently been becoming brighter in my eyes had returned to a hellscape: one that was quickly becoming uninhabitable. The leisurely lifestyle we had experienced these past six weeks vanished overnight, and anything not in our inventory at the time had been thoroughly destroyed.

"Looks like we're back to sleeping under the stars," I said. That got a sour look out of those within earshot. As a matter of fact, what with the lack of rain and the sunlight in the morning, I felt that my sleep the previous night had been the best I'd gotten in months. "What now?" I threw the question into the air.

I looked around at the faces of uncertainty. We didn't have any objectives to go by, nor any direction to travel. "Let's head for the road," Lucas said, "at least that gives us a direction."

No one disagreed. The road or here, there was no difference. At least traveling the road would lead us to the next city or town; we could see the scope of this event. We headed for the nearest highway, cautious of our surroundings.

Things became odd as we walked. The world had changed in more than just its destruction. The insects that had previously assaulted us were nowhere to be seen. The occasional singing of a local bird didn't bless our ears. All was silent. Dead silent.

"Has anyone seen any animals at all?" Jessica asked. I hadn't seen so much as a lizard, or any life form at all in fact. There was nothing... and even when I used my necrotic vision to scan for any life at all in any direction, it came back empty.

A looming dread spread over the group that Alan tried to quickly suppress. "Maybe they fled during the earthquake?" He offered up a solution.

My feeling of hope lasted only a brief moment before it was squashed by logic. "Was anywhere outside the earthquakes?" Glenn asked. "There was nowhere safe, clearly. We should see something."

"Are we the only ones left?" Maria asked.

"That's even more unlikely," Lucas replied, brushing her idea aside firmly, "this is a change in the system and the system wants players in this game. For them to eliminate all the other players but us makes no sense."

We paused in contemplation, and I moved towards the nearest tree. There was thick black dirt at the base of the trunk. Roots protruded out of the soil ever so slightly. Just enough to trip over if you were moving too quickly past.

I leaned down and dug my hand into the fresh soil, but scoop after scoop came up empty of life. Not the smallest bug, or worm, or even anything at all. There wasn't even fungus beneath the soil. Just a gritty, bleak blackness that sullied the hands.

I shook my hands and brushed them against my pants before standing and turning back towards the others. "Careful!" Jessica suddenly yelled at me. My heart started racing immediately as an ominous feeling rushed up through my legs. I leaped forward without the slightest bit of hesitation, barely dodging whatever was coming for me.

The earth ripped behind me as I tumbled forward. The dense roots ripped like paper and provided almost no resistance to whatever was forcing its way through the ground. I turned as I rolled to see a gigantic worm, towering eight feet high.

It swayed there like a tentacle. Something so simple looking was absolutely terrifying when such a great size. There were no eyes on its head, and its mouth was a closed opening that occasionally protruded with endless sharp teeth.

The body was sleek and pink. Black dirt fell off in sloughs that revealed its see-through skin. The veins where blood flowed were clearly visible, and even the heart pumping midway down its torso was easy to see.

Alan and Richard rushed past me before I could even get to my feet and by the time I had scrambled clear they had clobbered it into a bloody mess. While huge, it didn't seem to be very strong.

"Did monsters like this always exist?" Anna asked. I'd never seen one. Before this fiasco, worms had remained normal sized; the same with insects and birds and animals and everything else.

Several days ago the trees were filled with lizards and birds, and the soil had worms and fungus and mushrooms growing from it. Now it had a giant earthworm the size of a full-grown man in it. What else had changed?

"Is the entire world becoming gamified?" Alan disheartened tone indicated his belief things were changing for the worse. I felt that it could be true. Perhaps the whole world had been reorganized to become more of a challenge for those of us who had survived this far. If that was the case, the worm was just a signal that things were only going to grow more difficult.

Our trip to the road was made with heavy hearts. My hopes of finding some kind of shelter still standing disappeared as we walked past nothing but ruined farms and barns. The seemingly harmless day-to-day life fauna was now trying to kill us, and who knew what else had been added during this change?

The only silver lining currently was our new support class Glenn, whom seemed to have the ability to build structures. Looking at the debris around us, finding anything manmade now would probably be impossible.

The road was a cobbling of asphalt that was now uneven and full of deep fractures. It wasn't even possible to walk on it anymore. Instead, we walked alongside the road. It still provided a path forward, so that we wouldn't end up going around in circles. From the position of the sun, I estimated we were moving northwest.

No one even asked which direction to go. Going back towards our old haunts didn't seem like a smart option. Surely the city was more dangerous than what we'd face in farmland? Our party was stronger than ever. Jessica and I had reached level twenty-six. Everyone besides Mark and Glenn were level twenty-four or twenty-five. Mark and Glenn made some headway in the two weeks after hitting level ten and were now level fourteen each.

We were strong, strong enough to face whatever came...I hoped. "It looks like the world is forcing us out into the open," I said.

"They don't want us hiding away anymore," Jessica agreed.

"Anyone who was tucked away and surviving off supplies is probably a goner." There was obvious doom and gloom in Anna's voice.

I couldn't help but think about the trailer park. There had been a surprising amount of older folk bunkered down there. I hoped they fared better in those trailers than anyone hiding away in a city. I took one last look back at the ruined landscape on the far horizon and then turned forward—there was no going back now.

# Chapter 3: The Whispered Warning of a Dying Man

Two days passed, and there was still no sign of mobs reappearing, or even other people. As far as the eye could see, was nothing but a bleak landscape. Hunger was starting to get to me. Others could survive off Rations, but I no longer had that luxury. It was only hunger though. I wasn't starving just yet.

Based on my experience so far, I could go for quite a while without food, so I pushed the hunger to the back of my mind. The nearest city was still another hundred miles ahead of us. We wouldn't reach it till nightfall at the earliest.

On the way there were plenty of turnoffs that led to small communities: a farm here or there, and plenty of gas stations. None of them had survived the quaking though. They were shredded through and through. It was hard to imagine how the suburban areas would look, considering how devastated these farmlands were. Even the wooden fences for keeping cattle corralled were tipped over and more often than not destroyed.

Around midday we made it past the rural farmlands and now walked through a dense pine forest. There were no exits or turnoffs for miles. This was a timber farm that previously would have been producing lumber daily, but now it was desolate.

Many trees had fallen into the road and completely blocked the path for anyone not on foot. Not that there was a drivable road here anymore anyway. It still slowed us considerably, having to climb up and over each fallen tree.

"Did you guys hear that?" Alan suddenly asked while climbing up and over a log. He was the closest to where the forest edge once was. I paused for a moment and heard nothing at all before climbing over: nothing but the sound of roaring winds and crackling branches. So many branches dangled by a hair's breadth. The trees were full of torn remnants from the quaking, it only needed a single gust to send branches falling below.

"All I hear is the trees," Richard responded bluntly. They had walked side by side, and he was the closest to Alan at the time. When the last of us—Maria—had hopped over our current obstacle we all set off again; even Alan accepted he was probably just hearing whispers of the wind.

It wasn't even fifteen seconds after that when I heard what resembled a scream. Not heart wrenching, but definitely the sound of someone panicking, screaming for help in the distance. A trail nearby led to what looked like the clearing of a lumber yard and the cry was from that direction.

"See?" Alan said, "told you so."

Whomever was screaming was probably only a couple hundred feet away. That their cries sounded further away than the lumber yard was probably on account of how dense the trees were packed together.

"It's unlikely to be a trap," Lucas said, "thoughts?" I appreciated that he didn't look to me for a lead but made sure to include everyone. I could see that reactions were mixed. Everyone was battle-hardened by now, and some of the sympathy that I would have

16

previously experienced for someone in trouble had been washed away while watching hundreds die to the fiend. None of us were knee-jerk heroes in this unforgiving world. Help others? Sure. Run blindly into danger? We'd learned better.

"Let's go see," Jessica brought her bow around into a firing position. "It's not a big detour, and if there are mobs, I should be able to pick them up when we get close enough."

I was curious as well as moved by the shouts. As far as I understood, there weren't any monsters currently populating the earth, or at least we hadn't seen any. This unknown person meant at least we weren't alone. But what was the danger they were facing? "I agree." I pulled up my mask. "Let's go but at a steady pace, ready to back off."

Alan nodded and hacked a path through some branches of fallen trees before leading us along the trail and to the clearer area. Not that it was much brighter ahead, a towering canopy blotted out the sunlight. The echoes of the yells sounded out all around me, and they made discovering the source more difficult than I expected. Even Jessica needed several minutes to finally pinpoint the place it was coming from.

We walked in our regular formation: Alan and Richard at the front with Jessica just behind them; Thomas remained dead center with Mark and Glenn on his side—not to protect him, but to be protected as they were still too low level; I remained at the very back with Lucas, Anna, and Maria just in front of me. My near sixth-sense made me the safest choice for dealing with an unsuspecting ambush, as hopefully I'd feel something coming; that plus my undead squad provided a great buffer for our vulnerable damage dealers.

After three or four minutes from leaving the trail and entering the timber yard I was still struggling to see beyond all the debris and half-chopped logs scattered around the grounds. A sudden parting of the canopy and shaft of sunlight left my eyes stinging.

"Across," Jessica said curtly. Her bow gestured upwards.

A wide group of cut trees stood in front of us. Just stumps protruding from the earth, some with menacing splinters sticking out of the top. They formed a thicket more than a hundred feet across, and sure enough on the other side, twenty or thirty feet in the air was a man hanging for his life from a tree limb.

"Why's he in a tree in the first place?" Maria said with some haughtiness. I stepped out of the shaft of sunlight and back into shade. There was a spring to my every step, almost as if I were walking on marshmallows. The wood chips that lay everywhere had deteriorated and created a soft spongy surface atop the earth.

We only walked a few feet before Jessica stopped everyone. "He's injured," she said. Her intonation was clear: be careful.

"How badly?" I asked. "Is it from a monster?" A lot could be deduced from a wound.

"It's a slash or gash, potentially from a sword," Jessica answered.

"Other people?" Anna asked. Everyone immediately went to high alert. Humans were as vicious as monsters these days, and several times craftier. The possibility this was a setup increased several times over.

Everyone stopped speaking as we made our way through the damaged tree trunks at a snail's pace. It was reassuring that we had Jessica constantly scanning the surrounding and I spent as much time looking back as forward. As we came about halfway through the thicket the man noticed us. "Oh God, thank God! HELP ME." He screamed even louder.

18

He wailed nonstop for a dozen seconds but we remained fixed in place. Lucas's pleas for him to be quiet with our fingers and hand signs proved futile.

"PLEASE. SHUT UP!" Maria suddenly exploded. Her shout was no louder than his own yelling, but her outburst left the man stupefied. He didn't respond after that, so it seemed he got the point.

We were just thirty feet away from the tree he perched in and by now I could see him clearly. His face was dirt covered, or maybe blood covered. The brown, curly hair atop his head was tattered and filled with dirt and debris. His blue shirt was ripped clear down the side, exposing a massive gash along his ribs.

The wound was clean as Jessica said. A straight cut without much deviation, no doubt the work of a blade. "Can you climb down?" I asked him from below.

His face showed relief as he gave a nod. He made a move and a groan escaped his throat involuntarily. I could tell it was a fresh wound, but it still hurt like hell no doubt. "I can heal you when you're down." Thomas said. That wound wasn't life threatening now that we had found him.

"Wait!" Jessica shouted, spinning around. "Enemies coming! Five or Six." I looked in the direction she was staring and could see nothing, but soon I heard them. There was a menacing laugh, like the sound of a hyena, but a bit more high-pitched. Every little cackle ended up with a corresponding growl that made me shiver.

The man in the tree immediately hugged the branches despite the pain and stopped coming down. It was better for us this way anyway. Alan and Richard waited determinedly in the front for a dozen seconds before the trees in front began to sway.

Branches audibly cracked, and not from falling. My view was obstructed, but I soon sensed the incoming monsters with Necrotic Vision. They were man-sized dog creatures wielding swords, maces, and even bows and staffs. We faced a pack of them.

I could hear the man above me whimpering, "oh God, oh God, oh God." Over and over again. His eyes were closed as he prayed. The sympathy I may have felt months ago wasn't there. No God would save you now.

"Level twenty-eight gnolls," Jessica called out. She didn't have time to detail their skills, as they rushed at us without fear. Their cackling was skin crawling, more intimidating than any battle drum or war chant. It seemed that they had noticed us after we noticed them and perhaps it was the man's yelling which had drawn their attention; probably these gnolls were the cause of his current wounds.

They stopped as soon as they realized we were not running but stood braced, waiting for them. The hyena-like laughter ceased. There was a moment of dead silence, and then high-pitched yelping as if they were communicating. Then they started to snarl at us.

"These...might not be monsters." I spoke my thought aloud. "These are more like demi-humans." This was an entirely new race. A species intelligent enough to possess speech and culture. The re-structuring was turning into more than what I had bargained for.

"Don't hesitate!" Jessica yelled while releasing an arrow. There were six dog-men in total, four of those were melee, while two were ranged. It looked similar to a party you might see other players make. A staff-wielder wore tribal headgear, his staff was adorned with squirrel or chipmunk skulls. This was no doubt a shaman, which I equated to their healer.

The other ranged opponent was simply an archer, while the four melee in front were no different than Alan or Richard or Lucas. Two held thick maces, one wielded a sword, and the fourth wielded a sword and shield.

They had a slight height advantage, but we were the better prepared. They only had a moment to realize we were a serious challenge. Richard and Alan rushed forward on Jessica's call as my swathe of undead troops charged down either flank. My warriors skirted their melee types and headed for their backline immediately, and already there was no time for them to fall back in a protective formation.

Maria had already rooted their melee firmly in place while Anna rained glacial hell from above. The combination made it impossible for them to retaliate at all. Richard and Alan stepped in to lash repeated blows without fear, which kept the two sword-wielding gnolls fully occupied.

With no immediate threat, Lucas sent out Wind Slash after Wind Slash. With the restrictive movement caused by Maria and Anna, the two mace wielders were cleanly bisected and died almost immediately. This was the first fight in some time that I'd seen Lucas fully let loose, and he certainly did. Every swing saw blood fly.

In the backline, the shaman I set my sights on had his face explode into carnage. He was dead before my skeleton warriors could even reach him, which was a result of Jessica's marksmanship, specifically her Godless Arrow.

Merely three or four seconds had passed, and victory was already decided. I couldn't help but feel awed. We had taken a break for almost two months, and yet now we were better than ever. It seemed that during that time people were still thinking hard about the efficiency of their skill use, even though we hadn't had a single group battle since then.

My focus shifted to the archer, who to my surprise, was already darting off into the trees. "They're fleeing!" I yelled out. My eyes scanned the sword-wielding gnolls, who were firmly locked in place. They didn't make it past the ten second mark.

I was hesitant to chase the archer, as it seemed almost futile. The dog-man was faster than me without a doubt. No one else seemed to want to chase it through the dense forest either. We had a wounded man above us we needed to rescue, too.

"Aghh." Suddenly, our friend in the trees let out a strong groan. The gnolls had been dispatched and as a result I hadn't been as alert as I should have been. There was an arrow projecting out of the side of his ribs.

"Shit!" I couldn't help but curse aloud. I turned to where the archer had fled and started to sprint, calling my undead troops after me. Above me was another groan, and then another after that. The archer who had fled had turned around and put three arrows deep into the man's chest. I could hear the dog-man cackling as it raced into the distance. I couldn't keep up no matter how hard I ran, and any further away from my party among all these trees might find me lost.

I walked back in dejection. The actions of these enemies did prove one thing, though. This was a new race entirely. These were not pre-programmed AI. They did not fight to the death. They clearly felt fear, and could strategize. These were similar to the fiend in that respect, arguably even more intelligent as they had some form of language.

Despite Thomas's best attempt to heal the man I returned to find him on the ground, dying. The three arrows were deeply embedded into his chest, and no amount of healing would save you from critical wounds of that nature.

"Is everyone else okay?" I asked, specifically looking towards Mark and Glenn.

"Don't go there." The man on the ground managed to whisper. Each word came out slow and full of pain. He barely managed to raise his arm and point in the direction that archer had fled.

"Why not go there?" Lucas kneeled down and asked the man. We were all silent, listening as intently as we could. His breathing was growing fainter. Thomas repeatedly healed him to ease some of his suffering and potentially get a few more words out of him.

"...gnoll empire." His eyes closed gradually before he slumped and lay motionless.

"Gnoll empire?" Richard repeated. "An empire of these things?"

"That is what he said," Maria said sarcastically. Her fiery attitude had never dissipated despite all of our setbacks.

"Empire is a big word, though." Lucas said. "He didn't say camp, or city, or dwelling, he said 'empire,'" Lucas emphasized. That meant the scale we were talking about was astronomical.

Thinking about armies of these enemies left shivers down my spine. While we dealt with a small group quite easily, what would it mean if they had armies? If they had much higher-level classes? Here we had the upper hand completely. Our sudden appearance and swift action left them without much room for maneuver.

A pre-programmed monster would react instantly and, in fact, the fight may have been more difficult if they had been unintelligent. But what would the fight have been like if they were prepared, and if they had taken proper precaution to protect their healer? Their reactions would be more impressive, unexpected, and almost certainly deadlier than their scripted counterparts. As it was, the

gnoll group had maintained a basic formation when they approached.

I also had a concern about the gnoll shaman. Although it hadn't
healed or cast any ability, enemies that practiced voodoo-like rituals
often had terrible curse or debuffing abilities.

Thinking about hordes of these enemies moving through our
world… they could annihilate the remaining human population.
While I didn't think our group would be the highest level among
humans, there was no doubt we would be ranked in an elite
bracket. These enemies were level twenty-eight. Did that mean the
gnolls were well ahead of humanity?

# Chapter 4: From Fleeing in Panic to a New Strategy

We sat in a circle on benches improvised out of tree trunks and lengths of timber and everyone had a serious expression as we chewed over what we had learned. There were essentially two points of view: investigate the gnoll empire or turn around and head off in the opposite direction. Maria was the main person wanting to leave and while what she said wasn't particularly convincing, the fear behind her words was very persuasive. We could quickly find ourselves out of our depth.

It was Lucas who best put the other point of view. "We have to check this further. If the gnolls represent an existential threat to humanity we need to know. We didn't choose this responsibility but this is where we are. It might fall to us to rally other groups of survivors to create a force strong enough to defeat them."

"How's this," Jessica offered, "with my tracking sense we should be able to investigate carefully and we can turn back if I pick up large numbers of them."

My own view too was that we should check this out and after I said as much, there were nods and it was clear we had a consensus. Maria just shrugged.

We reformed our positions and followed behind Jessica as she followed the trail of the gnoll archer.

There was more than a hint of excitement alongside the nervousness I was feeling. The world had changed for the deadlier no doubt, but a budding excitement grew alongside my fear.

The truth was I grew bored easily. Ever since the apocalypse, I hadn't had time to even think about boredom…but a whole new world lay ahead of me. Literally, a new world. I was walking a path along a new frontier, and potentially I was going to witness things beyond my wildest imaginations. These gnolls might only just be the start of it.

With a cut from an axe, Alan marked the trees as we walked, just in case we somehow ended up getting lost. I was glad that he'd thought to do this; we were going into unknown territory; it was never bad to be overly careful.

"How's it looking up there?" Maria called from the back. "Seen anything?"

She put up a strong front, but I could tell she was hiding her nervousness.

"Nothing but trees," Alan yelled back. Jessica also looked back and gave Maria a thumbs up, which was much more reassuring.

We walked for at least an hour before coming upon a massive clearing. I'd have normally been in awe at the vast number of lumber stumps dotting the ground, or even the clear blue sky and beautiful view above, but my eyes were glued to something else.

"He wasn't lying…" Lucas could barely mumble. Others couldn't even find the words to speak. The empire he spoke of was there, and who knew for how many miles it extended? A bustling civilization grew out of the ground.

The construction was crude: boulders and rocks made up some structures, other buildings were made from lumber or even clay. Still, the sheer numbers of them were unimaginable. The gnoll community filled the clearing to the left and right up to the forest, and ahead it went for miles and miles to a very distant tree line.

There were so many huts and houses and strange buildings that I struggled to accept what I was seeing. A vast city, unexpectedly carved out of a forest. I felt like I was in a horde city playing World of Warcraft , that was the type of magnitude presented before me now. In fact, it would probably be considered bigger.

"We came, we saw…" Alan started.

"And we left!" Maria finished his sentence. "We are not going anywhere near that thing."

"I agree with Maria," I said. "How many gnolls could live in that?" My words were anything but eloquent, but I was shell shocked.

"Hundreds of thousands? Maybe millions?" Mark answered. "They probably don't care about the same luxuries that we do." Which meant they didn't need as much space.

Suddenly there was a blaring horn in the distance. The sound grew and grew to the point where it felt it was being blown all around us. I reevaluated my opinion that the gnoll cackle was the most intimidating noise you could hear before battle.

"I hope that isn't for us," Jessica said. "But there are gnolls exiting the front gate and heading this way." Her eyesight was by far the best of anyone's here. "We should run." Her words were as good as law right now.

No one remained for a second longer. We turned and raced back into the forest and out of sight. Alan's foresight in marking our path proved its value, as we made it to the lumber camp in just twenty minutes. No one had the breath to speak once we re-emerged. Instead, we raced back to the highway and away from the gnolls for another half an hour before deeming it safe.

"That was unexpected," I said, barely holding back the cough building in my throat. "But I think we should be safe here." We had moved far enough that it would be difficult for them to locate us, and even if they did, far enough where there was a good chance we could handle whatever advanced party came our way.

"There's no way that was there before the quakes…right? I'm not crazy for thinking that?" Anna asked.

"It's not impossible," Lucas said, "although it feels unlikely, because the insects and birds that used to be around before are no longer here."

"Is it possible that city is only the start of what's coming?" Thomas asked. "Like, the first wave of spawns?"

"What do you mean by start?" I asked. "Do you mean more monsters will be coming in the next few days…or long into the future." It was an important distinction to make.

"I mean in the next few days," he clarified.

"The world does seem a bit too barren," Jessica said. There was a unanimous agreement on that. We had grown so used to the constant background noise of insects and birds, that we didn't even realize they were there until they weren't. Now there was only an eerie silence broken by the occasional gust of wind.

"Everyone check their map?" I suggested before pulling mine open. We were in unexplored territory for us, so everything around us was grey. The forest was there, and the parts we hadn't explored personally were merely shadowy and unclear. Our path was visible, and even the clearing we reached was there.

There was a gigantic structure on the map where the empire was located, but as we hadn't approached or discovered it, there was no writing or indication of what it was. Just a hazy construction on the map. Seeing it from above like this really put into perspective just how large it was.

Everything else was undiscovered. It seemed without witnessing it or at least getting in a certain proximity, nothing else would render on the map. "So what do we do then?" Richard asked. "I'm tired of walking around without purpose. There's no guarantee the direction we're moving is better than where we are right now."

"Really? No guarantee?" Maria started on him. "Did you forget there's a gnoll empire some miles away from here? Surely there's something better than that?"

"Okay…besides the gnoll empire." Richard corrected himself. "I was trying to make a point. Without knowing what we're doing, we could be moving away from our goal."

It was hard to argue with that thought.

"Well…without knowing what's coming, the best and most logical thing to do would be to level up and get stronger," I said. No one responded, but I could tell they were hesitant as to what that meant. Leveling meant risking our lives, fighting monsters, putting ourselves in danger.

While hardened, the nearly two-month break had taken the edge off every single one of us. It would be hard to restore it. This was the opportunity we needed to get back on track.

"There's nothing to kill to even level up though." Alan said with some dissatisfaction. He was the most bloodthirsty one out of all of us, and our little skirmish with the gnolls earlier hadn't satiated him.

"There's gnolls," I suggested.

"What about a dungeon?" Glenn asked. "Dungeons should still exist." It seemed Glenn had one-upped my suggestion, and there were several nods.

"Why not do both?" Lucas asked. "We can wander the forest, killing any gnolls we encounter. At the same time, trying to find a dungeon." This was definitely the better suggestion. At least this way, if we didn't find a dungeon, we'd at least have gnolls to kill.

"All in favor?" I asked. Which got an agreement out of everyone. Soon we were heading back up the road. The plan was to hunt in the forest near the gnoll city on this side of the lumber camp.

Somehow, the anxiety I had felt about the existence of a huge gnoll empire vanished and was instead replaced by bubbling excitement. The prospect of exploring a new dungeon seemed to excite everyone, maybe me most of all. The idea that we were discovering an unexplored world was thrilling.

Everyone had grown a bit more accustomed to the forest environment and we made light work of the trip back. The gnoll troops we had been running from were now the thing we were eagerly marching towards.

No one wanted to remain stagnant. Every mob was another chance at loot and out of everyone, I had potentially the most to gain. I had an empty skill slot on account of the Fiend encounter waiting to be filled. If the right skill came along, of course. The rest we had enjoyed had been pleasant, but the skill I needed wasn't going to just fall in my lap.

It was if fate was on our side the entire time. We came upon a manageable gnoll party just after they had turned about and headed back to their fortress. With Jessica having whispered the information to us, Alan and Richard didn't need told what to do. There was an opportunity to get in among the weaker back line, and they took it instantly.

The back half of the gnoll group consisted of a shaman and three archers: support and damage dealers. Alan's charge separated them from their tanky frontline and gave us a huge opportunity. I didn't have to call out what to do anymore. We worked together like a well-oiled machine.

Jessica had already raced ahead and used her archery to drop a trap in between the melee types and their casters. Not only that, Anna had cast her AoE ability there as well, completely dividing their party. The tanks would be forced to struggle through a blender to defend their DPS.

With no warriors to defend them from our assault, their damage dealers lasted no more than a few seconds. Lucas was the star of the show in this fight as well. His Wind Slash was an exceptionally powerful ability against enemies with little or no resistance. These gnolls weren't wearing armor, and besides a light coat of fur and thin hide, they were largely defenseless.

The three archers and one shaman in the back group put up no resistance. The separated tank group didn't even attempt to fight after, and were already racing through the trees towards the safety of their city.

"Don't chase." I stopped Alan and Richard from hunting down the survivors. They didn't immediately understand why. "Let them report our existence, that way we have a constant supply of enemies to farm."

I could see a sparkle in Alan's eye when I said that. He truly was battle hungry. His bloodthirst had almost cost him dearly once, and that experience seemed to have changed him. I truly hoped that was the case, for all of our sakes.

We regrouped at the gnoll corpses and checked on the loot. It was a pleasant surprise to see actual equipment on a corpse again. The first pack of gnolls we had dispatched had dropped nothing, and the zombies and ghouls during our retreat were too low level to drop us anything as well.

"Looks like your hard work paid off," I said to Lucas before presenting him a sword.

**Brutal Katana: This slender, curved blade allows for swift attacks that deal devastating damage.**

**AGI +7, Attack Speed + 15%**

Lucas took the sword happily and then immediately tested it out. He slashed it through the air a dozen times, and then directly lopped off a nearby tree branch.

"How is it?" Alan asked.

"Sharp, it's already stronger than the nodachi, and this isn't even a two-handed sword."

"Does that mean you can dual wield them?" I asked. The Brutal Katana was a one-handed sword, and from when I passed it to him, I could tell it was a comfortable weight. Wielding it with one hand shouldn't pose any problems in terms of strength requirement.

"Probably, but I doubt I'd be very good." Lucas said and I accepted his answer.

I saw plenty of dual-wielding characters in video games, but those were just video games. It was likely to be exceedingly difficult to master using a sword in each hand. The dexterity required to do so would be daunting no doubt. It was a conversation for another day, or at least until Lucas actually had two one-handed swords to potentially equip.

After tidying the remaining morsels of loot: some rations, one healing potion and one bandage, we slipped away to the north east. While we did want to encounter more gnolls, it was safest to do so on our own terms and that meant being at sufficient distance. We needed to keep moving.

# Chapter 5: Ambushing Gnolls for Levels and Loot

We moved north and east for about an hour, so that if we had been directly south of the entrance to the gnoll city before, we were off to the side now. Our hope was that this would be far enough away that no large forces would come our way, ideally we'd come across small patrols which were complacent and unaware.

Our goal was to look for easy fights while we could. No doubt, once the gnolls came to terms with our existence we would be facing serious challenges and probably would have to retreat. But in the meantime we were on the lookout for low hanging fruit.

Thanks to Jessica's tracking, we discovered that there were a lot of small gnoll groups moving around the forest that we could ambush. She reported that their standard patrol was just three gnolls in size, or at least that's mostly what we ran into at the start. These groups consisted of one tanky melee—which was almost always a mace-wielding gnoll—and two ranged units. More often than not these would be two archers. Very rarely it was an archer and a shaman. Of the ten patrols Jessica spotted, only one of them contained a single shaman Gnoll.

Although we were confident of victory over such groups, we didn't rush. We spent a long time scouting the patrolling gnolls. Only after we had a decent lay of the land, and a basic understanding on how they moved and crisscrossed with each other, did we dare engage any. The point was to work out a place for our ambush where we wouldn't get unwanted adds. Even then, there were still some unknowns.

The gnolls we had fought before were more like vanguard units than these patrols: these small groups seemed to be scouts rather than fighters. There was a good chance that once we pulled them they would make the biggest ruckus they could to alert everything around, and try to flee rather than stand for a confrontation.

"All we can do is try it and find out," I said. There was no real way to know how these gnolls would behave until we pulled the trigger. No one took much convincing, and in the worst case, we had planned an escape plan and it seemed to me that everyone was on the same page.

I was mentally prepared for battle, and now it was just about timing. Taking a position downwind of an approaching group of gnolls, we tucked ourselves away as a group in the bushes between two trees. Although we'd done our best to get the advantage of surprise, I was anxious: it was likely that these canines had an exceptional sense of smell.

With every step and grunt as they grew closer and closer though, that anxiety changed to anticipation. An unsuspecting patrol group were feet from us when Jessica released a hellish blow to the gnoll brute at the front. To my great relief, none of the gnolls howled or called for help at all. Instead, they each let out a menacing cackle and rushed in Jessica's direction.

The rest of us were still hidden. I was well aware the intelligence of these enemies made it likely they would flee the moment they saw our numbers. Standing alone, however, Jessica seemed like easy prey, and they took the bait flawlessly. Their charge was halted the moment they stepped over her Quagmire trap.

By the time they realized they were slowed, vines encased them and a Glacial Storm sent ice ripping across their flesh. The slows from each ability stacked, which meant it was nearly impossible for them to get out of the devastating AoE. The three abilities combined had managed to fell every foe we used them against so far.

The battle ended so swiftly that my summoned undead squad hadn't even time to reach the enemy. Our ranged DPS was a scary force to be reckoned with.

Despite feeling somewhat useless, I wasn't dejected. Fast engagements like this were not my forte anyway. Large scale, drawn out battles was where I performed best. In those situations my undead troops could continue to deliver damage as long as they were alive, regardless of my MP.

We quickly repositioned and prepared for another patrol group. In just a matter of a few minutes, another pack was cleaned out just like that. Only after we had taken out five gnoll patrols did we hear the sound of horns blaring in the forest and howls in the distance. The remaining patrols must have noticed something was amiss and sounded the alarm.

Immediately, we retreated east for a good half hour, before pausing and waiting to detect just what we were now up against. Their response was quick, and it wasn't long before Jessica reported that squads of ten gnolls were moving around in the distance.

"Let their urgency cool off for a bit," Lucas said, "we should pull back further." I felt Jessica's hand land on my shoulder as she urged me to turn away and follow. Ten was probably too many, although the experience and loot might be good.

This reminded me to use the downtime to distribute the recent drops. From the five patrol groups we had dispatched, we had gotten another two pieces of gear.

### Blessed Light: A holy hammer imbued with the power of god.

### STR +5, WIS +5, Holy Damage +15%

"I'm not a man of god, but I do deal holy damage." Richard couldn't help but chuckle as he snatched the one-handed mace away. It was a perfect fit in his hands.

### Maiden's Veil: A beautiful veil that specializes in blocking unwanted attention.

### WIS +6, STAM +2, Sense does not work on you.

I handed a veil made of a deep blue, see-through fabric to Anna and it waterfalled over her face as she put it on. Her eyes remained fully uncovered, and somehow the veil seemed to enhance their beauty. The draping sides connected via a single cloth that clipped across the mouth.

"Can you sense me?" Anna looked at Jessica. She did have the skill, and had leveled it enough to get a basic reading on players.

"Skill has failed," Jessica responded.

"What about blocking unwanted attention?" Lucas asked.

"I'm not sure," Anna said. "It seems pretty see-through to me." And she wasn't wrong. Just looking her, it was obvious the thin material obstructed very little in terms of unwanted gazes. Anna continued to play with the item until something happened.

She fully fitted the veil, even going so far as covering her mouth. Her only visible feature was her two piercing eyes. I could still see her face behind the veil, but something miraculous happened: my image of her was completely obscured in my head.

It felt to me as if nothing had changed, and yet the facial features I was expecting were not there. The eyes seemed almost blurry but at the same time completely clear. There was an imaginary fog that covered her face, and even from one second to the next, I could not confidently say it was Anna standing in front of me.

"That is terrifying," Maria said. So it wasn't just me having this experience. Even though my brain knew it was Anna standing there, a strange power seemed to interfere with that information. I felt that the veil was similar to my mask and inflicting fear upon those who stared at it.

"Is it that bad?" Anna asked. Those words sent me for a loop as well. Even her voice, while completely normal, warped in some extraordinary way. I was listening to a stranger, and for a second, I fully believed someone had replaced Anna.

"It's not bad per se…" Alan said. "But it's really, really confusing my brain."

"How could it be doing that? Last I recalled you didn't have a brain." Maria didn't forget to throw in her jabs. Alan would usually retort, but the fact he didn't made wonder did he feel he deserved the attack. The two had been spending more time together as of late, and I wondered if a growing relationship between them was affecting their public banter.

"Let's keep going." I tried to steer the group back on track. Nothing else needed to be said. Alan and Richard led the front as we got away from the gnoll city for the time being. Now it had gotten too hot to ambush gnolls and was a good time to explore for dungeons.

My eyes constantly scanned my map as we made our way north. By now we were at least three hours east of the gnoll empire. Nothing new was revealed on the map as we moved, and our search for a dungeon remained fruitless.

We settled for a break after walking for nearly an hour. There were still gnoll groups here but perhaps they had not been recently sent from the city in response to our ambushes, because they were roaming around in packs of five. Our hit-and-run tactics continued to prove incredibly effective against these gnoll groups. In fact, the majority of the work was being done by Jessica, Maria, and Anna. They set up the pulls and basically spoon-fed mobs to us.

The EXP was plentiful as well. Mark and Glenn were receiving a penalty, but even they had both climbed to level 18. Somehow Mark still hadn't chosen a class. He was on the fence, and since he wasn't fighting right now anyway, it wasn't an issue.

The rest were all closing in on me and Jessica, and we were both steadily closing in on level 27.

**Name: Mike Reynolds Class: Necromancer**
**Level: 26 EXP: 72%**
**HP: 1290/1290 MP: 485/485**
**STR: 5 Fear Resistance: 5**
**AGI: 2**
**DEX: 5**
**VIT: 29 +14**
**WIS: 27 +26**
**Available: 15**

**Skills:** [A] **Summon Skeleton LV.** 10 | [A] **Summon Skeleton Mage LV.** 4 | [A] **Decay LV.** 3| [A] **Reanimate Dead LV.** 3 | [A] **Bone Armor LV.** 2 | [A] **Vast Shadows** | [A] **Temporary Grave LV.** 1 | [P] **Sixth Sense** | [P] **Bravery LV.** 2 | [P] **Mutated** | [P] **Pain Resistance LV.** 2 | [P] **Skeletal Mastery LV.** 4| [P] **Intimidate Living** | [P] **Inner Calm LV.** 2 | [P] **Necrotic Vision** | [P] **Blood Thirsty LV.** 1 | [P] **Cold Hearted LV.** 1 | [P] **Poison Immunity**

Since we had started grinding gnolls I had gained a total of thirty percent of the EXP I needed to level, which was impressive considering it hadn't even been a full day of fighting yet. We were also taking it easy. If we went all out, I felt confident we could fight up to ten gnolls at a time. Even these groups of five weren't an issue and I hadn't cast a single ability yet.

My fifteen stat points were still sitting there waiting to be used. Unfortunately, or fortunately, I didn't have any need for them, yet. With my extra skill slot, I definitely had a lot more leeway on how to build myself. I wasn't sure if I should take a support skill for my summons, some form of CC so I could lockdown enemies better, or just take some long-range damaging nuke.

All I knew in the moment was that if my undead warriors weren't dying, I had a whole lot of MP sitting around. Bone armor also provided me with a lot more tanking ability than other casters. There was a good amount of freedom to either get WIS or VIT as well.

# Chapter 6: Not the Ambush We Planned For

For the next two days we continued our hit and run tactic. While displaying a certain amount of strategy, it seemed there was still some minor restrictions on the gnolls that made them seem more like pre-programmed mobs than a rival species to humanity. They couldn't just up and mobilize their entire army to deal with us, nor did it seem like they were setting ambushes or adjusting to our activity: the size of their patrols stayed at five. Also, they seemed to replenish the patrols less and less often.

On the second day, both Mark and Glenn had managed to hit Level 20, which was closing the gap between us. Jessica and I managed to get to 27, while the remaining members all reached 26. We powered up as a group, and this far our decision to take on the gnolls had been smooth sailing.

There was so little risk involved in this strategy that it seemed almost pointless to do anything else. We had stopped searching for a dungeon and focused on grinding via gnoll patrols. We moved along the paths of the forest and tried to be unpredictable, working our way around the outskirts of the massive city, heading north, reversing south, going to the east and then to the west, trying to keep moving while also maintaining an efficient kill speed.

"Getting harder to find patrols," Jessica said from the front. She was our scout, and almost always gave us the advantage when it came to encountering enemies. We were never caught unprepared, always being able to set up against the incoming patrol, and usually making quick work of them.

By mid-day I felt that our rate of EXP gain was really going downhill. And then it became clear that ninety-five percent of the patrols were gone, maybe even ninety-nine percent. There were virtually no gnolls available for us to hunt. We moved around constantly searching for them, but the gnolls were no longer coming out of their settlement.

To us the hundreds of gnolls we killed was a huge number, but had it really been enough to trouble the empire? Given the massive population that must reside in the city, these patrols we'd been picking off were just a fraction of the cost to them of a real battle. Assuming they were not fully sentient and independent but some kind of spawns, why would the patrols dry up?

We maneuvered around east of the city for most of the afternoon before finally finding a new patrol pack to slaughter. At last. It should have troubled me that this was the only patrol we'd seen in hours and why it was here now. We just...pulled.

In fact, we pulled and dealt with the pack as usual. No one questioned the changed pattern of behavior as we stood over the corpses gathering the miscellaneous loot. It was only after the rations, bandages, and potions were distributed did things go terribly wrong.

"We're surrounded," Jessica suddenly looked at me, face pale, "they're on every side." I couldn't hear or see anything at all. It was that empty forest all around us, and yet I could imagine how the gnolls were stealthily creeping in. "We have to go now or we won't have any chance otherwise."

No one questioned her. The expression on her face was stern, which meant the situation was probably worse than what she let on. She picked a direction and started to run, "Get ready to fight," she yelled at us. We should never fly too close to the sun, yet this was one of those moments we had slipped up and were doing so.

I didn't hold back at all. Sprinting, I raced towards the front while bringing my undead squad out. "Killing or running?" I yelled as I passed Jessica. I couldn't see how many enemies there were; I didn't know how hopeless fighting our way out would be.

"Just run!" she cried. Things went from bad to worse. As soon as the first pack of enemies came into view I realized why we couldn't try to make a stand. There was a sea of gnolls in front of us.

"Support me!" Alan yelled at us, and then charged in without fear. He directly crashed into the first row of attackers in our path. The frontline of the shield wall the gnolls had put up crumpled in an instant. "I'll open a path!"

Richard joined directly beside him as the two began to bulldoze a path through the ranks of gnoll troops. Maria shot out explosive arrow after explosive arrow as close to our tanks as she could. Gnolls were sent flying through the air as we struggled to carve out a path through their army.

My undead warriors reached the gnoll line, and like a row of linebackers, they rushed into the breach in the wall of gnolls like a crashing wave. Metal hitting metal rang out, and those gnolls that weren't knocked aside by the physical force of impact were stabbed and pummeled by my skeleton troops.

I channeled Decay at the closest gnolls. Their faces aged rapidly, and the clarity of their eyes faded until it was a murky gray. Despite experiencing what was no doubt incredible pain, the gnolls didn't break rank, and fought with everything they had.

"FASTER!" Jessica yelled. The gnolls were closing in on all sides, and as soon as they reinforced the troops in front of us, we would truly be at a dead end. We were making progress, even though the advance of Alan and Richard had slowed; we were about two-thirds the way through these mobs and I could see spaces between the trees beyond their back line.

The cackling of the gnolls as they fought raised every hair on my body. Despite them dying in droves, despite their flesh being rent, their howls sounded ecstatic.

The situation was not looking good. "Have your skeletons support me!" Richard suddenly yelled back to me. There was no time to ask in what particular way he meant. His shield started to glow white-hot as he leaned forward. I understood; he was going to plow on through behind that shield with sheer force.

On my command the undead melee classes sheathed their weapons and then balled behind Richard. There was no other way to offer support except to push him forward. His shield glowed as bright as the sun, and every enemy it touched screamed in agony. While the gnolls weren't undead, touching something filled with so much holy power still seemed to be able to deal terrible damage to them.

Lucas was in the fray as well, doing whatever he could to assist in breaking through. He took the easy kills when presented with them, but otherwise worked on maiming enemies: breaking or slicing the tendons in their legs, or removing arms. Without the support of those appendages, they couldn't defend against our push.

With Richard barreling forward, the final rows of gnoll soldiers didn't last more than a few seconds. Richard came out beyond them and nearly faceplanted on the ground from the force of the push from behind him. My skeletons, however, were recovered and I immediately had them form a wall on both sides to keep the gnolls from closing in on us as the rest of the group dashed for freedom.

Paired with the support of Anna and Maria, keeping the opening wide was easy. "Rush through!" I yelled at everyone, holding back so that I was the last through the gap we had made. "Keep running! My undead troops can hold them off for a bit."

Without hesitation, the others raced off in front of me, and I didn't wait around either. My undead soldiers could be re-summoned, there was no point in being frugal about the MP in a life-or-death situation. We got about a hundred meters clear from the precious seconds my undead bought us, but it didn't seem to be enough.

"They're gaining on us," Jessica called back, "closing in on all sides." This was their territory after all. Expecting to outrun them on their own turf was a laughable joke. Not only that, their powerful legs were perfectly suited to move through the forest at rapid pace.

I could hear a growing cackle of canine laughter as they raced after us. The sound grew louder and louder in my ears; they were getting closer with every passing second. My undead had mostly been destroyed and there was no opportunity to resummon them.

It was a miracle that none of us had tumbled and fallen so far. The forest floor was covered with thick tree roots that protruded from the ground, creating uneven footing every few meters, and the vines were everywhere. Getting stuck and tangled up would have been incredibly easy if Alan wasn't hacking away like a madman at the front.

Time seemed to slow down as the beating of my heart filled my ears. My fingers were icy cold and I could barely breathe. We hadn't stopped running for over ten minutes in such a challenging area. My legs were screaming.

"We aren't losing them," Jessica forced out the words. Her voice was dry, like me the constant running must have sucked every drop of moisture from her mouth. My nose ran a like faucet and my face felt flushed and sweaty.

"Don't stop." Lucas yelled out. We ran and ran, and eventually we exited the forest and into an open field. This was both a blessing and a curse. The footing was more even here, which allowed us to move faster, but we were fully exposed. There were no trees or cover for us to hide in, and as soon as the gnolls exited the forest and joined on the grassland, they drew their bows.

First it was five or six, but soon dozens had accumulated there, and the number was climbing. The twang of their bows filled the air and drowned out everything else. Arrows whistled past us, every single one a potential kill shot.

"Are we going to die like this?" Anna cried. The archers had gathered in such numbers, it was only a matter of a few more seconds before it would be raining arrows. There wouldn't even be a gap between the arrows to dodge into. Their oncoming melee classes gave us no time to stop either. All I could do was prey their aim was poor today.

"There's something ahead!" Jessica was leading the front still. I couldn't see what she was referring to yet, but a surge of hope immediately bloomed inside of me. Every one of us put a hundred-

and-twenty per cent into it and pushed ahead, and after I breached a small hump of a hill, I saw it.

There was a black circle in the middle of the grassland. A giant hole had opened up in the earth, except it was too clean to be natural. It was a perfect circle, the edge wasn't dirt or grass, but some form of tile or stone with intricate carvings lined the outside.

# Chapter 7: Chased by the Arrows of Gnoll

It took me only a moment to reach the circle in the ground and stand with the others around the carved stone edge.

"What is it?" Lucas asked. We were all asking ourselves the same question, and of course no one could answer it. The darkness below me wasn't completely uniform, occasionally I saw a glimmer, like a reflection of sunlight on a gem below.

The gnoll archers were setting up on the hill, and within a few seconds we were going to look like porcupines. The number of gnoll archers hurrying up the hill was in the hundreds, the melee classes were closing in on us too. "I think it's water," I declared to everyone. I couldn't be one-hundred percent certain, but that flicker of light was familiar: like the sun shimmering off a water's surface. "We're going to have to jump in: we don't have much of a choice." I looked around and saw only doubt and hesitation.

There wasn't enough time to argue. Spending even a few seconds trying to persuade the others would lead to deaths. Our enemies' bows were now drawn. "Good luck and I'll see you all below," I said just before jumping. I had to prove by demonstration that this was a liquid. If it wasn't, if it was a deep pit, I'd be responsible for everyone's death.

The freefall lasted a very long three or four seconds, and then I plunged into icy, cold water. Splashes sounded all around me as my party members joined me. I could even look up and see the others still in free fall. None of them had doubted me, jumping before I'd even confirmed if it was water.

"It's SO COLD!" I heard Maria yell out.

"We aren't safe yet," Jessica warned us. "They're racing to the edges." I looked up to see their shadows appear above. Their bows were visible too as were the arrows beginning to hit the water around us.

"Dive down!" shouted Lucas.

I hugged the wall's edge and then dived down a few feet, periodically holding my breath. The arrows only made it around two feet into the water before losing all their force. We were safe, but still trapped like fish in a barrel.

The gnolls above continued to shoot more arrows for several minutes before it seemed they might have given up. It was impossible to see us below and while we were trapped, the hole in the ground was anything but small. It was bigger than any swimming pool I'd ever been in by two or three times.

"There's something over here," suddenly Mark yelled out. He was across from me, against the far wall. I couldn't see anything at all from where I was, but I could hear how everyone was slowly converging on him. Only when I reached the wall could I see what Mark had found, thanks to reflections on the surface of the dark water.

There was a passageway, half submerged in the water. "It's the only way to go," Lucas looked at everyone. "Who wants to go first?"

"I'll explore; wait here, I won't go far," Jessica promptly swam into the tunnel. With her improved physique, her physical ability was through the roof, which included her lung capacity. During that entire sprint, I hadn't noticed any sign of her being winded at all.

She started her swim into the tunnel and then disappeared into the darkness. I waited anxiously there, hand on the cold, rough stone of the wall. It would be cruel if there was no way out once inside, but I was confident that whatever she found, Jessica's awareness would keep her safe. She would turn back if things got bad...

Two minutes passed that felt like an eternity, and I was growing increasingly nervous. Maria had her fingers in her mouth, biting her nails with anxiety. Suddenly, there was a faint light in the dark water, and then Jessica emerged. "You'll have to swim for about a minute underwater," she said while taking a deep breath of air. "Just on the other side is an open cavern that leads somewhere."

"Is it...possible to get lost underwater?" Maria asked. She seemed nervous about swimming in. the dark, as was I.

"It was just a single tunnel; you can't get lost." Jessica clarified for everyone. "There's enough space to turn around if needed as well."

"That's good." Lucas wiped his head. "Underwater is already ick; claustrophobic and underwater..."

"Nightmare combination," Maria agreed.

"Okay, who is first?" Jessica asked. "I'll bring you." Once again my admiration for my closest friend and comrade soared. She seemed completely at ease in the water, and expertly guided each person who wasn't comfortable going alone through the underwater tunnel. After a dozen minutes, everyone had passed through the sump without a hitch.

I arrived on the other side of the cold swim in a cavern, completely plain and pitch black as could be. Lacking magical light, or old-fashioned torches, there was no other option for us but to feel around blindly with our hands.

"Here," Richard called out at last. He had found an opening in the cavern, forward and right of the tunnel we had swam out of.

The walls of this new area were jagged and filled with cavities. It was easy to hold on and use the projections of stones as support, but a budding fear that something would pop out of these holes and bite my hand started to grow. I said nothing as I brought up the rear.

We wound through the dark corridor for several minutes with Richard leading at the front. The corridor was unchanging and just as I heard a few grumbles about this, the scenery changed.

The winding tunnel came to an end and we entered an even wider cavern than the first. We were on a ledge in fact, and there was light. Glowing algae spotted the outline of the cave in front of us.

"Those plants are creating their own photosynthetic reaction," Glenn said like an absolute nerd.

"That's good for them," Maria said sarcastically, but I was just happy I could see. I could see the gleam of light in the eyes of the others as they took in our surroundings. The cave below was beautiful in an utterly unexpected way, the perfect sight to take in after experiencing nothing but pure darkness.

"Careful," Lucas warned us. I had been pushing to the cavern ledge to take a better look below, "there's something there."

None of us had noticed it, but there was a small thin film in the air. Like a portal or a pool of water. Lucas tossed a small pebble over the ledge and the air in front rippled and blurred before going back to perfect peace. Even the view behind it blurred, and seemed to be an illusion.

51

Were we merely sitting in an empty boring cavern? Did the beautiful cavity in front of us even exist?

"Is it a portal?" Anna asked. She tossed a stone as well, and even shot a spell through the film.

"Isn't this just a dungeon entrance then?" Jessica asked.

Several of us pulled out our maps and checked for any changes, and sure enough, there was something there. "The Hole." I read the name out loud. On the map, the name was posted above a simple black circle.

"Doesn't sound very inviting," Thomas said.

"Well, this is what we were looking for," I said. "Even before the gnolls took our choices away. We've stumbled upon our original objective. And it goes without saying, but I think we have to go inside."

Unless we somehow obtained the ability to climb up the side of the hole and out, our only option was to go into the dungeon. I had only been in one dungeon so far, and my experience that time was that we had been trapped inside and only could leave after defeating the boss. If that was the case here...we could be stuck for months or even years.

The more I thought of that, the less worried about it I actually felt. Retreating into a dungeon for several years might be a good thing, especially with the world changing as it was. There was potential for this to be safer inside than outside.

"Is anyone against going in?" I looked around and double checked. It was only now possible to see the faces of my party members with the—possibly illusionary—algae providing some light. There was a hint of hesitation on a few faces, not everyone seemed fully prepared to go. Jessica, of course, gave me a determined look. She was ready for the dungeon.

"There's nothing for us out here anyway. Why the hell not?" Glenn broke the silence and his words seemed to encourage the others.

"True enough," Anna agreed. She hadn't been with us in our original dungeon exploration. Neither were Richard, or Glenn, or Mark. This was a brand new and possibly frightening experience for them.

"Alan in first," I said. "Count to five after he enters and then go." This was just in case there were enemies and he needed time to pick up aggro before we arrived.

"See you on the other side," Alan said before dashing through. There was no hesitation on his face, just a thirst for battle.

Five seconds later, all of us pushed through the portal in front of us.

The situation I had expected to see was nothing like the reality in front of me. We weren't in a cave, nor was it dark and damp or moldy. Instead, we had appeared on a beautiful grassland.

The land ahead of me was luscious and green with grass and colorful flowers. The sun shined happily above me with vibrant intensity. A cool breeze washed over me, and the sound the racing wind made across the fields was heavenly. It didn't seem like we were in a dungeon at all.

"This looks a bit similar to where the Hole was, no?" Jessica asked. She had come out in high alert, instantly taking in everything around us. Nothing escaped her vision, and thank goodness for that.

"I think so," I answered, "the hill there is almost identical." I was even more certain than my words indicated, because the situation when we were being chased by gnolls was burned into my mind. We'd survived without any casualties, or even damage, but the heightened level of stress had fixed the details of that encounter into me. I'd be seeing dreams of it in the future for certain.

"Did it just spit us back out?" Lucas suggested. "Where are the gnolls then?"

"Could be…" Richard was on proceeding cautiously as we slowly made our way to the hill. "You said we have to defeat a dungeon boss to get out of here?"

"As far as I'm concerned, this place is paradise!" Maria had made it to the top of the hill and gazed into the distance. There was the forest behind us, and then green grass as far as the eye could see.

"It's hard to believe a place so beautiful could still exist in this hell," Thomas said.

"Let's be careful. This can't be the world we just came from." Jessica gave everyone a stern warning. Being the one in charge of detection had slowly morphed her into an almost motherly figure in the group. The downside was she never had a moment of reprieve. Constantly scanning for danger and being responsible for our group had to be taking a toll on her.

I approached her from the side and wrapped an arm around her, "Are you okay?" I asked.

I received a tender, but extremely rare smile. "I'm okay. You know we can't be careless."

"I know. I won't forget what happened to Maria." Our carelessness back then almost got her killed. The green fields looked harmless, but who knew what was lurking beneath. "Try to relax just a bit. We can set the pace here."

I turned my attention back to everyone else. "I know this place looks like paradise on earth, but we have to remain vigilant, so I'd like to lay down some ground rules." I paused and made sure I had everyone's attention.

"First of all: Never ever wander off alone. Under no circumstances is anyone to go anywhere without being in view of the
group. If you need to use the bathroom, find a partner." This rule
was almost humiliating, but the possibility of someone slipping
away randomly through their own mistake or being hunted by a
malicious entity was high. And if one of us did disappear, finding
them again in a world of this size might prove impossible.

"Second: if you discover something strange, or even THINK it's
strange, say something. The world can play with our minds. If
something doesn't seem right, speak up about it."

"Third: We are a single entity. We work as a group, and we do
everything as a group. That means, regardless of how you feel about
something, we all follow the group's decision. With that being said,
we will vote and discuss pertinent issues if they arise. That's all, any
questions?" I finished.

No one seemed put off by any of the rules. They were created to
ensure the group's survival, and keep every person in the party alive.
Perhaps because the others appreciated the spirit behind them, no
one complained. "Now that that's out of the way, we should talk
about how to get out of here."

# Chapter 8: What Kind of Dungeon Have we Found

*Where do we go from here?*

"It seems like there is no rush, but we shouldn't be complacent and we should think about what to do next," I said.

"I'm betting on gnolls being a part of this." Lucas said. "If we return through the forest, we'd probably come upon their city again."

"Can we like…not, though?" Maria asked. "It's so nice here and we aren't in a rush." She had a pleading expression. "Let's go explore that way." Her finger pointed towards the endless expanse of grassland and flowers.

Again, I studied the two directions we could go in: the beautiful grassland that seemed heavenly, or the dark and uninviting forest that no doubt held considerable danger.

"Maybe there's some treasure waiting to be discovered out there," Maria added to sweeten the pot for everyone.

There was no good argument for going into the forest, besides the possibility that if our main challenges were there, we would get out of the dungeon faster. The reality was though, there was no guarantee we were able to tackle what lurked there anyway. Also, staying here for a while might allow whatever turmoil was currently brewing outside to subside a bit. Maybe if enough time elapsed the gnolls who had been chasing us would return to their empire.

"I don't pick up any reason to prefer one way over the other," Jessica said.

No one seemed to be in a rush to leave, especially after our recent brush with death. Those fifteen minutes of running for our lives shaved a few years off all of us.

After enjoying the calm for a few more minutes, I said, "Lead the way, Maria!"

She rushed to the front with Jessica and the two talked as they walked. I returned to my position at the back and re-summoned my undead troops by using Temporary Grave before putting them away with Vast Shadows. I didn't need them right now, but they could be called in full at a moment's notice.

Strung out along the field, we had broken formation for the first time since we departed the apartment complex, but I didn't feel particularly worried about it. There was nothing in sight for miles, and with Jessica detecting even those enemies that might be beneath the ground, nothing could come close to us without her being able to warn us.

The forest edge was never far away, extending to the horizon, always there reminding us of the possibility of dangers within. We walked and walked and yet the scenery in front of us never changed. Endless blue skies, green grass and beautiful flowers for eternity. "Haven't we been here before?" Mark asked. He had been brooding silently, and wasn't distracted by the conversations of others. "This is familiar." He seemed to have noticed something no one else had.

Everyone paused and looked around carefully, "Wait, this is the hill," I said. "We're back where we started?"

"Unless the scenery just reuses itself and we truly are moving," Lucas pondered.

"Are we slowly moving in a circle?" Glenn asked.

"The forest edge looks as straight as can be," said Jessica, "so it can't be that."

"We can test it," Anna said. "Half stay, and half walk." Her suggestion was a good one. If some kind of teleport was putting us back here, the group that departed would pop back shortly after leaving.

"Let's move away from the forest edge first," I suggested. There were no guarantees that while we were divided some monster might burst out and attack us on a whim.

"I'll go, who else?" Jessica said. "Mike you should stay, your undead are worth several people. If I detect any problems, we'll come back immediately so there should be no danger." It was a good assessment and sound plan.

"Fair, who wants to go with Jess?" I asked. In the end, Thomas and Alan were her companions. Their group now had a tank and a healer, so a small skirmish shouldn't end up deadly if something happened. The rest of us moved a bit further away from the forest and then patiently waited for them to disappear over the horizon.

We watched them walk for about ten minutes before they went beyond a rise. Without an accurate way of keeping time it was impossible to tell exactly, but after what seemed like half an hour, Anna spotted them coming up from behind us. That pretty much confirmed the landscape was sending us for a loop.

"Seems like the forest is our only option," said Lucas.

I felt he was right. The dungeon itself was forcing this decision upon us. "Let's take the remainder of the day off, sleep well tonight, and we'll start exploring the forest in the morning?" I suggested.

There was no guarantee we'd have the opportunity for a proper sleep once in the forest. I was assuming it was safe enough here, but who knew where we actually were and what the dangers were?

No one complained about spending the night in this lovely place. Even the scents were refreshing and new compared to the staleness outside the dungeon that I'd become used to. The entire place smelled like fabric softener, and I couldn't get enough. Sleep didn't come easy that night for me, but unlike the previous dungeon there was at least a day and night cycle.

I was woken for my shift on guard duty by Jessica, first thing in the morning with the sunrise. Even the grass and flowers around us had a layer of dew upon it, nothing I could see was fake or artificial. It was miraculous to think all of this was created at the whim of some powerful being. A snap of their fingers could erase us, or give us paradise. A bittersweet thought. After enjoying the dawn for a couple of hours, in the company of Alan who was sharing the shift with me, it was time to wake everyone. We breakfasted on rations and got ourselves ready to explore the forest.

"Formation from here out," I said as we set off, noticing that Maria was chatting to Jessica at the front.

"Fiiine," Maria moped before taking her place at the back again. I summoned my undead squad and followed the group into the forest. The mellow sun above disappeared from sight and the temperature dropped several degrees. We were on high alert, and any needless chatter disappeared.

The area we entered was silent. Not a single branch creaked or swayed, as if there wasn't the slightest breath of life in this land. "I'll retrace the way we ran," Alan whispered. He led us in the direction we originally fled from, which would take us to the east side of the gnoll empire.

"If there are gnolls here, they might be elites," Lucas warned everyone. I understood why he said that. From our previous experience, dungeon monsters were a step up compared to their worldly counter-parts.

The forest around us was starting to look familiar and if it was a copy of the outside world, then the first gnoll patrols would be coming soon. My body tensed in anticipation.

We traveled close enough to where the city was to be in range any patrols, and yet we found none. By the time we reached our hunting grounds to the east of the city we still hadn't seen any monsters. A feeling of déjà vu struck me, and I became even more alert. "Careful of an ambush," I said.

Everyone tucked in even tighter. We were nearly shoulder to shoulder as we moved, eyes scanning every direction. We walked slowly with Jessica constantly scanning our surroundings. The ambush I feared never came.

Instead, we breached the forest edge and entered into a muddy and murky land. A civilization was there, but it wasn't a gnoll empire. It was a majestic city, like something out of medieval fantasy. The walls were pure cobblestone. Towering structures of impressive construction dotted the distance.

The walls were dozens of feet high, and below them were fortifications: pits dug deep enough to swallow a man, and wooden stakes just behind them, for anything able to cross that gap and reach the city walls.

There were watch towers at every corner, and most surprising of all were the people. There were humans garrisoning this section of the wall. Even crazier was the caravan of goods venturing through the front gate.

"Are those merchants?" Alan asked.

"It looks like it," I said. "Assume they are human and not enemies for now." My mind was telling me they were NPCs, but without knowing for sure it was best to not make any move that might trigger a hostile response.

"A civilization? I can get a shower?" Anna seemed the most jubilant of us, jumping to a conclusion that I wasn't so sure about.

Richard couldn't help but sniff under his armpit, "I think we all could use one." Which got a light laugh out of a few of us. The situation in front of us was daunting and unknown, but at least it was a city of people and not gnolls.

"Let's go around to the front," Jessica suggested and I agreed. Walking up to the wall would come off as suspicious, and the guards above wielded longbows as big as a man. An arrow from one of those could be lethal, and I was sure saying 'whoops sorry I got lost and nearly breached the side of your fortress on accident' wouldn't be enough to get out of the resulting trouble. I put my undead troops away too, to avoid any trouble.

We moved across the muddy and murky ground. Pits bigger than bathtubs gave us trouble every few feet. "Careful," Alan warned before gesturing below. Half a rusted sword poked through the mud, and anyone unlucky enough to fall on it would be in for some serious trouble.

"It looks like a battlefield," Lucas observed. There were pieces of half broken armor, shields, swords barely breaking the surface. Some of the craters in the ground were pitch black, evidence that something of extreme heat had burned in them and scarred the earth.

"That would explain the lack of grass," Maria said, perhaps it was stating the obvious, but she liked to have something to say. "I just hope we can get into that city."

That slowly became my own fear. Merchant carts were lined up in the distance in front of us, hardly moving beneath the city gate. A dozen or more guards in silver armor with long spears moved carefully through the front caravan lifting tarps and opening hemp bags and wooden crates.

"This one's good." One of the guards patted the ass of a horse. "Move along." Which got the entire cart moving through the gates.

"They're careful," I noticed. I watched to see if anyone slipped by, or even got through without inspection, but every cart without fail was thoroughly inspected. Three guards would clear a merchant at a time before ensuring him and only his goods made it through the gate.

"They're charging a fee for entry," Jessica said as we walked towards the line of carts. Her vision was the best, and while I could see the wider picture, the minute details of gold exchanging hands was not something anyone else would have been able to pick out.

It took us ten minutes of walking through this pock-marked land to read the back of the queue, and it became obvious why the guards were so careful. Battle had been recent in this area. The rusted swords and equipment were obviously older, but fires from whatever had happened recently still smoldered below the walls.

# Chapter 9: Entering a City of the Rigar Empire

There were no corpses on the landscape around us, but I did see the bones of animals occasionally, and oddly shaped skulls.

While I was studying the ground around the city walls, Lucas had been watching the merchants. "They are using coins to get in and the merchants have small bags of coins."

"We have no money, so we are going to have to talk our way past the guards," I said. So far, silver and copper and gold pieces hadn't dropped yet, but I could see Lucas was right: these merchants were clearly exchanging them as currency. Perhaps coinage was a feature of this pocket dungeon? On the other hand, the world was constantly changing outside and coins might have been introduced somewhere. As far as I was concerned, it felt like we were in a form of beta test.

We patiently waited at the back of the queue. Ahead of us were individuals on foot and horse as well the carts full of goods, but the caravans of the merchants were the majority. I could see they had hired guards, which probably meant monsters lurked in these forests, we just hadn't encountered them.

"BACK TO YOUR PLACE." I heard a guard start arguing with someone at the front.

"Please, it was a misunderstanding." The man who was being yelled at was pleading. No matter what he said though, his words fell on deaf ears. Arguing even seemed to get him into more trouble. "Is there nothing that can be done?"

"TO THE BACK WITH YOU THEN." And then several guards surrounded him before physically forcing the man away. He was pushed down the queue until he ended up behind us, clearly angry and dejected. It seemed the guards weren't to be messed with, and causing any disturbance was a definite no.

"Are you okay?" I scooted a bit back and tried to strike up a conversation with the man. His black hair was shoulder length and a bit greasy. The clothes he wore were low quality, definitely on the side of lower class. "They didn't need to be so rough," I tried to sound sympathetic.

"Tssk." He clicked his tongue. "You're right, they didn't. I just wanted to get in to see my wife and daughter as soon as possible."

"I'm Mike," I said while reaching out a hand.

"Rhood." He had a firm grip and callouses covered his hands. Paired with his shoddy appearance, he was definitely a part of the lower rung of society. He worked hard for a living, doing physical labor no doubt. I'd been there too, and this gave me a bit more confidence in my approach.

"This is gonna sound really crazy, but we aren't from around here. Is there any chance you can give us some advice?" Sometimes, it was best to be straight up. I couldn't even think of a story that might get us information without revealing we were strangers.

What was the country we were in called? The name of the city? I had nothing to construct a lie out of, so I just went with the direct approach and hoped for the best.

Rhood looked at me appraisingly, and seemed to have a question on the tip of his tongue. He held it back though. "Must have come from afar," he said instead. "Welcome to the Rigar Empire." There was a tone of awe and reverence in his voice.

I couldn't help but follow his gaze towards the flags over the gatehouse before my eyes came to rest on the guards, "Are they always this strict?"

"Usually no, but there was a battle just recently. Security always goes up right after. Neighboring empires try to sneak in spies; smugglers try to sneak in goods; the guards get shouted at and they take it out on us; you know the drill."

He had mentioned spies so deliberately that I felt a bead of sweat run down the back of my neck. "We aren't spies." I assured him, whatever good that would do. "We're just a wandering group of mercenaries." I looked over my group. "We go where the battles are."

Some of the suspicion in his expression eased up. "They are recruiting for their corps. Might be some glory to be had there," he paused, "but also just as likely to be death."

I let out a breath of relief, "Openly recruiting?" I asked.

"Right," he said. "Even then, there ain't no reward for reporting spies. I don't care whether you are or not. Just listen to what they say when they talk to you, and don't say nothing else." We were slowly approaching our turn to be inspected. "You don't know me," Rhood added and then scooted back about ten feet, clearly distancing himself from us.

I moved a few feet back to the group, "I'll do the talking." It was best one person took the role of leader in the group. If everyone started yapping we might find ourselves in trouble. "We are mercenaries," I told everyone.

The only issue now was our backstory, but I prayed the guards would be lenient enough in their prodding for us to slip through. By the time it was our turn, my back was drenched in a layer of sweat. The dungeon surely wants us to enter the city.

"State your business." A single guard approached us. Through the gap in his helmet I could see a deep scar that ran across his face. His eyes were apathetic, and I knew instantly that no sob story would gain his favor.

"Hello, we're a traveling mercenary group looking for work," I said. "We've heard of the recent battles and were hoping to be hired to help your defenses."

"All of you?" he asked suspiciously. I noticed his eyes wandered to the women in the group. I couldn't be sure if special powers or spells even existed in this dungeon world.

"All of us," I said firmly. Everyone behind me played their part and stood ramrod straight, and when I looked over the group, I couldn't see the slightest hint of nervousness on their faces. We looked so natural that it was hard to find fault in our demeanor. A battle-hardened group of mercenaries through and through.

"Give me a moment." He turned and walked back towards the gate.

"If things go south, run," I said to everyone. There was no reading the expression on the guard's face. They could come back to welcome us with open arms, or archers could perch upon the walls and litter us with arrows. The only assurance I had right now was my sixth sense, which typically would be screaming for me to run if things were going south.

The guard stopped at a towering wooden door and gathered two or three other guards with him. They talked without much haste, and the two he was addressing didn't run off, which instantly took the weight off my shoulders. The three of them turned and walked in our direction.

"Come to the side." The guard beckoned us out of line. "These two will record your details and if they are satisfied, they'll escort you to the barracks."

"Understood." I didn't ask any questions on account of Rhood's advice. I looked at everyone and gave a nod before leading the group over to the two guards. Sixth sense was calm; things were okay.

An older guard walked around the group, looking carefully at our gear. His younger companion had a parchment in his hand. The older one spoke at last, "We're going to need your name and your specialization; any other spells you may be able to use can be recorded as well. Your usefulness determines your salary, so keep that in mind before trying to hide your cards." He didn't wait for any questions and simply pointed at Lucas. "You go first."

One by one we gave him the most basic information for ourselves, with the younger guard writing on his scroll with a quill that he dipped into an ink bottle on a table beside him. The older guard's introduction cleared up one thing: there were spells in this dungeon world. Our classes wouldn't out us, and could potentially gain us favor.

There didn't seem to be any particular order in which we were called to account for our classes and skills, and it seemed like they were purposely making the process a slow one to shake our nerves. Would a group of spies give themselves away in this situation? It would be hard to act natural while the young guard took his time writing and the older one stared at you with unwavering eyes. When my turn came, I gave a basic description of myself: that I was a summoner and could spawn undead allies.

Everyone did the same, describing their battle specialty—either ranged, support, or melee—and something about how their class functioned. It seemed spell users were not common, and I caught the two guards exchanging glances more than once. They were warming up to us.

By the time the process was done, the manners of the guards were no longer severe, but had softened, "Alright," said the older one, "you'll be escorted to the barracks where you'll be tested to prove what you've just said. After which, you'll receive some basic briefing about the duties and responsibilities of being mercenaries in the cause of Rigar Empire. Normally, mercenaries are confined to barracks for two weeks, but you probably heard that people with special abilities like yours get privileges. After your briefing you'll be allowed to spend time in the city. Just mind that you are back before moonrise and accounted for in the morning. That's the rule for everyone."

We moved through busy streets with two new guards as escort, which got quite the stares from locals. The area we were in was bustling with activity. Vendors lined the streets selling all sorts of wares: weapons, armors, jewelry and collectibles. Food like bread and vegetables, even cattle tied to posts, weren't an uncommon sighting.

It was a marvelous feeling, being around people. Whether they were NPC or human didn't matter in the moment. There was a budding comradery growing in all of us: this was what the world could look like in the coming years if we could manage to take back a bit of power for ourselves.

The wonders disappeared just as fast as they came. Only three streets over and in a little under five minutes of walking was a compound. It connected to the south eastern wall and had entrances to the guard towers in that area. Training dummies lined the walls with racks of weapons hanging nearby.

One-handed axes and swords, long swords and two-handed swords, battle axes and maces and morning stars, daggers and scimitars—there was no end to the assortment of weaponry waiting to be grasped and used to kill.

The barracks wasn't busy by any means, with only a few soldiers wandering around the compound, seemingly randomly and without purpose. The reason for that came shortly after Jessica asked a question about it.

A grinning guard said, "After a battle we all got a few days of freedom. All who fought." The local bars and brothels were probably packed to the brim right now.

# Chapter 10: Frustration is a City Full of Magic Items for Sale and an Empty Purse

We moved through halls without conversation until coming upon a steel door, the only one we had seen in the barracks thus far, "Be respectful," the guard with us warned before using the door knock.

"Come in," a deep and tired voice welcomed us inside. The room was spacious, an office of sorts no doubt. While the rest of the barracks had been plain, this room was full of life. There were two paintings upon the walls, both portraits of stoic men who held a striking resemblance to the man seated in front of us. The head of a buck of considerable size was mounted on the left wall, there was even a potted plant in the window.

"This is General Rhugar," our escort said, "he's in charge of the south east walls and a force of five-hundred men." The general was burly and intimidating. His entire body was covered in armor, as if he just came out of battle. Only his hardened face and head of dark, greasy hair was visible. His eyes lifted and met mine, they showed no emotion, only indifference.

Our guard walked over with a parchment and handed it to Rhugar before standing to the side, head tilted down and hands behind his back at perfect attention. There was silence as Rhugar studied the parchment and glanced over each of us.

70

"Seems we've gotten quite the catch this time," he looked to the guard, "you did good today Donivan, you'll be well compensated."

"Sir! For the empire! Sir!" Donivan responded without showing the slightest bit of emotion on his face. There was definitely pleasure in his eyes, though.

"Spellcasters and magic users are quite uncommon, and for a group such as yourselves to show up on a whim is suspicious in and of itself," Rhugar began. A bead of sweat dripped down the nape of my neck and ran cold down my back, my Sixth Sense wasn't picking up anything, but I was still on high alert. "With that being said, your assistance could be extremely valuable."

"How can we be of help?" I spoke up, glad to hear that my tone sounded neither servile or overbearing.

"Lately, gnoll invasions have been coming here more frequently. We need all the mercenaries we can hire and normally we distribute them throughout the army. But seeing as how you've come as a group, I presume you fight best together?"

There was a bit of a hidden threat to his comment. Splitting us up was well within his power, and would definitely hinder any nefarious plans we potentially could have if we were spies. "We fight best together," I said firmly, "but we will follow your arrangements."

He didn't seem to think too hard about the decision, "Good. You'll stay in a group together, for now you'll be your own squad. Donivan will lead you to your rooms so you can get situated. ID cards should be available for you by tomorrow. Your freedom won't be limited, but you must always be in the barracks by moonrise."

"Is there a curfew in place?" Jessica asked.

"There is, and will be for the foreseeable future," Rhugar said, "The times are tumultuous; crime goes up rapidly after these battles and to ensure there are no riots, curfew is enforced. Only shadow guards are allowed to roam freely at night." He looked at each of us, with a calculating expression as if gauging our interest in the role of shadow guard.

"We have no interest in being night watchmen," I assured him.

"That's a shame." His gaze settled on Jessica, probably because her tracking ability would prove invaluable for detecting those sneaking around in the night. "Meal time is in an hour, and there is breakfast at eight-thirty in the morning. If you hear an alarm while out and about, return immediately. Dismissed!" He waved his hand.

We followed behind Donivan, who was no doubt in a jubilant mood. It seemed his reward for recruiting such a powerful force wouldn't be small. "It turned out to be the gnolls," said Alan.

"It's always the gnolls," Anna joked.

Donivan didn't say a single word the entire walk back out of the garrison. Instead, his hands flickered in front of him as if moving invisible abacuses or counting handfuls of coins.

The barracks were lined with bunk beds and when I took mine, Jessica threw her gear on the one below me. Having clarified we were free to go into the city, subject to emergency recall and the requirement to get back by curfew, we didn't hang around the minimal facilities of the barracks. We got envious looks from some of the soldiers present in the room, as those without special abilities were stuck in the barracks for a beginning period of at least two weeks. We had been given a lot of freedom on account of our special classes.

"We should assume we are being watched," Lucas warned once we were clear of the gates of the barracks. 'They might be giving us freedom in the hope that if we were spies we might slip up and be exposed.'

"Let's just enjoy the next few days," I said to everyone. As far as I was aware, there was no time limit on this dungeon. Not only that, the potential for the dungeon to bring the danger to us after a certain time here was also true. We might just be along for the ride; no one could know for certain.

"I'll go to the seedier areas of the city to gather information," Glenn said. Richard, Mark and Lucas decided to join him and they set off towards the east, where the houses we'd passed had been smaller and more crowded together than they were in the vicinity of the barracks.

The rest of us headed back to the main street. I was extremely curious what this dungeon world had to offer by way of magic items and gear.

I felt like a kid in a candy shop as we got closer to the bustling main road. More and more side stalls lined the streets as we walked. Some merchandise was set out on rugs or sold out of a wagon, some of the buildings even had huge fold outs or wide window sills lined with wares.

"Isn't that an equipable neck slot item?" Maria asked while looking at a particularly shiny necklace. It was pure silver, and definitely caught the eye on a day like this one. There was also a single ruby sticking out of a bell cap that also drew the eyes. It felt out of place on such a plain looking rug.

"Have a look if you want," the shopkeeper said, she was an old woman who seemed to me to be nearing the end of her life. It was hard to even tell if her eyes were open and looking at us under the brim of her cap.

Maria looked back at Jessica and I, as if to ask, 'Can I? Jessica gave a nod and urged her to do so, I was curious as well. Was it an ornament, or did it actually give stats? Maria took the necklace into her hands. "It's magical and equipable," she said excitedly.

"How much is this necklace?" I asked. Accessories in particular were incredibly rare, at least they had been up to now.

"One gold," the shopkeeper responded.

We didn't have any gold at all. Not a single piece of copper or silver, either. "Would you take any trades?" I asked. There was surely something among our spoils we could potentially trade for this item.

"Unfortunately, I can't do that young man. I can only pay for my medicine in gold." If she had made any other objection to trading I'd have pushed the issue and tried to barter, but since this was a matter of her health, I realized we'd have to leave it until we'd obtained a gold coin.

"Alright, thanks for your time," I said before leading everyone away. "There will be more opportunities," I said to Maria who seemed the most dejected.

"The stats were really very good…plus five on Int and Dex."

I was actually glad I hadn't taken the opportunity to look. Maybe I'd have been as dejected as her if I had to hand back a useful item like that for want of one coin.

"We just have to make some gold," Alan said. "We get a salary for being mercenaries at least." He tried to comfort Maria.

"Agreed." I was also happy that there was finally a currency. The post-apocalypse world seemed to be developing into something more similar to that of actual games.

"There was even an active ability…" Maria turned her face away to hide a sob. It seemed the necklace was exceptionally special. As we continued along the main street, it was clear the opportunity to get good items to fill our empty slots didn't just stop at the necklace, there were innumerable equipable items available from the stalls lining the streets. Something for literally everyone, and a good portion of them had unique active abilities or buffs.

I had agreed with Alan that we needed to make some currency—not entirely serious about it being our priority. But now? I eagerly wanted to get hold of a large quantity of coins. The gear here was no worse than the secret shop we'd previously accessed. There weren't any consumables for purchase, but the gear was several steps above what we were currently wearing, and the quantity…There was enough gear available for purchase to supply a small army.

We hadn't made it very far when Jessica stopped us, "If we want to eat tonight, we have to head back soon." She was right. Dinner time was coming upon us, and night meant the arrival of the curfew as well. "We'll have more time in the morning, and we need to meet up with the others again. Maybe they've found out something interesting."

Of all the group, only Jessica seemed unmoved by the tantalizing presence of items that would make a great difference to our strength and ability to survive. Even I felt a bit dejected at having to walk past so many gear upgrades. We hadn't explored more than five percent of what this city had to offer us, and had found so many potential upgrades.

"There's probably somewhere that sells skill books and potions and stuff, yeah?" Maria was glowing like a flower in sunshine.

"Hopefully," Anna said.

The walk back to the barracks took one tenth the time as our outward journey as we didn't stop and browse any wares. The dead street of earlier was now bustling with soldiers also making their way back to the garrison for dinner.

The pitiful amount of people in the large dining hall was surprising, though. It seemed the previous attack did quite the damage to their numbers.

# Chapter 11: Reputation, Professions, and Gear Upgrades

The reason for the ease of our recruitment to the city's forces became clear after ten or fifteen minutes in the dining hall. Soldiers stopped arriving, yet the slop hall was nearly half empty. Some may have eaten while out, but the overall mood wasn't great. The number of soldiers was pitiful. This room could surely hold the five hundred soldiers Rhugar was supposed to command—there weren't even a hundred.

There was no jubilant atmosphere over a successful battle recently won, or an excitement at surviving to enjoy life—it was downcast. Empty seats where friends once sat were evident throughout the hall. The soldiers sometimes looked around at their still living comrades, and I could see their gaze pause on empty places that would have been filled just nights ago. Agony.

This is real war...This wasn't the fantasized and glorified TV version that I'd been shown in the past. There was nothing glorious about what I was feeling inside right now. The grim atmosphere etched itself deep into my heart. Death was the only certainty that came along with war. I carved that inside my heart and knew I wouldn't forget it.

None of us spoke much over dinner, which was a meaty stew served with a small loaf of bread and some butter. I ate out of habit.

Something to fill my mouth with so I didn't feel the urge to talk. It felt like nothing when it went down. Sorrowful and slightly bland, enough of it to fill a belly for the day, just not mine.

"Let's talk later, before bed," I said to everyone. I didn't have any urge to speak about our future plans right now, not here in earshot of these disheartened soldiers. Our rooms were all next to each other at the end of the hall so it wouldn't be inconvenient to meet up and then sleep after.

"I want a bath." Mark looked up. "There's a bathhouse," he reminded everyone.

"Is there one for ladies?" Maria asked. Heads turned and I took a look around the room. Not a single woman sat in the hall besides the three at our table. She didn't wait for an answer and simply started grumbling under her breath. The mood in the hall was like a dark miasma bringing down everyone.

"We can go a bit later tonight, together," Jessica said. "After Glen and Lucas give us a rundown of what information they found. We need to tell you about the gear that's on sale in this city. As long as we survive we can come away with some serious upgrades."

She was right but making money to buy the gear was the issue, and I hoped Lucas had found something while gathering information that would help us do so.

We left the hall in ones and twos, to not draw too much attention to ourselves. Not that it mattered, but leaving early as a group somehow felt a bit disrespectful. We gathered at the end of the hallway to our rooms.

"We need gold. ASAP," Maria blurted out before anyone else could pitch in. As if she had photographic memory, she listed off every item she had seen that she wanted, making sure to emphasize the amazing stats and abilities they had.

Everyone was wide-eyed by the time she finished. "Okay...we need gold," Lucas agreed flatly. "For our part , we found out some decent information." I focused on him, as his news might be essential to our survival and successful completion of the dungeon.

"Gnoll attacks started about six months ago and have been ramping up ever since. There's a nearby gnoll empire that's been expanding and pressuring the surrounding kingdoms. They're so numerous that even a city of this size has been struggling to fend them off.

"They reproduce very quickly, and they mature into fighters capable of killing a man in only a few years. They're naturally gifted at moving through forests and dense foliage, and they can even have magical powers."

"Are all the kingdoms working together to fight the threat?" Alan asked.

"Good question. Unfortunately, I don't know the answer to that but as far as I'm aware, the surrounding kingdoms aren't on good terms. It's likely they would rather sit and do nothing in the hopes that each other are destroyed, and that the resulting territory that opens up is enough to satiate a gnoll expansion."

"Rolling the dice on their survival?" I asked. "Sounds like something greed would cause idiots to do."

"Right," Lucas agreed. "Although it might be that there are limits to the size of this dungeon and really there is only this city and gnolls, the rest being spoken about but not affecting our main challenge. My understanding is this dungeon is fully functional as a game world. We encountered more than one person that offered us quests in exchange for goods. Leveling, collecting items, obtaining skills—all of it should be possible here."

"So, treat it no different than our own world," Thomas said.

"Are the people here NPCs or human?" Jessica asked.

"That...I don't think it's possible to know, but at the very least our interest coincides, so we aren't enemies."

"For now." I warned everyone. We had no idea what the city rulers wanted us to accomplish. Until we understood that, our group had to look out for ourselves first and foremost. "What about the quests? What kind of quests are they?"

"Mostly gathering materials, helping with manual labor, those types of things."

"Anything about battling monsters?" I asked.

"Mostly involving gnolls, which only appear during their invasion periods."

"So we wait, then," I said. "Shall we go looking for quests tomorrow?" I asked everyone.

"Let's do that," Jessica agreed. "We can explore and gather more intel while forwarding our progress." We could never stop improving.

The girls went to their rooms while the men headed to the bathhouse. I was glad they didn't get to see the chaos there. As might have been expected for a time after dinner and just before bed, it was packed.

There wasn't a spot for us in the whole room. We waited outside for over ten minutes half nude, and we were too committed now to go back. Eventually a little corner opened up that we flocked to and claimed as our own.

The washroom was primitive, to say the least. We sat on stools while the majority of bathing pools were taken. Some type of cloth that fluffed like cotton rested on wooden counter tops around the room were our washrags. Richard walked without fear around the room, filling up three full buckets of lukewarm water for us.

It wasn't hygienic at all by modern day standards, but this would get the grime off. Better than nothing. For once, we didn't talk strategy or future plans. The women weren't here, and anything we discussed would need to be conveyed a second time anyway. "How's it going between you and Maria?" Thomas suddenly asked Alan.

I was surprised by the question. Alan and Maria weren't exactly a secret, but it wasn't exactly talked about. Alan looked like a deer caught in headlights, "How? You? ..."

"It isn't hard to tell she's interested." Mark laughed. Even though he was a newer member of the group, he'd picked up on it in just a day or two of traveling. Maria was sarcastic and fiery, but when it came to Alan she took it up a notch. He also took the beatings quite well.

"Don't know, to be honest," Alan shrugged. "I can never tell when she's just joking or actually mad. Sometimes she's mad and I don't even know what I did."

Richard couldn't help but start cracking up laughing. Alan was young, to be fair. "Her type is just like that," Richard said. "My best advice, don't take it to heart. It's as likely that you did nothing wrong as that you did. You'll never know."

"Then what do I do?" Alan asked.

"Don't read into it," he said. "Let the criticism roll off you like water off a duck's back."

"Right," Glenn said. "You can either take the heat, or you can't."

Alan looked around, a bit confused. I kept my mouth shut, as my relationship with Jessica was very different and I didn't want to talk about it. It would feel disloyal to her.

"Just don't overreact to her provocations," Lucas said, "if you think she's mad, but don't know, be calm. If she's mad, she'll let you know about it soon, and if she isn't, well forget about the situation and keep going."

The same message was coming across. Maria was fiery whether mad, sarcastic, or sad. Alan just needed to be there for her with a calm and unyielding demeanor until she made her deeper feelings clear.

"That's probably why you guys are fighting so much," Lucas added. "She's just being herself, and you're reading into it and reacting in a negative way."

A smile formed on Alan's face as he listened. Perhaps he thought that what Lucas had said was pretty much spot on. It was though dozens of situations where the two had bickered and argued were passing through his head as he tried to confirm if there was truth in what he was being told.

We washed while chatting about nothing at all. Nothing of any real importance.

"Alright, which one of you is scrubbing my back," Richard suddenly said. He turned around on the stool. I don't know what I was expecting, but my God was it hairy. It was like a carpet had grown on his back.

"I think I'm all washed up and ready to go," I said. Almost everyone agreed with my sentiment and stood up, leaving Richard to it. We all headed back to our rooms separately.

I made a stop on the way back at Jessica's room. "There were maybe a dozen or so people left in the bathhouse when we left," I told her. "Maybe within the hour it will be clear."

She was still fully dressed in her day attire, probably thinking there was no point in changing while still sweaty. "I'll chase the remainder out if need be." There was a devilish smile on her face as she approached me for a hug.

"Make sure to chase them far away," I said before giving her a kiss. "We'll probably have long days for the next while, so don't stay up too late."

She walked with me back to my room while gathering the girls to bathe. "I'll join you after I'm clean," she said when I got to my room.

I slept in the next morning, just enough to miss breakfast. I was hungry, but regular meals no longer did anything for me. It was such an unsettling thing, but I needed to be killing monsters to survive. If…one day monsters didn't exist, would I need to turn to humans?

The thought passed quickly, or rather I pushed it out of my head by thinking about equipment. Today would be a group exercise in quest and information gathering. That was exciting in and of itself.

I truly felt like I was in a game inside this dungeon. It was different to the real world in some way, even though death was permanent in both. It felt more like there was a script to follow.

We met as a group just outside the training courtyard and I was the last to arrive.

"Took you long enough, sleepy head," Richard said in a cute voice, which got a laugh out of almost everyone.

I scratched my head in embarrassment. "I hope you didn't wait long, sorry."

"Just a few minutes," Lucas said seriously. "Let's go then?" He motioned to everyone and we took to the streets and deeper into Rigar.

"Are these the items?" Mark asked as we made it down the street. He picked up a pair of boots off a stall, then passed them to me.

**Green Boots: An exceptionally crafted pair of leather boots. Their nature essence makes them the color of grass.**

**AGI + 5, STR +2**

**Grants the user Growth.**

**Growth: You feel one with nature. Grass grows with your every step granting +2 HP regeneration per five seconds.**

I read out the description of the skill.

"Regeneration like this actually exists?" Glenn seemed the most excited. He and Mark were the least familiar with equipment. The stats and effect were amazing, but not surprising to me. I had seen plenty of equipment yesterday with similar or even better effects.

The boots were only 75 silver, which didn't seem like much. "Is that a leatherworking shop?" Alan asked.

"I think so." Lucas said while heading inside. He was somewhat of an assassin type, so leather was his preferred base type. Jessica and Maria shared that with him. They followed him inside while the rest of us browsed the street around us, taking in all the sights.

The three returned just five minutes later, "We can learn crafting professions here," Lucas said with excitement I'd never seen from him before.

"You can create leather gear?" I asked.

"Potentially, but the apprenticeship is one gold." It seemed every opportunity presented to us required gold or silver or copper.

"Guys," Richard said, "I just told that shopkeeper she was beautiful, and I got something called Reputation." Our eyes turned to see a blonde-haired barbie with a lithe figure selling bread.

Things were becoming interesting. "We need gold," I said seriously. "We should put our full attention towards that." This entire dungeon was a miraculous opportunity for us. This was an opportunity to put us well ahead of the curve for our return to the post-apocalypse world outside the pocket dungeon.

"We can take individual quests for coin rewards, which require luck to find," Lucas explained, "or we can head to the mercenaries' guild and take quests from there."

# Chapter 12: Where are the Worthwhile Quests?

"Let's just go to where we know there are quests for us," I proposed. There was no point walking around randomly if we could start picking up quests immediately.

As we moved on through the city, the number of stalls we saw quickly decreased and were replaced with well-established shops. Not all had to do with leveling goods or even game-world type items. It felt like we were walking through a mall.

Food stores, clothing stores, jewelers, even just miscellaneous pubs and places of 'entertainment' were abundant. Any temptation I had to visit them were trumped by Maria's constant commentary about the need to earn some coins. "I can't wait to buy that necklace," she would say, or, "those earrings in that window would look so good on you Anna." I was definitely seeing a more girly and feminine side of her.

We walked for at least thirty minutes before Lucas pointed to a line of a dozen people outside a large building that reminded me of a town hall and which had a sign outside: 'Mercenaries Wanted: Missions for all Levels.'

"We were told there were quests available in here, but we didn't go in," said Lucas.

"Let's go see, even if we have to wait," proposed Jessica. In fact, the line of entry moved quickly enough that we crossed through the doorway in under ten minutes. Ahead of us was a counter with two clerks, who were making a note of the levels and classes of applicants. The entire process was quite informal. We weren't asked any awkward questions, our clerk simply pushed over a parchment with a few questions about our abilities and after Jessica had filled it out, the clerk gave it a cursory glance and told us return in a few hours.

The wait was frustrating. I could see beyond the registration desk was a room with noticeboards and I could almost make out the missions that were being advertised. But we were forced to go back out to the streets. We browsed the shops for only an hour before returning, hoping the fact that the missions building wasn't busy would mean we could get permission to browse the quests sooner than later.

There wasn't even a line when we returned and we walked directly up to the front desk. Right away, I got a nod from our clerk that pointed in a direction off to the side. There was a stack of certificates there, made out in our name with the seal of the Rigarn empire, as well as a card that accompanied each one: identification cards.

It went without saying we were at the very lowest rung of the ladder in terms of reputation. Still, these cards allowed us past two guards and out of the lobby and into the quest hall where we could read the quests that had been posted. "Let's spread out and read them all," Maria urged us, "and call out any good ones."

I was excited for what we would find, this could be the right way to go about earning coins.

"Ugh. Help me birth my newest calf—two silver," Anna read a mission with a shake of her head.

"Part-time chef wanted—five silver per week," Mark read off another.

We continued to read them and realized there was almost nothing anyone was qualified to do, or would even want to do. There was a few that just about anyone could do—carrying heavy goods or clearing up trash.

"This is pretty disappointing," Jessica said as she scanned a board.

"Excuse me," Maria went back out to the reception desk, "is this right? There is some mistake right? Where are the good missions that reward gold?"

The clerk looked at her in utter confusion and seemed to have no idea what to say in response. "Sorry, I don't deal with putting up missions," he eventually said. "If these quests aren't to your liking, you can acquire them from private citizens as well. While less strict on their recruitment, you can still receive reputation credit for them." Without waiting for a response, the clerk stood up and disappeared in a backroom, clearly hoping to avoid dealing with us.

"Maybe it's always this slow after a battle?" Lucas suggested.

"Does anyone want to help birth a calf?" I jokingly asked. It didn't seem like any of the missions available for us as first timers was going to be lucrative enough to sway us. A few silver wasn't a lot: surely we could make more putting our fighting skills to use.

We left the hall with heavy heads. Disappointment was evident across everyone's faces. Getting the money we wanted clearly wasn't going to be as easy as we had expected.

"We need a new plan," I said to everyone. "Any suggestions?" I left it open ended, mainly because I had put all my eggs into one basket, having fully expecting the hall to provide us with the income we desperately needed.

"Find someone who needs help," Alan said.

Which nearly got Maria to smack him upside the head. "Clearly...But how do we do that?" she asked instead.

"I...dunno," Alan admitted.

"Our best bet might just be asking the general," Richard said. "I'm sure he has connections to people interested in receiving escorts or protection."

"That's a good idea," Jessica replied, "that would be right up our alley, using our fighting power to make money."

"Any thought about getting a regular paid job?" Anna asked.

Which got unanimous opposition from everyone. No one wanted to spend their time working if we were in a race of some sort to level up and master the post-apocalypse system.

"Someone is following us," Jessica suddenly said, "act natural." I felt no urge to look around, with her tracking abilities I had complete confidence she was right. "Follow me," she moved to the front and abruptly rushed us down a street alley. We turned a sharp corner at the end of it and there she held up her hand. "Let's wait and confront them," she whispered.

Not even fifteen seconds passed after we had stopped, waiting quietly, when someone turned the corner. "Oh...excuse me," a thin man in cheap robes looked surprised. "Just trying to pass through." Jessica walked past him swiftly and turned to trap him from the far side. "What're you doing? What's the meaning of this?" His voice was calm no more, turning to panic.

"You've been following us for three blocks," Jessica stated, "care to explain why?"

"I don't know what you're talking about..."

"No one would notice your disappearance here," I said while summoning my undead soldiers. They immediately filled the alley and left no gap for him to run through. Nor for peering eyes to see inside the huddle. "Spill it."

The man showed a hint of dread and then excitement filled his eyes. "Ah, I wasn't expecting to be seen through so easily." He wiped his brow, probably a habit to help calm himself down. He inhaled deeply, "I'm looking for some able bodies to complete a mission."

This sounded promising. I wanted to maintain our intimidating approach, but Maria's enthusiastic response betrayed my efforts, "You have a quest?" She pushed through the skeletons towards the man. "Tell us!"

The man cleared his throat. "I do have a mission, but don't know if you're qualified." He looked over his shoulder at Jessica, and after seeing the arrow gripped between her fingers, weighed his words carefully. "My master is in need of some goods that aren't easy to come by."

"We aren't interested stealing or robbing," said Lucas and I nodded. Regardless of the value of the offer, we had to stay in good standing with the city authorities or this pocket dungeon was over for us.

"You don't have to steal anything," he added quickly. "What we need are bodies. Specifically, the bodies of gnoll shamans."

"Gnoll shamans?" Lucas asked. "What use do you have for them?"

"I can't say that as I don't know for certain," the man replied. "I would assume its for research, though. That's all I can tell you."

"What are the specifics of this mission?" I asked.

"One gold per body," he said, "it needs to be intact enough to be studied. You can't blow it up or damage the head. Even better if its captured alive."

"How do you suppose we do that?" Jessica asked, albeit sarcastically.

The evident comfort the man had been feeling while steering the conversation disappeared in a flash and a bit of nervousness came back, "I don't know, I only deliver the message. You guys can fight, that's for you to figure out."

"If we capture a shaman alive, how much?" I asked.

"Three gold."

"Seems terribly low," Lucas said, "if it was alive, then clearly we would have to smuggle said gnoll into the city, which no doubt comes with a hefty punishment." He made a slicing motion across his neck.

"None of that will be your concern. If you can get the bodies and captives to the eastern gate before moonrise, we have men in place to take them."

"How will we get paid?" I asked.

"I just need an address and we can deliver the gold next day," he said.

"Not good enough," answered Jessica. "We don't know anything about you. You might disappear without payment. Bring the gold tonight. Bring lots of it."

"Wait, hold up," Richard said. "Where are we even supposed to find these shamans, and capture them for you?" It was a good question, as we had moved through the forest on our way here we had found nothing, and the plains we walked looped for eternity. Unless this dungeon world morphed its structure to follow the dynamic of our decisions, there was no way to fit a huge gnoll settlement inside the limited space we had seen.

"Ten miles east of the eastern gate you'll start seeing gnoll patrols," the man said.

"They're that close?" Lucas asked.

"Right, they dare come this close," he growled. "They've been moving west every year and taking more and more of the forest. You should be able to find them there. One gold per body; three gold alive. Payment on delivery. A deal can be worked out if you're more impressive than expected and bring more than we have gold for."

"Fair enough," I said.

The man paused for a moment. "It goes without saying you can't discuss this with anyone, ANYONE."

"How will we go about reporting our battles against the gnolls for an increase in reputation then?" asked Alan. I could see that it would be valuable if we could get both gold from this mystery quest and official approval for ambushing gnolls at the same time. If we were here for any extended period of time, a reputation increase would be important, not least because I hoped for better quests.

"Usually people hand in canines," he answered. "As for the bodies, you saw you left them on the ground. And you definitely don't say if you bring back a gnoll to the city alive." This time it was the man who made motion of his hand towards his neck. "Contraband like that will get you executed."

"As of right now we don't know if we're allowed to venture out of the city," I said, "we've only just been conscripted."

"For that problem I cannot help you," he said with evident disappointment, "I suggest you find out and you leave a message for

Lazemus at the hall if you are able to go outside. Then we'll know to meet you afterwards. What name will you use on your message?"

"I'm Mike," I said.

"Leave a message for Lazemus from Mike and the subject as 'gnolls'. I'll be in contact." He turned towards Jessica whom raised her bow as if she had no intention of moving. Putting his hands together, like in prayer, he silently pleaded for her to move, which, after a dozen seconds, she finally did.

"He runs like a rat," she said, watching the man flee back down the alley.

# Chapter 13: Standing Before the General

"What do you think?" I looked at Lucas as the man who had given his name as Lazemus went out of sight around a corner.

"I don't see why he has a reason to lie to us about paying for gnoll bodies," Lucas said. He gave a shrug. "There is always the possibility this is a setup or trap, but why us? Perhaps it has something to do with the overall goal of the dungeon. Something we have to solve before we get to leave?"

"Or it could be a test to see if we're spies?" Anna suggested.

"Potentially," Lucas agreed.

"I'm conflicted," Jessica said. "As far as we're aware, this dungeon world has a limit to its size. I find it hard to believe there are multiple empires and kingdoms dotting the distance. That's all probably just a sort of lore to frame whatever it is we are supposed to achieve here."

"Right, but the mission still came down to gnolls, which as far as we're aware is the entire subject of this dungeon," Glenn pointed out.

"We could also assume the dungeon is simply moving us in the correct direction. We reached the checkpoint of making it to Rigar and now we've unlocked some new space?" This may have been the first non-sarcastic thing I'd ever heard come out of Maria's mouth and I agreed with her.

"Is it possible this is the main questline we need to address in order to finish the dungeon?" I thought aloud. "There could very well be a gnoll invasion happening in the lore of this world, but at the same time, that could just be background for a small group mission like the one we've been offered."

The more we discussed it aloud, the more we couldn't wrap our heads around it. Without enough clues, we really couldn't figure out one way or the other, and eventually decided action was better than standing and twiddling our thumbs.

We headed back to the Barracks with the intention of speaking with General Rhugar. He would have a grasp on the surrounding area and let us know if this quest was even something we could accept while signed up to the defense of the city. We didn't know the rules.

For my part, I hoped we could take on the quests and earn some gold. The bubbling excitement I had for gear—both for me and for all of our group—was starting to boil over. As a group we potentially needed hundreds of gold to acquire new gear and gain skills in the professions we would need for our future survival. That was a lot of shamans to kill or capture.

While on the streets we walked in a reasonably effective formation. A more loose one than when we were moving into confict, but if things went south, we were prepared for a battle even here.

Jessica fell back to my side, "I hope we can take the quest." Her hand reached down and her fingers locked between mine. We had grown closer these past few days.

"If we can't, I'm afraid there will be hell." I looked at Maria, and Richard, and Anna. They all had a very keen eye on the loot they wanted. If they were suddenly told we couldn't take the quest and our money making scheme was out the window…I didn't know what they'd do.

"I have a feeling it will work out: that the dungeon is designed for this to happen." I gave a nod and then cherished the silence as we walked hand-in-hand. Some of that emotion I felt was slipping away from the both of us had come back, or both of us had better learned to control it.

Frankly, the increase in gentler feelings between us was probably a result of the long period of peace. We hadn't needed to kill another person in months, and that was the hardest part of this ordeal. The true believers forced us down a potential path of slaughter, and until we got out the other side, we truly couldn't see an end. The thought of taking life still wasn't something easy to swallow, and yet I had needed to do so to survive.

Reluctantly, I let Jessica's hand drop when we arrived at the barracks. It felt too soon, but this matter had to be taken care of. The others went to get lunch while I went to meet the general. Our ability to prosper entirely depended on this interaction. My hands were suddenly more clammy than when I was holding Jessica's hand.

The door to General Rhugar's office was cracked, and I couldn't hear any talking. I suddenly felt emboldened as I approached. My hand knocked on the edge of the door. "General Rhugar, are you free for a moment? It's Mike. I'd like to discuss something with you."

I heard the ruffling of papers for just a moment before a coarse voice came through. "Come in Mike, I have a few moments to spare." I grasped the handle and pushed inward. The creaking of the doorframe broke the silence and he looked over at it, "I'll have to get that fixed." He gave a light laugh.

"Good to see you, sir," I said respectfully while raising a hand. Regardless of the difference in our strength, I was still a subordinate here.

"Be at ease," he said. "What do you need?"

"I'll get right to the point sir. We were solicited for a mission today, and the mission requires us to leave the city for a short time." My eyes were locked to General Rhugar's face the entire time. Any change in expression I'd immediately notice. Even my sixth sense was primed to read the room. I didn't continue talking but allowed him to speak.

"What kind of mission is it that it requires you to leave the city?" The severity of his voice let me know he was fully in control, and that I needed to choose my words carefully or he could reject my plea with no explanation.

"It's a killing mission sir, to kill gnolls," I answered, "there is a camp about ten miles east of the western gate, with the gnolls pushing closer to Rigar every day."

His eyes flashed between doubt and excitement for the briefest moment. That flicker of emotion on his face would have easily been missed but it gave me hope. "I've heard of this," he said, "and someone wants you to kill these gnolls?"

"Yes sir. We were looking for missions to acquire gold and stumbled upon this one." My explanation wasn't a lie, and as long as 'Lazemus' wasn't up to nefarious deeds, this was a win-win for the empire.

"And your goal for this is simply gold?" General Rhugar asked.

"Right, sir," I said. "As you know we are traveling mercenaries. In the end, our main goal is gold. If we can make some extra while we wait to be of use to the Rigar empire, then we don't see any reason to say no. We're good at killing gnolls and we'd all love to buy some new equipment."

I felt I'd done my best. That there was nothing I'd said which would make him doubt my explanation. The entire time I'd been in the office, I'd been focused on this, on preventing a curt refusal. Even the way I presented the information to him was calculated: breaking it into chunks and talking in a monotone, so as to hide my excitement. It was as if his rejection or acceptance didn't matter to me.

There was a moment of silence as the options played in his mind. I didn't know if he was picking apart the conversation to find a reason to reject, or to see if I was being untruthful in some way. I waited in silence, trying not to show any eagerness or expectation.

"I don't see any issue with it, so long as you don't go too far and we can recall you quickly," he finally said. "I would like to know when and where you go though, so run it by me beforehand, or my assistant. This way if something happens, we can send people to retrieve you." He paused for a moment. "No doubt you've seen how many men we've lost, and the fact you've signed up for duty matters." He spoke as if he was explaining a rule to me.

Lucas had briefly talked with me about some possible outcomes from this meeting and what General Rhugar had just said was our best-case scenario. Freedom to move without surveillance. There had been the chance he would give permission for us to take the quest but send someone along with us, and that would make moving bodies nearly impossible.

"Absolutely sir," I said. "I'll get in touch and let you know every time we plan to go and hunt gnolls and where we can be found."

"Good. Then I have nothing to worry about. Dismissed."

I saluted again to show respect and then walked out to the find the others. I had put up a strong front, but every inch of my body had a fine layer of sweat on it. General Rhugar was an intimidating man. His presence was commanding and unyielding, he had seen much more death and life than I had.

As I walked the halls I reviewed our conversation and especially that moment when I mentioned having been solicited to attack the gnoll camp: he'd grown excited before hiding his emotion. It was possible he even knew what we were going to do: even the part about gathering gnoll shaman bodies.

The family or person requesting this mission from us was clearly not short on money to do so. Going off that logic, it was completely possible General Rhugar had been either offered, or knew someone who had also been offered our same deal. The rich had very little fear of authority, especially when those enforcing the laws were in their pockets.

Our biggest hurdle was gone now, though. I was excited to find the others and break the news. It took just a minute of brisk walking to make it the slop hall where everyone was waiting for my return.

For some reason I was feeling a bit impish, and shrouded my face in a downcast expression. The jubilant mood of my party slowly dwindled as I approached, sure that I had failed. "It... WORKED!" I blurted out as I reached them. "We have permission to leave the city."

"You are an ass," Maria said flatly, but then it was clear the anger she felt had washed away as she realized this meant she might be in line to buy the new gear she wanted.

Lucas let out an exhausted sigh. "Was it difficult?"

"Not at all, he didn't interrogate me or suspect anything was dubious, at least on the surface. I had been expecting a no, full stop. But it didn't come."

"Someone will need to visit the mission hall again and leave a note addressed to Lazemus," Jessica said while walking over and wrapping an arm around me.

"About that," I replied, "I assume everyone wants to get going as soon as possible, so I was planning on going back there now." The day was still young, and the sooner I had delivered the note the faster we could get easy access out the west gate.

"Do you need anyone to go with you?" Jessica asked.

As much as I wanted to bring her along, I actually felt it was best I went alone. Less distractions meant I would be as fast as possible. I'd have time to spend with her tonight, anyway. "I'll go quickly by myself."

Jessica nodded and the others agreed. With that, I took to the streets as fast as possible and made quick pace. Without stopping and looking at wares, or the wonders of the Rigar empire, it took less than twenty minutes to get back to the town hall.

"I'd like to leave a message for someone," I said to the front clerk.

"Their name?" he asked.

"Lazemus," I said. Which caused his pupils to constrict ever so slightly.

"And yours?"

"Mike."

"Understood." It was if he already was informed of the situation and didn't even ask for the message contents. I stood there baffled for a moment before realizing what that meant. Lazemus had connections even in the mission hall, which meant his sphere of power was large.

# Chapter 14: Will Lazemus's Quest Let Us Complete the Dungeon?

A lot was on my mind as I walked through the city back towards my group. The quest we'd been given probably went much further than Lazemus had led us to believe and I didn't know if this was bad or good. This was possibly the catalyst for progressing this dungeon and ultimately moving on.

I didn't waste my time in the darkening streets and the entire trip took me only around an hour total. I was getting to know my way around. All we had to do now was wait for Lazemus to be informed about my message and reach out to us at the southern barracks.

With nothing left for us to do on our end, I just relaxed and enjoyed the city of Rigar. It was exciting being around other people, even if they were probably NPCs of a limited dungeon. The desolate world outside was daunting, unforgiving, and truly uncaring. Here, an old lady would wish you a good day as you walked by. In fact, I started to dread the day we would have to leave the dungeon for the race to survive outside.

Two days passed in a flash, and on the third day, early morning, a note arrived for us. A messenger specifically asked for Mike, and we met him as a group outside. The young lad who was waiting for us didn't show any emotion or indication that he knew the contents of what he was delivering. The messenger was holding a small parcel the size of a notebook, bound in golden thread.

"I'm sort of excited," I admitted while taking the package and turning it around in my hands. My party members' eyes didn't betray my expectations either: they were vivid with interest.

"Quick! Open it up!" Maria said. Even Anna's eyes were glowing, no one was calm right now. This could be the next step to earning gold and some vital gear.

"Let's head back to a secure place first." Thomas said, just as I was about to rip the light thread holding it together. He was right, it would be bad if there was sensitive and incriminating evidence inside.

"Good call," said Lucas, even he had lost himself in the momentum of Maria's eagerness. We moved to Jessica and I's room and stuffed inside before closing the door. For everyone to fit in was a squeeze, but no one would bother us here. My hands carefully undid the golden thread and unsealed the parcel. The top of the pack flipped open like a bag and I tipped the contents into my hand. It was a wooden box, clearly made of some fine wood. The deep polish glistened in the dim light and had intricate and beautiful designs.

I opened the box carefully while everyone crowded around. There was a letter that acted like an inlay, and another bundle within the paper, that I couldn't yet see.

"Dear Mike, the contents of this parcel should be well enough to put you on the right path.

"Work hard." I read the letter aloud.

"Is that all it said?" asked Maria.

"That's all." I put the note aside and scanned the contents of the box.

There was a letter inside for each of us, I passed them out and it quickly became evident that each contained a card with our identification and also a special badge, whose purpose I could only guess at?

Besides that, there was a pouch with over five gold in it.

"That's all?" Maria asked, clearly expecting more.

While I didn't disagree with her, I could also see that any more detailed instructions or explanations could potentially be dangerous to us and them. A simple and precise message kept us both safe, if there was some kind of political battle going on within the city that we had yet to appreciate.

"We'll make it work," Jessica said.

Lucas took the bag of gold. "We'll need a carriage and some horses if we want to transport the goods." Even he was circumspect about what our goals were. "This should be enough, for that, from what I've seen in the markets."

"Do you remember where the stables were?" Glenn and Mark both asked him at the same time. They had gone with him first day to gather information.

"Yea," Lucas said, "I should be able to buy the horses at the very least, or at least rent them."

"I saw a cart-makers when we were headed to the mission hall," Anna added in.

"Really?" Lucas was excited, "That saves a bunch of time then, cause if the stables don't have some connection, I was lost on how we'd get the carriage."

"Can I trust the two of you to take care of it?" I asked them both, which got a nod. "Good, you two take care of that. If we can get the carriage sorted we're good to head out tomorrow." I paused, "How is our supply situation?"

"We have four or five days of rations left." Lucas said. "We should probably stock up more on food."

"I agree," I said. "If we somehow get stuck out there, we need food. Otherwise, we can eat our dinner here."

"Right," Lucas agreed. "Anna and I can take care of that." He waited for a moment to see if there was anything else before leaving with Anna.

"I need to inform the general that we're departing in the morning. I'll do that now," I told everyone. The sooner that was out of the way, the better. We moved as a group back into the hallway and I split off without them towards the general's room.

It wasn't too far of a walk, and after just thirty seconds of twisting and turning through hallways I was there, outside. I knocked, "Are you available general?" I asked.

"Mike? Come in." It was a quicker response than I was expecting and I hurried through to him.

I stood before the general fully at attention. "Tomorrow we'd like to make our first trip outside the city walls." I informed him.

"Sooner than I expected, but granted," he replied at once. There were stacks and stacks of papers in front of him, and the dark under his eyes grew deeper than they were before.

"Thank you, sir," I said and then saluted.

"Be safe. The gnolls will attack again sooner than anticipated. Dismissed." There was a hint of melancholy in his voice. I could see how tired he was, but I refrained from saying anything. I made my way out and met the others at the end of the hallway.

"Did it go well?" Jessica asked.

I gave a nod. "Seems the gnolls will be attacking again soon." I said. I couldn't help but wonder what our objective in this dungeon actually was. Were we meant to stay inside the city and defend against gnoll attacks? Venture out and fight some gnoll boss? Too many questions and not enough answers.

I spent the rest of the day in a hurried stupor. Nothing was left to arrange at the barracks, and Lucas and Anna returned a little under two hours later. There would be a cart available for us tomorrow at the western gate as well as two sturdy horses. None of us had any experience with carriages, or horses, but we would make due.

It was like the next day was Christmas morning. I went to bed with a bubbling sense of excitement; there would be no presents under a tree, but instead gold to buy amazing equipment, possible professions, and maybe even skills.

The skills weren't something we ever confirmed, but without money there was little point in looking unless we wanted to go on a robbing spree. Not exactly a wise decision if we wanted to clear this dungeon, especially if this city held the rewards for us.

The following morning was quiet; a fog hovered over the cobblestone paving as merchants and vendors brought out their goods for the day. There was serenity in the quiet hustle and bustle of a new day.

I couldn't find any words to say as we walked and from the silence among us, nor could anyone else. Perhaps it was nerves—a lot could happen on a whim. We were potentially entering the lion's den and didn't even know it. A steady pace brought us to just outside the west gate checkpoint after thirty minutes.

There was no line at this time, and no incoming traffic, just a few clearly tired soldiers. The top of the wall wasn't even visible in this fog; a dreary atmosphere that wasn't the least bit inviting pushed us forward.

"Halt! State your business!" A call came through the fog when we were just ten yards from the towering gate. Two guards didn't wait for our response and made their way to us. Their armor rattled and the spears held firmly in their grip glistened with danger.

All I could do was trust in Lazemus right now. Whether we could return with the bodies and enter the city afterwards depended on him in the end anyway, or at least whoever was behind him. I removed the special ID card given to us in the letter and handed it over to the guard.

I could tell by his demeanor he was ready to berate me, but the words caught in his throat as he looked over the ID. "Just a moment," he said. His voice had already taken a more placatory tone, clearly he was not inclined to offend me anymore. Lazemus's status in my mind rose a point or two.

The guard rushed away in haste before disappearing into the small side building meant to house documents and other important information acquired at this gate. After that though, time seemed to pass in a crawl and after nearly five minutes there was no sign of the guard returning.

I started to have a bad feeling in my gut, and then I heard the clopping of a horse's hooves, more than one actually. A cart rolled towards us and then stopped behind us. We moved off the road and out of the way when the driver called out. "Mike?"

"That's me," I said, slightly confused.

"We'll be your escorts for today," the man said and the armed soldier in the seat beside him saluted me. "Climb up. There's room for you all."

"These are the horses and cart we purchased," said Lucas.

This was odd. Presumably the two guards were sent by Lazemus but how had they known about our purchase? And were they coming along because we weren't considered trust-worthy, or because this was his way of giving us the most help possible?

Exchanging a look with Jessica, I returned the salute and then moved with the others towards the back before clambering into the cart. Despite my calm demeanor, I was a bit riled up inside. The atmosphere had been too weird, too unpredictable. "It looks like things are fine," I said to everyone.

"Make way! Lord Lazemus has special business to attend to!" The two guards at the front shouted, and didn't even wait for the guards at the gate to give the go ahead. There was no room for discussion, and to my surprise, the gate opened with no qualms from the other side. We rocked uncomfortably in the back as we raced into the distance and towards the gnoll encampment.

# Chapter 15: The Tactics of Attacking a Gnoll Camp

I had underestimated Lazemus, clearly. The fact these guards were driving the cart Lucas had prepared meant his information gathering was beyond what we had realized. The danger level he represented went up in my mind at this moment as well. We were dancing in the palm of his hand.

"How far is it?" Anna whispered to Lucas, whom clearly had no idea.

"Excuse me, how far is the journey?" he called forward as a proxy in her place.

The guard on the right side of the seat turned his head and shouted through the clattering sounds of iron-bound wheel on cobbles, "About ten minutes due east." He turned forward again. Neither of them had any interest in small talk, or even us for that matter.

This was to be a shorter journey than expected, which was a pleasant surprise. My entire body was being rattled as if in a washing machine, and the ache in my backside was growing steadily. Hopefully, a few gnoll bodies would weigh the cart down and stop some of this incessant shaking.

We had discussed our tactics already, and had a contingent plan in place—mainly for how to capture gnolls and bring them back alive. First, though, we needed to confirm the difficulty of the encounter. The guards, too, might play a factor, but looking at their indifferent demeanor I expected they would have nothing to do with the combat.

The cart came to a stop after a dozen minutes of horrible rocking, "This is as close as we can bring you. The gnoll camp is through the trees east of here. The horses and carts will go no further, but I will accompany you," the guard who had spoken to Lucas got off the cart. Presumably, the other would watch our transportation.

I accepted this statement without any objection. The forest was no place to bring a cart and horses. Moreover, even if we could have found a path wide enough, the gnolls weren't without intelligence, and anything to hinder us was on the menu, and that included killing our horses if they came across them.

The cart wasn't exactly the cleanest, and I found myself brushing off straw and chaff immediately after hopping out. Just east was a daunting forest, and the sun didn't fully penetrate to the forest floor. It was dark and uninviting, but we needed to move forward. I reminded myself that getting paid for this work was our best bet at acquiring new gear.

Jessica led the front and our guard stayed at the back. His indifferent demeanor vanished as we entered the forest, replaced by a look of caution, anxiety even. There was no road, and I suspected this was the most likely reason the cart had stopped where it had.

The sound of the guard's armor clanked behind me constantly as he checked every direction. His head was on a pivot, and although he tried to look confident whenever he caught my eye, he failed. I couldn't help but take a few steps back. "We have someone who can track, nothing should be sneak attacking us," I told him. He gave a stern nod, but didn't make any change to his behavior. I smiled to myself and then moved back into my position in the center of our own party.

Jessica stopped suddenly and raised a hand before looking back at us. "Dozens of enemies just ahead," she came back and whispered. We grouped together around her and peered through the dense foliage, barely able to make out the encampment ahead.

There were dozens of gnoll warriors and just few shamans. It was clear getting a large harvest wouldn't be so easy, and this was probably why the gold offered was so generous. Jessica then pointed out the gnoll scouts that were perched in trees around the area, each held a heavy bow with long arrows that would pin a man to the ground.

We had discussed our plans ahead of time, and on the assumption there would be guards around the outskirts of the camp, determined they would be the first and best targets. I used Vast Shadows and went to pull my horde of undead out: the abominations, however, didn't appear. I had never experienced this phenomenon before. Was there a time limit on them? They had been my reincarnations for quite some time, and they'd never failed to appear.

I shook off the dismay and told myself it was for the best, as even in this densely packed woodlands the large abominations would stand out like a sore thumb. Staying lowkey was the best way to stay safe, not just for us, but also the guard behind us.

If push came to shove, I was confident we could get out unscathed, especially given how we had an unthreatened line of retreat. Nothing could keep us here if we wanted to leave, except perhaps a boss with unexpected powers.

We activated protocol and moved forward slowly as a group in formation. The plan for these scouts was to approach as carefully as possible, and then see if Anna and Jessica could dispatch them in an instant with Anna's glacial spells and Jessica's Godless Arrow. It all depended if these gnolls were any tougher than those outside this dungeon. If they were the same, they could be taken down by the ranged attacks. We opted as a group to leave Maria's attack out of it, as her explosive arrow would cause too much destruction and noise.

According to Jessica, there were three scouts, and the closest was just fifty or sixty yards away. The gnoll scout's relaxed body language told us they didn't get many visitors, and their scouting was almost a formality. In fact, this first scout may have just been completely asleep.

There was no reaction from our enemy when we were just thirty yards away from him, which was amazing news for us. Jessica stood next to Anna and allowed her to begin the process of attack. Her Godless Arrow materialized, which meant it could reach the target in an instant, and as of now we had seen nothing that could counter it. The name Godless Arrow was extremely fitting for the ability, and it matched its high coin cost from the secret shop.

An ice spear whistled through the air a moment later and landed directly on the neck of the gnoll. Its eyes opened in fear and no voice could escape its already mangled and destroyed throat. The confusion lasted merely a moment before its face exploded into a mess of gore from Godless Arrow and the body fell to the forest floor with a thud.

The guard behind us finally stopped rattling and I couldn't help but look back and see the shock in his eyes. We must have been much stronger than he was expecting, and his expression changed immediately to one of respect.

This reaction was odd, because he didn't show the same admiration when I summoned my army of undead, which I felt was

111

particularly intimidating. I guessed seeing was believing. "The next is around eighty yards away, opposite side," Jessica whispered and slowly led the way.

As I had done no damage, reincarnating the gnoll was out of the question, which was unfortunate. I did have an idea I thought might be interesting, something I'd not considered until part of my undead squad didn't appear from Vast Shadows.

We moved like assassins as we rotated around the small camp. Jessica checked the gnoll scout for loot as we stepped over the lifeless corpse. I tried to reincarnate it out of sheer determination, but received an unwelcome message:

### Skill has failed.

It was expected, though.

The second scout was dispatched as easily as the first, and we moved towards the third, which was surprisingly far away. It seemed this camp was less like a circle and more oblong-shaped. I didn't mind, it just meant that many more enemies to dispatch and more gold to gain.

Some of the unease of our guard escort subsided, and the noise of his turning head disappeared completely. Our abilities had bolstered his confidence, surely? Especially when the third scout was dispatched as easily as the first two. We had infiltrated the camp with great success.

Given the shape of the encampment, we determined that this far end of the oblong was the best location to begin. Not only was the area of the camp before us less concentrated with gnolls than at the other end, but the forest here was less open, our likelihood of being outflanked or swarmed was low. As I studied the gnolls in the camp it seemed from the ones moving around that the mobs weren't tethered or in groups, which meant pulling single mobs was probably possible.

The question was: how to pull them? Similar to before, we didn't know how these enemies would react to our presence. Pulling one might mean pulling fifty, and continuing to sneak attack them would only get us so far.

"Let's lure them out with some noise," Mark suggested after a back and forth discussion. Alan wanted to rush right in, and Maria was all for picking them off one at a time from a distance. The reality was though, we needed to separate the shaman from the camp and other gnolls.

"What about a fire?" Thomas asked. It was another good idea, but could also backfire. If the flames drove the shaman away from us, chasing them down would prove difficult in the smoke. Despite how strong we were, I doubted we could handle heavy smoke inhalation and fire.

"Let's just go with the noise making and see what happens," I proposed before turning to Maria. She had a skill that literally exploded with a bang. It wasn't so loud as to alert the whole camp, but all the gnolls within a good twenty or thirty feet would hear it clearly and perhaps come look out of curiosity. From there we could start a manageable fight.

"What are you looking at me for?" she asked, evidently feeling nervous. That just got everyone to look at Maria and Alan even took a step towards her, which turned her face ugly. "I'm not being bait no matter what anyone says! I WON'T DO IT." She put her foot down, which got a laugh out of everyone.

"Relax, we just want you to use Explosive Arrow," Jessica assured her.

"Oh…okay." Her face went from fiery to embarrassed in a moment. I was amazed at how fast she could switch gears. Alan was in for it, no doubt.

We moved a good thirty feet away from the edge of camp and concealed ourselves well. Alan was crouched on one knee with Richard just beside him. My undead soldiers had been spread around the woods to our left and right, their job was to catch any runners and encircle our enemies once they came close enough.

Our teamwork was phenomenal and everything was put into place. Maria nocked an arrow and then let it loose. The fiery arrow distorted the air from its heat before landing on the trunk of a tree that reminded me of an oak.

The arrow exploded with a bang but the fire was extinguished immediately. I stared at the impact in surprise, as the tree had not the slightest bit of damage, nor was there even a scorch mark. It seemed that burning this forest would have proved difficult if we tried.

Still, the noise had been effective. I crouched even lower, and then the cackling came. First it was just once, and then as if contagious, dozens of cackling sounds echoed through the forest and disappeared, diffused in the dense foliage.

# Chapter 16: A Job Well Done

"Incoming," Jessica warned everyone. We were so low to the ground our knowledge of what was happening was entirely dependent on Jessica. Branches cracked and bushes rustled as the gnolls moved towards us. "Eight of them are in range. Let's go!" Jessica shouted and stood up, pulling back the cord of her bow.

I sprang to my feet and ordered my undead squad to come out of the shadows and flank the incoming gnolls from the shadows to cut off all paths of retreat. Even as I did that, Alan and Richard sprinted forward like track and field runners before plowing into the closest gnoll warrior.

Entangling Arrow, Blizzard and Wind Slash flew out in quick succession, immediately dispersing the first and closest enemy. Alan jumped over the falling body and slashed his sword against the shoulder of a mace-wielding gnoll while blocking the strike of another with his shield.

That second gnoll was immediately rammed by Richard and let out a horrible and excruciating sound as the white-hot shield singed the fur completely off its skin. "They're non-elite!" Jessica yelled at everyone, which gave me a bit of reassurance and relief.

There were eight enemies in front of us, and after just two or three seconds, two had already been dispatched. I channeled Decay on an archer in the back and instructed my undead squad to dog-pile it.

The skin of the archer gnoll's face 'melted' as it aged rapidly. Its eyes turned grey and even the skin on its face pocked with wrinkles and moles reminiscent of the passing of decades. It had no chance to retaliate while fully blind, and my zweihander-wielding general lopped its body cleanly in two.

Anna swapped from casting single target abilities and instead opted for a Blizzard directly in the middle of the pack. Maria also shot out two Explosive Arrows back to back, one to herd them into the blizzard and the other directly into the clump of enemies.

It was an absolute slaughter, and merely thirty seconds passed before all eight foes were dead. I had personally dispatched two, and opted to reincarnate them as part of my undead squad. I picked the first gnoll archer and then a mace-wielding tank—unfortunately there were no gnoll shamans in the pack. For now, this was the best I could do.

We each looted a corpse and I reminded everyone to focus on the mission. Our goal was loot, but we could distribute the loot after this mission, right now we needed full attention on the camp. The loot from these would probably not be nearly as good as the loot we could purchase, not until we were fighting elite or boss-type gnolls.

The gnoll archer I had reincarnated slowly stood off the floor as its body reformed. The gash across its chest slowly vanished and even the signs of age on its face disappeared. Instead, its originally brownish body had become a dull grey. Its eyes were fully cloudy as if nothing existed behind them, but from a distance it was not easy to distinguish the undead gnoll from a living one.

"Can I try something?" I asked everyone. It was the idea I had originally—using my own reincarnated mobs to infiltrate and coax other gnolls to leave the camp.

My question got a few curious stares, which wasn't surprising to me. There was almost no hesitation though, as a resounding 'yes' came from the group. I wasn't risk averse, but I was calculated. I could feel the trust my group had in me.

I grouped the gnoll archer and mace wielder together and slowly walked them into camp. There was a special connection between us—a feeling that was there at the moment I chose to feel it. I could see through their eyes even though they were both clearly blind, this bond with my undead was something that had developed over time.

Once I attracted the attention of a few gnolls, I made a mad dash with my reincarnations to the northern edge of the camp where we were waiting patiently. I was relieved that no alarms had been sounded, but the gnolls who had seen my squad members couldn't help but chase in expectancy and curiosity. Although intelligent, they were still dogs in the end.

Just four gnolls came chasing through the low brush and into our ambush. Still no gnoll shaman, though. We couldn't go back empty handed, no matter what. "Is anyone low on rations?" I asked after looting a corpse. I felt it important to keep the group talking and moving.

Morale was good, but if we continued to fight without a sign of a shaman, I could tell it would decline fast. The EXP was only so-so, merely a percent per gnoll kill. While not bad, it couldn't compare to the gains elites would give, nor the loot.

"I have only two rations left," Glenn said. Both him and Mark had the least supplies of all of us, which made sense. Glenn still hadn't taken a class and had no skills. He was currently satisfied stabbing a longsword into the unsuspecting gnolls while Mark wielded a spear.

There was almost no difference between the two of them currently, so no one took any issue in it. Glenn was non-combat, and all of his skills had no effect on our battle plans as of yet. They didn't get in the way

"That seemed to work well," Thomas said. "Let's just do that again." He cut off any negotiation before it could take off.

"Agreed," Maria added. Anything to keep her from being bait was a good choice, and my expendable undead were the obvious candidates to lure more gnolls our way. No one had any qualms and we moved slightly closer to the larger clump of this gnoll village.

In between battles, I kept a close eye on our guard the entire time. His facial expression had gone from weary, to surprised, and now to a contemplative one. He hadn't done anything to warrant my unease, but I couldn't trust him, not fully.

"Stay close," I told him under the guise of care. Seeing how strong we were could have easily changed Lazemus' plan, and whatever his plan was, it was unknown to us.

"This one has an armor on it," Alan said while looting a corpse we were about to step over.

He hadn't had a chance to read it out before Anna was nearly on top of him, eyes sparkling gold. "Well, let's see it then!"

### Barbaric Vest: STR +5, VIT +2

**A vest made of some sort of animal hide.
Wearing it makes you feel more feral.**

The only people really lacking in gear right now were Mark and Glenn, as everyone else was wearing somewhat decent gear in most slots, albeit some of this was jewelry. I looked towards them first, and it was Mark who spoke up. "Give it to Glenn. I may end up being a caster."

While Glenn was non-combat, he was able to wield a weapon in melee, and, if he wanted, he could potentially learn to use a bow, but he would never be able to cast magical damaging abilities without learning a new skill for it.

Alan handed the vest over without hesitation and immediately took to the front again with Jessica right behind. Her tracking allowed us to find the best openings in the camp in which to infiltrate my undead without much suspicion.

It was a huge boon that the gnolls had some level of intelligence, but not enough to realize things were going awry. Even more so was their lack of comradery. I witnessed more than three or four nasty scuffles between them in just a short fifteen-minute window, and each drew blood.

They didn't kill each other, but maiming wasn't out of the question. They thought nothing of their fell gnolls disappearing, which was a boon to us. Was this a rogue tribe of gnolls completely separate from the hordes that had laid siege on the Rigar empire? I couldn't be sure.

"There's a shaman ahead," Jessica told everyone.

"Is everyone clear on the plan?" Lucas asked. We had planned on how to capture a gnoll shaman alive—whether it worked or not would now be tested.

Anna, Lucas, and Thomas all gave a nod. They would be the main players in accomplishing that feat.

"I'm going," I said then sent my gnoll infiltrators forward.

Jessica gave a glance. "Try to make it small." The smaller the pull, the easier controlling the shaman would be.

My undead gnolls tiptoed forward and crossed the threshold between our hiding places and the pathways through the tents of the main camp. I spotted the shaman just a dozen feet in the distance and waited for it to notice the presence of my squad members. Once it did, I allowed one to pull back and the other gave a nasty snarl and a low cackle.

This was something I had been fortunate enough to witness: the gnoll battle challenge. That nasty snarl followed by a low cackle always preceded those fights that left fingers or limbs dangling from half-mangled flesh.

The shaman was confused, and then immediately infuriated. It reciprocated and then rushed after my gnoll archer without the slightest indications of fear. I hadn't seen a gnoll shaman challenged before now, and I realized only then that maybe their status was much higher than these fodder.

It wasn't my intention, but somehow only the gnoll shaman came running, and I realized at that moment we might have found the goose that laid the golden egg. "Just one shaman coming," I annouced to everyone.

There was a bit of surprise followed by bubbling excitement. This was the best case scenario, and the only way to truly test the effectiveness of our strategy. "Are you good, Alan, Richard?" Lucas double checked.

"We can handle it," Alan said, which got a stern nod from Richard.

The shaman came racing through the brush and faced off against my gnoll archer. The moment my undead soldier turned around to face the shaman would be our best chance. While they seemed stupid, they respected this little ritual.

I led the shaman as far away as possible without causing suspicion, which was around twenty meters or so. Too much commotion might alert other gnolls, but if we were fast it wouldn't be seen as too much of a concern. Cackles and yelps sounded out inside the camp almost constantly, and this would be drowned out or ignored like the rest.

Once my archer stopped and made eye contact with the shaman, Alan and Richard burst from the brush on either side of it. Their hands held no weapons, and instead they each grabbed a shoulder and shoved the shaman body to the ground.

The shaman, while gifted in magic, put up little resistance to their physical assault. It was on the ground in a mere moment. Alan didn't hesitate to shove his arm guard into the mouth of the gnoll as hard as he could. Only one simple yelp escaped before it was muffled growling that traveled only a few feet.

"Ready," Alan and Richard spoke within seconds of each other, and Anna came forward in a moment. She pressed her hands against the base of each limb and channeled her frost magic. An ice crystal that encased the flesh inside and out appeared and the growls of our prisoner turned into whimpering.

Lucas didn't hesitate to Wind Slash through the ice, cleaning bisecting the limbs off that had already been frozen solid. The blood flow was almost nonexistent, and Thomas was up next.

He quickly channeled heal several times, until the frozen openings had closed completely and become smooth stumps. After that, Alan carefully grasped the snout of the shaman and removed his hand before wrapping twine around it to keep it shut.

"Did it work?" I asked excitedly. It was a plan we came up after careful deliberation, and only after going through the scenarios did we come to this sequence of events.

Originally the plan was to simply secure its mouth and then drag it back—but in the case of some unfortunate incident, we would have had a fully able shaman against us. With that out of the question, we decided removing its limbs would be the next option.

Thomas assured us he could heal the wounds, but the amount of blood loss in just a single moment after Lucas's clean cut would be tremendous, and the possibility of the gnoll dying while being transported was high.

It was actually Maria who suggested freezing the limbs. That would completely stop any blood flow while Thomas healed the wound, and it would allow for the cleanest cut. The gnoll would definitely be very ill, but it shouldn't die, not with Thomas administering a heal when needed.

"I think it worked," Richard said. He was the closest to the shaman, and was getting nasty stares only second in intensity to Alan. "Job well done everyone." The fact it hadn't passed out and was still conscious was a good sign.

Everyone let out a breath of relief, and even the guard couldn't help but mumble, "What in the world..." under his breath. I barely heard it, but I knew Jessica would have caught it as well. Somehow that put a smile on my face. We'd done it! We had our shaman prisoner and if we got the reward as promised, that would mean being able to purchase a magic item from the shops.

# Chapter 17: Professions or Rare Magic Items? Planning Our Future Spending

"What now?" Lucas asked. I was of the mind to keep going, but hauling the gnoll shaman around with us was out of the question. Even just a torso weighed around one-hundred pounds, which wasn't exactly light.

We hadn't discussed what to do once we were successful, I just knew we needed more shamans. "Let's get it back on the cart and go again," I said. I was just about to assign two people to bring it back when Jessica interrupted me.

"Let's not split up. If the next pull goes poorly, we will be down members and that's a risk we don't need to take."

I caught her eye and gave a nod, "Agreed."

Lucas and Alan ended up carrying the shaman between the two of them all the way back to the cart. It wasn't a long walk by distance, but the terrain proved annoyingly difficult to traverse quickly. I could just make out the break in the forest ahead when a horn bellowed behind us from the direction of the gnoll camp.

"That's an alarm," the guard warned us. No one was of the mind to question him and we picked up the pace immediately.

"Give it here," Richard said to Alan, before hoisting the entire shaman over his shoulder like a sack of potatoes. Trying to maneuver while sharing the awkward burden with another person was harder than him just bearing the entire weight temporarily.

A quick sprint had us at the edge of the forest in merely a minute, and we spotted our cart in the distance. No one held anything back anymore, and the guard we came with was left in the dust, even by me.

"The gnoll shamans don't go unnoticed," I said. It was the only explanation I could offer for the alarm. Presumably, there were so few of them that they held a special position in their tribe. The alarm had sounded quickly though; which meant capturing more shaman in the future would be equally as difficult.

"This sucks," Maria said. "Now what?"

"We call it a day and collect our earnings," Lucas said before Jessica or I could answer her. "We'll have more chances in the future." Maria gave an unhappy hmph before running a bit faster towards the wagon.

The reins snapped and both horses let out a neigh while kicking the sky. The carriage was already turned around and ready to go before we had even arrived. This clearly wasn't the guards' first encounter with this gnoll behavior. And I was thankful, because gnolls had finally breached the forest edge and were running in our direction.

We surely weren't the first to attempt to catch gnoll shamans, but maybe we were the first to get one alive. Ahead of me, Jessica reached the cart, followed by an annoyed Maria. After that it was Mark and Glenn and then Anna. Richard, Alan, and I were in the very back, and I made sure to keep watch on the guard who hadn't managed to match our pace.

Burning any bridges right now wasn't a good idea. The fact was that we could pull up to Rigar and be immediately arrested for contraband goods. A living gnoll shaman would probably be a death penalty.

I waited for the guard to pass me before keeping pace with him, "Are you okay?" I asked. This got a nod in return. We were the last to arrive, and the face of the guard controlling both horses was hilarious to see. It was pure shock, as Richard loaded an armless and legless living gnoll shaman like he was placing down some apples in a farmer's cart.

"Ask…questions…later," the panting guard who had arrived with me said, before jumping onto the front seat. "Fast! HYAH!" he yelled while whipping the reins, which got another neigh. The horses took off and kicked up a trail of dust and dirt. In just a few meters it was impossible to see the gnolls behind us.

"Out of sight, out of mind," I said aloud.

That was easy to say, until the bumps from the wood under my ass grew so intense I could barely bear it. This cart needed more weight, which meant a whole lot of gnoll shamans. That was the goal, at least.

"I'll never miss this," Anna complained, bracing herself against the shaking of the cart while trying to find a comfortable sitting position. No one disagreed.

"Let's try and find a more suitable carriage when we return," Lucas suggested.

"Thicker wheels provide more stability!" the guard yelled from the front. They were a bit more secure as the front part of the cart was weighted more heavily than the back. Any bump would send us a foot in the air and then we slammed back down our ass, often times we would get hit again by the cart before we even fully came down.

I constantly glanced at the gnoll shaman laying there. Its breathing was stable and there were no signs of anything untoward happening with it. As far as Richard was concerned, that was a bag of five gold right there. "That's probably the heaviest five gold I'll ever carry," he laughed.

"Until we get more," Maria reminded everyone. She was right though, this wasn't over. We would go again tomorrow. It didn't need to be said, it was a given.

"What should we spend the gold on?" I asked. "Besides the carriage." There were other options besides just gaining items. Professions were extremely enticing and surely everyone wanted a profession for themselves. No doubt adding them would increase our overall power.

"The carriage will probably cost over a gold," Lucas said. "It's likely we'll have three gold remaining at most. We should consider starting two or three of us on a profession." The two professions I had seen were leather working and tailoring, and each cost a gold minimum to learn. Whether there were more expensive tiers to purchase was currently unknown.

Typically, in games, the cost to level a profession was much higher than what it took to learn. Assuming there were profession levels that required more training, we could be in for dozens of gold per person. The number of shamans we needed to catch suddenly became unfathomable. The gnoll shaman bouncing around with us started to look a lot less valuable than it actually was.

"I hope granny still has that necklace," Maria said aloud. "That's been in my dreams every night since I saw it." I could see Mark and Glen exchange looks, like they wanted to laugh, but her deadpan expression told us all she wasn't joking.

"Leatherworking appeals to me," Lucas said. "If we can afford it, I may even be the first person in this new world to ever learn it." No explanation from him was needed. He needed to wear light-weight and easy to move in armor to maximize his potential.

"I'd like to have tailoring, and maybe spend a little money tasting some of this world's cuisine," Anna said. "I know what you're thinking…that it's selfish of me to suggest it. But maybe with tailoring I could make clothes that earn back the money." I was actually impressed because Anna wasn't someone familiar with games, and then she came up with a good argument as to why my initial thought was correct: professions were likely to be better value for us than items.

Casters usually wore cloth because their stats specialized in non-physical traits. Carrying around plate or even leather would hinder them greatly. They were squishy, low health classes. Standing still for a cast was fine, but being able to move swiftly and easily was important when a single hit could be your death.

I thought about what profession I wanted, and realized that my case was a tad special. While somewhat of a caster, I had an army of undead at my beck and call, and the majority of my spells were related to them.

Besides channeling Decay, I didn't need to stand still for any other reason. My undead troops also meant I didn't exactly need to move that much either. In the off-chance Alex or Richard let a mob through, my warriors could act as tanks in their place.

I wasn't nearly as fragile as Anna, and my limited number of spells meant as long as my minions were alive, my MP expenditure was low. That freed up a lot of stats to go into strength. Would that qualify me to wear plate armor?

I thought back to the secret shop and regretted greatly not taking Drain Life. The potential it had now would be huge. With bone armor, full-plate armor, and my army of undead to bolster my attack and defense, I could fight on almost endlessly.

Small attacks would barely scratch the surface of bone armor, and big attacks would be avoided when possible, and then Drain Life would sustain me back up when I did take damage. This was all hypothetical of course, but the possibility was there.

"What about you Mike?" Jessica suddenly asked. It seemed in my daydreaming I was the only one who hadn't voiced an opinion on what they wanted. Even now I wasn't sure, but I thought a profession was the best investment in our future. "A profession or new skill."

There was a lot of unknowns still, and until I was better informed I couldn't make a good decision. What if only one profession was learnable? What if there were professions so out there I'd never even dreamed or imagined they could exist?

I'd never anticipated that the class Glenn got—Apocalypse Architect—would even exist, and that was a perfect example. The possibilities that could harm or benefit us in the future were really endless. I doubted the beings toying with us started on Earth. How many hundreds of planets across the stars had fallen to a fate like this?

Surviving was the most important thing, and unless I was forced to make a decision haphazardly, I wanted to make the right one. Every face around me had a smile on it. Morale was at an all-time high as we daydreamed about making some progress.

"Another minute or so," the guard at the front said. By now we could see the walls of Rigar appear over the hill we were cresting.

This was only my second time seeing it from the outside, and it was just as magnificent as the first.

# Chapter 18: A Power Struggle Between Princes

"Is everything going to be okay?" I asked the guards. If there was any sign of unease or nervousness on their faces I was prepared to bail on the mission. There were still many unknowns here and we could be about to get into a lot of trouble by bringing a gnoll Shaman into the city. According to my Sixth Sense there was no obvious danger. The skill wasn't perfect though and it only worked for my own safety, not necessarily that of my party.

The cart came to a crawl as we reached the eastern gate. You could cut the air with a knife the atmosphere was so thick. We were breaking the law, and looking around I could see that each and every one of us knew it. I gave one last look at the guards before deciding to stay in the carriage.

Their calm and relaxed demeanor gave me a bit of courage. One of them even cracked a joke at the other, "You ran like granny Rhees tried to get in your bed again!" He slapped his leg. "I've never seen a face like that in all my years."

The other opened his mouth but the only thing that came out was a laugh. In fact, he started laughing his ass off along with his companion. "You'd run too if you heard the words that came out her mouth that night!"

The cart came to a slow as did their laughing and then we all had to wait patiently for two guards to come out and inspect the goods. My heart was in my throat even though Sixth Sense wasn't giving me any warnings. "Special goods for Lazemus!" The front guard said, which caused an immediate change in the approaching guards' faces.

"Understood, carry on." The two guards that had come up to us didn't even bat an eye at the cart. They clearly had no intention of inspecting it and the gate rumbled as it opened before us. We passed through at a steady pace and were just about to disembark on the other side when a voice echoed down the street.

"HALT!" Two guards with an insignia on their breastplate that I'd never seen before stepped out from beside a building. Their faces were anything but friendly.

"What's the meaning of this?" said our driver. Our escort and watchmen came forward to stand between the newcomers and the cart. Their cheerful mood was gone and instead replaced with a threatening anger. The veins of our escort's arm bulged as he squeezed his spear.

"We've been commanded to inspect this cart for contraband goods!" One of the new arrivals yelled and then made to force his way forward despite the response they had gotten.

"YOU DARE?" The second guard finally couldn't hold it anymore. He jumped off the carriage and pulled the spear from across his back without hesitation. "On whose orders?" I was anxiously, hoping our guard could restrain himself from attacking and causing a headache for sure.

"Marquis Edward," said the newcomer flatly. That name meant nothing to me, but the faces of our guards turned even more hostile.

"This is a shipment for Marquis Lazemus," our driver said. "You dare to seize what belongs to him?"

The two scoffed and the nearest said, "We would search even if Lazemus was here in person." Whoever Marquis Edward was, it was clear that his relationship to Lazemus was unfriendly. It looked like there would be bloodshed at any moment. Even we on the carriage prepared for a fight. Turning over this gnoll shaman would implicate us.

"Is that so?" a familiar voice sounded as Lazemus himself walked out of the storing facility near the gate. "I could have your head for that comment." He spoke matter-of-factly.

Edward's guards turned ashen, but there was nothing they could say in return.

"In fact, the king would probably give me a medal for it, too." The roles had been reversed in a single moment, and presumably without Edward himself being here, we were in the clear. "So? Are you going to try and seize my things?"

The guard nearest us had a big mouth and he bared gritted teeth and a frown as he forced out the words, "We would never dare! This was a misunderstanding!" They gave a half-ass salute and then rushed away with their tail between their legs.

"Shouldn't you stop them?" I asked, jumping down onto the road near Lazemus.

"No need. I knew they would be coming," he shrugged, "this is just a warning." Lazemus peered into the cart a moment later and recognized the gnoll shaman. When its eyes opened up and showed it was alive, his diffident demeanor changed to one of respect. "You caught it alive?"

"We did, but only the one," I said.

Lazemus paused in contemplation for only a moment, "Right. I forgot to mention they are very protective of their shamans. If one goes missing, they kick up a fuss." He detached a bag from his waist band, "The gold you were promised."

I took it without hesitation and then passed it to Lucas. Jessica jumped out of the cart and approached Lazemus. "How did you know?"

"Those men were coming?" Lazemus asked but didn't wait for an answer, "Edward has had spies in my regiment for a long time. What he didn't know until now is that I already knew each and every single one of them."

"After this, won't Edward realize you must be on to him, though?" Lucas asked, leaning from the cart. "You might have given up the valuable ability to be able to feed an enemy the information you want them to know."

"Well, it's a warning. I know all of the spies in my regiment, but Edward definitely has secrets even I don't know. All I did was scare him a bit, which may make him second guess the plans he's set in place. If it makes him pull back a card I didn't know about, that may sway things in my favor and in the favor of the Red Prince."

I was starting to feel a headache come on. The rank of Marquis meant that Edward and Lazemus were not low-ranking officials. In fact, they were extremely high. Two of them battling it out while including us in their duel was dangerous for us and it probably meant there was a power struggle happening, one that affected the rule of the city itself.

It wasn't only me thinking this, "So you're supporting a prince then?" Thomas asked.

"That's right. The Red Prince."

"And Edward is backing another?" Thomas continued.

"And how many are there?" Lucas asked.

"Just two, but that isn't currently important right now," Lazemus said. "Edward is quite a vengeful and underhanded man, so I'll have a few guards keep close watch on you all. You will need to be a bit more careful after today."

"Compensation," Maria suddenly said. "COMPENSATION," spoke even louder. "You can't put us in the crossfire of your rivalry with Edwards for free." And this was one of the few times I found myself wholeheartedly agreeing with Maria.

Using us to a degree was okay, but putting our lives in danger to potentially throw his rival off a little bit was out of the question. "I agree," I said, "we expect to be compensated for being obliged to take your side in this feud." I didn't leave any room for discussion. "I suggest you speak with your guard and get a report of what happened in the woods, then come speak with us." I left it at that and then beckoned everyone to follow. We left in the direction of the barracks, keeping a slow and watchful pace.

I wasn't worried about Lazemus's response. Once the guard that had been in the forest with us had spoken of our battle prowess, Lazemus would come running back. Power was king when it came to becoming the...king. It was true, regardless of how funny it sounded.

We weren't to be toyed with or messed with, and this would show that to him now. Lazemus didn't put up a fuss with our quick departure and left it at that. There was something brewing beneath the surface that left me feeling uneasy.

"This might go way over our heads." Lucas said after we walked two blocks more, away from our escort. "Monsters...I'm not so scared of," he paused, "but humans...I don't want to die from poison or in my sleep."

"Agreed," Jessica said. "Lazemus paid us, but now I feel there's a level of untrustworthiness about him. It's more than just the gnoll shamans. We are his chess pieces."

"I understand where everyone is coming from." I said. "but how else can we attain the gear and skills we want?" I looked at every worried face. "Time is not on our side, and I think this power struggle might be part of this dungeon clear requirement, or at least part of it. Not to say I don't agree with all of you, but we have to see where this goes."

Although it was dangerous, at least staying by Lazemus put us in a position of knowledge. We would hopefully have some heads up if something bad was coming our way, instead of being completely blindsided.

"I agree with Mike on this," Thomas said. He was a man of few words. "We're already in it whether we want to be or not. Those guards saw our faces, and Edward will make quick work of finding out our identity."

"I fear Lazemus already thought about this, and this is part of his plan," Anna chimed in.

"So we've already been stripped of our choice?" Maria groaned. "The payment better be a good one." She harrumphed in anger and then stared daggers straight ahead.

Somehow the jubilant mood when we had received the five gold disappeared just like that, and no one was much in the mood for talking on the way back. Jessica assured us when we made it back to the barracks that no one had followed us.

It was an early night for everyone. Physically we hadn't been pushed too far, but the stress of the struggle we were coiled up in left everyone feeling lethargic. Our understanding of the power structure of Rigar was too small, and tomorrow I hoped to find out more.

# Chapter 19: When Princes Feud

The following morning a messenger from Lazemus came with another wooden box, inside of which were ten gold coins. This was the same value as bringing in two living gnoll shamans, which felt like inadequate compensation for the trouble he'd got us into considering the situation.

"We need information," I said to everyone over breakfast. We couldn't dive head first into this power struggle without knowing where we stood.

"Should we seek out Lazemus?" Anna asked.

Lucas shook his head. "No, let's not seek him out on our own accord. Plus, I don't fully trust the information he would give us."

"We should subject everything he says to careful scrutiny. Everything that comes out of his mouth will be in order to benefit his cause. We need to know our angle in this struggle. Why did he seek us out?" I posed the question to everyone.

Gnoll shamans surely couldn't be the difference between his prince becoming king or him and his prince being killed once his rival took power. Also, where was the king in this picture? We didn't know enough.

"I met someone while purchasing the carts," Lucas said. "He seemed to be a crafty individual, maybe I can find something out from him." I could always count on Lucas' intelligence and expertise. He seemed to be naturally gifted in this role.

"Only if you feel confident," I said, "the rest of us should lay low for a few days."

"Do you think there's a target on our back already?" Jessica asked me.

"It's possible," I said, "Edward wouldn't be so bold to act upon us inside a military barracks, not when Lazemus is surely keeping an eye on us. As soon as we leave the safety of these walls though, that would be a different story."

"Lazemus would have no recourse if we were to vanish in a puff of smoke," Alan said.

"Let's give it a day or two," I said. "Lazemus may come see us to figure out why we haven't gone out for more gnoll shamans. In the meantime we are best staying out of the battle between the two factions." I turned to Lucas. "That goes for you as well. There's no need to take any risk by leaving the barracks."

"I can do it." Lucas said with hardened resolve. "And the sooner I go, the better. If we've made an enemy out of Edward we need to know what is in store." Once he made that point, it made sense to me, just letting Lucas go and slip through the cracks would probably be okay.

"What about the rest of us then?" Maria asked.

"Sit tight and wait for good news." I shrugged. At the risk of us all becoming terribly bored, it really made sense to me. Let the two factions fight it out without bringing us into their feud. And hope that Lucas could come through with more information.

"I'm going," Lucas announced before rushing out and into the morning sunset.

"I'm already familiar with everyone who comes and goes to the barracks," Jessica said. "I'll keep watch from the courtyard."

Richard and Alan went for a shower while Maria and Anna both opted to get some more sleep. I followed Jessica out into the courtyard.

Not a single soldier was practicing when we stepped outside. A table off to the corner was our only place to sit as we perched and waited for Lucas' return.

"Lazemus gives me a dangerous feeling," Jessica said, "he's not trustworthy."

"I know, but he's the lesser of two evils right now," I said, "we take his comments with a grain of salt, but for now we have to go along with him." She gave a nod of understanding as we watched the sun slowly rise into the sky.

Several hours passed without my being at all bored. There was no need to fill the air with noise when Jessica was beside me. She rested her head on my shoulder as we sat and waited patiently. This was one of the only times I still felt human.

It was close to lunch time when Lucas finally made his reappearance. "He's back," Jessica said well before he had reappeared in the courtyard, "but something is wrong."

"Wrong?" I asked, confused before looking at the gate. Lucas staggered through the gate a moment later. There was blood on his face and he was holding his side while barely being able to walk.

"Are you okay?" Jessica and I immediately rushed to his side and supported him. "I'll get Thomas!" Jessica disappeared into the barracks in a flash.

I suddenly felt my blood boiling. "What happened?"

Lucas coughed. "I got the information." He forced through a bloody smile. "But I got jumped."

"Edward?" I almost couldn't stop myself from shouting.

"I don't know if it was on his order, but it was one of the guards from that day, no doubt." There was always the possibility the guard was acting alone, but it still pissed me off no end.

Thomas came a moment later and started to cast Heal. Alan and the rest were directly behind him. Anna carried a bowl of water and began to tend to the wounds on Lucas' face while allowing him to get the blood out of his mouth.

"I'm okay everyone." Lucas brushed off their doting hands and sat up straight. "I think you'll all want to know what I found out."

He groaned when he sat but began narrating what he learned, "Besides the two princes, there was also a princess," Lucas began, "in fact, she was the most loved child of the king, but she met an unfortunate end." He paused.

"Whether this is true or not, the rumor was she was brutally murdered, but what is known for certain is that she is gone. Whether dead or captive, she has made no appearance before the king in many months. The king himself also remains cooped up in his room and refuses any visitors.

"Because of her disappearance, the two princes have begun a power struggle for the throne. The whole situation sounds dubious, and foul play is in the air. Some say her maid killed the princess and fled, and others say one of the princes killed her and dispatched her maid." Without speaking to Lazemus, we couldn't confirm the actual situation.

"How do the gnolls tie into this?" I asked.

"That...I don't know," Lucas confessed. "However, there have been others recruited to gather shamans before as well, but nothing has come of it." Regardless of how I wrapped my head around it, I couldn't figure out that angle of this situation.

"We are in danger, though," Lucas said. "They know we are here, whether Edward has issued them to act upon his behalf or that guard holds a grudge for his humiliation, we are considered to be on the side of Lazemus and the Red Prince and we are targets."

"How about we give Lazemus three days while Lucas recovers," I proposed. "If he doesn't come, we leave the barracks in the night and kill anyone in our way as we go look for him." I still felt my blood burning over the attack on Lucas, "Would you recognize the guards that jumped you in a lineup?" I asked.

"Ninety-percent confident," Lucas replied. I nodded and then gathered everyone to return to their rooms and allow Lucas to rest. Even though he was healed and his life was safe, the aftereffects still left him in pain. He would be bedridden at least two days.

"If the opportunity arises, we will make them pay," I said. I presumed the only reason they hadn't outright killed Lucas was because of their fear of Lazemus. That thought led me to believe Edward hadn't issued the order. They were poking a hornet's nest and were about to find out.

"Keep an eye on each other," I said. "Relax for a few days." All we could do was wait to see what Lazemus would make of the situation.

That wait finally ended three days later, when I was nearly bored out of my mind. An entire guard escort came to our barracks. "Orders from Lazemus to escort you to his quarter." Men on horses wielding long spears lined the street, at least a dozen of them. There was a cart for us to ride, and we all jumped in without hesitation.

"Took him long enough, tsk," Maria hissed. It really had taken Lazemus quite a while to get in touch with us. Fortunately, Lucas was in decent condition now. Besides the bruising of his skin, you couldn't tell he had been badly beat up just a few days prior.

"Be on alert," I warned everyone. It was a leisurely ride, at least an hour north of our current location. His quarter was along the west wall and occupied quite a large chunk of land. A towering mansion rose in the distance and we steadily made our way towards it.

Guards patrolled on horses while gardeners rushed here and there. The raw smell of fresh cut grass was heavy in the air. Butter-flies fluttered from bush to flower, many I'd never seen before. It was a rainbow of color and a sight for sore eyes.

If I didn't know a bloody war was happening between Edward and Lazemus, I'd feel this sight was quite beautiful. But there was a dark storm brewing under this colorful scenery, and I'd not be fooled by its appearance.

"He's quite rich, isn't he?" Anna asked.

"He's a marquis after all." Thomas said. If I recalled the documentaries I'd watched properly, a marquis was one of the—if not the highest-ranking—most important officials in a kingdom like this. Lazemus was no small fry, which made him dangerous and fitted with what I'd seen in terms of him being ambitious.

"He should pay us more." Maria groaned. Lately all she could think about was the money we could make. Anna and her seemed to bond on that front. I knew Anna liked nice things, but it seemed Maria was also going down that same route.

The guys were much quieter about it all. Alan and Richard both talked less and less, and I wasn't sure if that just came with the territory of being a tank. Something about fighting with your life in constant danger changed you,

I understood that at least, and it didn't help that there were also passives working against us, too. Working against us might not be the right words to use, because it was all pushing us towards survival.

Jessica and I seemed to find an equilibrium, at least somewhat. I noticed it in myself, even when I wanted revenge for Lucas. My ability to jump to an extreme conclusion came easily, too easily. I was able to be rational about it though, I wasn't overly impulsive just yet.

"I'm the manor's keeper." A white-robed man approached on foot and beckoned us out of our carriage. "Lazemus is waiting for you all at the hall; I'll lead the way." He turned and walked ahead at a leisurely pace.

We followed behind on a finely crafted stone path. Bushes, perfectly cubed, rested on either side and rose into the sky, a maze of life that provided a great amount of privacy for anyone spending time here.

It was a short walk and in just a few minutes we found ourselves face to face with a staircase leading us up at least one floor. A magnificently crafted mansion with stained glass windows and tall towers stood just in front of us.

"He's waiting just in the hall." And then the man moved to the left and bowed while extending his left arm, as if beckoning us in.

An assortment of delicious smells rushed at us the moment the door opened. An entire feast laid out first for our eyes and then no doubt our stomachs. "Welcome!" Lazemus shouted while standing up. A golden goblet adorned with gems gripped tightly in his right hand. "Come, sit, eat!"

Maids came from the sides and pulled out chairs for us to sit, and then bowed and backed away without the slightest change in expression. Alan was the first to find a seat, and before the rest could sit, already had a piece of chicken in his hands.

"It's not poisoned!" Lazemus said jokingly. "The rest of you, come sit." I was expecting some sort of positive welcome, but this was too much. The table must have been twenty feet long, and could easily serve forty people.

"I don't sense any danger from my Sixth Sense," I whispered to Jessica before taking a seat. Her hesitation disappeared as she took a seat beside me. Everyone else settled in and began to eat.

Maria grumbled through a half-full mouth, "This doesn't mean you shouldn't pay us more." I ate slowly while waiting for Lazemus to speak, it was him who called us here after all.

"I heard that you had a run in with some of Edward's men," he began.

# Chapter 20: Out for Blood, and Maybe Some Loot too.

Lazemus was smiling as he asked us about our run in with Lord Edward. It was a cold smile.

"Well, Lucas met them," I replied while chewing on a piece of unknown meat. I couldn't get any nutrients from it, but I could taste it. Not only that, surprisingly the food gave me stat bonuses, which I was not expecting.

Lazemus looked towards Lucas and I could see his reaction as he studied the bruising around Lucas's chin and eyes. Lazemus couldn't see the bruising around the ribs though, which was where Lucas took most of his beating. "I've already had my people find out who did this," he said, "I can have the man, if you want him."

"Have the man?" It seemed Maria didn't realize what Lazemus meant.

"That guard acted on his own accord, and Edward didn't know about it at the time," Lazemus continued. "Not only is that extremely disrespectful to Edward...he's proven he can't control himself." He looked hard at Lucas, "If you want the guard, Edward won't fight me for him. Do you?"

It almost felt like a test. As if Lazemus wanted to see how tough we were, how easy to push over we were. Lucas was the only one who could answer this question, and none of us spoke while we waited.

"It's okay. I assume Edward and all his men will be taken care of once you win the crown?" Lucas responded. Even Lazemus wasn't expecting such a response, and his gaze lingered on Lucas as though seeing him properly for the first time.

"Interesting!" Lazemus laughed. "It seems there's not much point in beating around the bush then. How much do you know? We can save ourselves some time." It was weird to see Lazemus like this. He was completely different from the helpless man that chased us into an ally and left with his tail between his legs. Something must have changed that gave him a sense of firm ground beneath his feet, but what?

"We know you support the Red Prince, and are in direct confrontation with Edward and the prince he supports for the throne."

"Go on."

"We also know the princess has been killed or at least imprisoned."

"Right," Lazemus looked downcast, "she is indeed deceased." There was some sorrow in his words. "I suppose you've heard the rumors about that as well then?"

I gave a nod in response. "Only rumors, though."

"Do you believe the rumors?" he asked, showing no care or caution in finding out what side we stood on.

"Like I said, only rumors. Look, don't worry. We are with you. We don't exactly have another side to join regardless of what people say about you." While that wasn't strictly true, because we could decide to become neutral, it wasn't like we could just go join Edward's side. Well, we could probably make a pitch to him, but

Edward had already shown hostility to us through his men, intentional or not. My own pride wouldn't allow me to just swap sides.

"Well said." Lazemus nodded. "I wasn't wrong in thinking you all have good heads on your shoulders. The princess is indeed dead, and she was killed by Edward himself."

"How can you know?" Lucas asked.

"The princesses' aid was an honorable man and a good friend of mine," Lazemus began, "he was there that night on the balcony outside, and witnessed the killing." He sighed. "However, almost immediately after, as if Edward knew he was there, guards were tipped off and swarmed the room. The aid was caught near to her body: and with no explanation he was blamed immediately."

"Was he executed?" I asked.

"Actually, in a stroke of genius on Edward's behalf, the aid escaped."

"So, he was kidnapped?" Jessica asked.

"Right. He was kidnapped and removed. This served two things: to further his guilt in 'running' and to disallow the man to ever even bring up the claim Edward was the murderer. Fortunately, he wasn't a stupid man, and left a note for me."

"What did it say?"

"In the most frantic handwriting I'd ever seen from the man. 'Edward did it.'"

"Just that? And you believe it?"

"The man had been with the princess her entire life, and was like a father, in some ways even more so than the king," Lazemus replied, "he wouldn't have the heart, and if he did, he would accept death alongside her, never run."

"Is he dead? Surely Edward would have killed him?" Glenn said.

"I believed so, but apparently my friend had secrets he kept from even me. I have found from one of my spies he is alive, and his life is safe as long as he does not reveal this secret to Edward."

Suddenly there was a terrifying gong from the distance, and bells began to ring.

"What is that?" both Alan and Richard asked.

"Gnolls. You must go, my men will take you back in haste," Lazemus replied, "I will continue this story another time; until then stay alive. I will make sure you are safe to move through the city." He turned to focus on Lucas. "That man you didn't want will still die. It is the price for harming a trusted ally." Lazemus left no room for negotiation and swiftly walked away, to make his way deeper into his estate.

The white-robed man escorted us out to a carriage as quickly as possible and rushed us to our barracks. The drums of battle had been sounded, and we were finally going to see what we were up against.

The streets were barren as we traveled, every shop covered up and every cart pushed out of the way. Guards patrolled every corner as they congregated towards the south east wall. That was also our position in this fight, and the barracks buzzed like a swarm of bees.

"It's good to see you made it back." General Rhugar waited at the front gate, ready to lead his men.

"We wouldn't miss it," I said. "How far away are the gnolls?"

"Our scouts give us a little under two hours. We should see them breaking the tree line by then."

"How many?" Lucas chipped in.

"It's impossible to say for certain, but they number in the thousands."

"Have you fought off that many before?" Jessica asked.

"The scouts have informed me that it's a larger army than any we've faced before, and by a significant margin. Your orders are to act as a special forces unit beyond the walls. I won't tie you down, but hope you'll put as much effort into defending Rigar as you can. You will be responsible for yourselves out there, and from what I've heard from guards you're quite formidable on your own." He grew solemn. "Even so, I think there is a high chance that some of you will not make it back alive." The dark circles under his eyes were creased, and his voice grew tired as he spoke. "I have things to attend to before the fight, but I will bring you out of the walls before their arrival." He didn't wait for a farewell before hopping upon a horse and galloping away.

"Is this our fault?" Glenn asked the group. "Our arrival is most likely speeding up this world's timeline."

"Probably, but we can't change it now," I said. "No one should forget the circumstances that got us here." We had been chased by gnolls with bows and swords and spears. The difference between life and death had been merely a dozen seconds at that point.

"Even if we have triggered a bigger attack, we're only doing what we needed to survive by coming here. We are not evil," Thomas said. I could tell there was a rage hidden under his calm demeanor. He said the least out of all of us, and yet I could tell he was the most emotionally invested out of all of us.

"I will do whatever it takes to ensure we survive," I said to everyone. "No matter what that means. The people here have been good to us but our priority is to each other. If we can help them out there, good; but we are not going to sacrifice ourselves for this city. The time for softhearted indecision has long passed." A moment of hesitation meant the difference between life and death. I had seen this at least three times already. Maria, myself, and our entire group had almost perished for that foolishness.

"Stay together," Lucas said. "We help when we can help, but we will not stick our necks out."

"Understood." There were nods all around and the heartfelt solidarity in their eyes was powerful. We stood together or would fall together.

Lucas began handing out excess rations to ensure anyone who needed to eat could fill up. Rhugar hadn't said how long these sieges could last, but I imagined they could last several days if the gnolls were persistent.

I opened my stats for the first time in what felt like forever.

**Name: Mike Reynolds Class: Necromancer**
**Level:** 26 **EXP:** 91%
**HP:** 1290/1290 **MP:** 485/485
**STR:** 5 **Fear Resistance:** 5
**AGI:** 2
**DEX:** 5
**VIT:** 29 +14
**WIS:** 27 +26
**Available:** 15

**Skills:** [A] **Summon Skeleton LV.** 10 | [A] **Summon Skeleton Mage LV.** 4 | [A] **Decay LV.** 3| [A] **Reanimate Dead LV.** 3 | [A] **Bone Armor LV.** 2 | [A] **Vast Shadows** | [A] **Temporary Grave LV.** 1 | [P] **Sixth Sense** | [P] **Bravery LV.** 2 | [P] **Mutated** | [P] **Pain Resistance LV.** 2 | [P] **Skeletal Mastery LV.** 4| [P] **Intimidate Living** | [P] **Inner Calm LV.** 2 | [P] **Necrotic Vision** | [P] **Blood Thirsty LV.** 1 | [P] **Cold Hearted LV.** 1 | [P] **Poison Immunity**

Besides dispatching the gnolls and retrieving the singular shaman, we hadn't done any grinding or leveling at all. I was honestly growing weary of the politics. I wanted to learn new skills, purchase new gear, and get the hell out of this place. Carving out a place for ourselves inside a dungeon wasn't my goal. Earth was my home, regardless of the situation it was in. I would live or die there, and this dungeon would just be another stepping stone on our rise.

The sooner I could pick my next skill and determine my professions, the sooner I could put in the remainder of my stats. An idea I hadn't shared with anyone, even Jessica, had been slowly blooming over the course of a week—strength was the only thing that mattered.

Nothing mattered more than grinding levels and getting gear. Overwhelming strength would ensure a place for ourselves on Earth. We could carve out a home—a community—with that power in the future. Power was wealth, and I had learned from experience that the rich ruled the world.

# Chapter 21: Encountering the Red Prince

"Look," Mark said, "over there." He pointed to an official towering on a horse larger than a man by several feet. I'd only ever seen a creature like it before in pictures. His blue attire shined with jewels and guards surrounded him. "Edward?" Mark asked.

The man's eyes looked in our direction and I met him stare for stare. His face slowly grew into a smirk before he turned the massive war horse around and trotted away. "Must be," I said. A bad feeling had crept up my neck when I looked at him. It was clear his intentions weren't good. "It's unlikely he'll act against us during the battle, but keep an eye on everyone around us, even Rigar bannermen."

Everyone gave a nod.

"Check your stats; check your gear; check your consumables," Lucas reminded us. "Have them ready to pop when we depart. I've also brought along some stat food from Lazemus."

No one held back with false politeness: each of us grabbing a snack that corresponded to our best stats. A single mouthful gave +3 to a certain stat for thirty minutes. I opted to take VIT and WIS food, which turned out to involve eating a hearty piece of steak, and a light blueberry muffin. Besides that, I also had some elixirs, passing them out as desired.

With nothing left to do, I summoned my undead squad from the shadows, feeling it was best to go to battle with them out, and myself at full MP.

"ENEMY ATTACK!" a guard screamed out, and in moments we were surrounded by men with spears drawn. The atmosphere was thick enough to be cut, as everyone in the party pulled out their weapons.

"What's the meaning of this?" A shout echoed through the street, loud enough to silence the clattering of armor and the mumbling of confused men. "Disperse! These men and women are ours!" the voice yelled again.

It was only after the sea of people parted could we see him. A young man no older than twenty appeared before us. His dark curly hair bounced with each trot of his horse. A hint of stubble speckled his chin and cheeks, but it didn't take away from the dominating presence he gave off. "It's nice to finally meet the Red Prince," I said when he came close to us.

"You must be Mike?" he asked, taking a glance at the numerous skeleton warriors and mages surrounding my group. "I've heard of you from Lazemus. You know me as the Red Prince, but can call me Arthur."

I wasn't some mastermind. From the moment the prince had arrived it was as obvious as day who he was: his entire attire was themed in red. The rubies that neatly and perfectly adorned his red velvet outfit must be worth a fortune. Paired with his young age and a presence that said 'no' was not an answer, he was clearly someone of great influence in the kingdom.

"That's good. I'm glad to see the prince is an upstanding gentleman," Lucas spoke flatteringly. "Will you be joining us on the battlefield?"

"Unfortunately not, but I will be here for morale support. I can't safely leave the walls, even among my own bannerman I'd not be safe."

"Very wise of you," Maria said sarcastically. Fortunately, Arthur took this as a compliment though, as he didn't know her temperament. It seemed she had unintentionally gained some brownie points without intending to.

"Lazemus says you're quite formidable, I'd love to see you in action," Arthur added.

I was about to speak when Maria started again, "We are good too! You should pay us per gnoll commander we take out, how about it?"

"Commanders? You're confident in killing commanders? Plural?" Arthur seemed surprised then glanced at my undead squad, maybe gauging what his expectations should be.

"Of course. I'm confident." She crossed her arms to emphasize her belief.

"Fantastic," the prince said. "If that's the case I'll give you twenty-five gold per commander." His tone of voice implied that was a good price. Maria kept her arms crossed without responding. The silence became awkward. "Thirty?" the prince suggested; again with no response. "Thirty-five?"

Maria didn't seem to want to speak up, clearly she intended to milk Arthur for every bit of gold she could. "Ahem; thirty is plenty." I stepped in before she potentially burned an important bridge. "We make no promises, but will do our best." I side-eyed Maria to stop any further mischief.

"Excellent. I'll be looking forward to it."

"Of course, your excellency. It was a pleasure to meet you." It was Anna that spoke up this time, clearly looking to gain some benefits. I had to side-eye her immediately after.

"Very good. I have to go, but it was nice to meet you all. I hope for your safe return," Arthur spoke before turning his horse way, his personal guards following close behind him.

"God, this is too much," Jessica complained. I couldn't help but agree. Politics was not my favorite activity and I decided to let Lucas handle conversations with the prince in the future as he seemed to enjoy it. "Let's just kill some gnolls; figure out what in the hell we gotta do, and get out of here."

There was an hour or so left before we needed to depart, but I opted to head to the gate anyway. I didn't want to deal with another ambush or political encounter. The guards at the gate stopped us, but provided a room for us to wait in where we couldn't easily be attacked by Edward's followers.

"I still can't figure out how the gnoll shamans tie into this?" Glenn said. "I've been thinking about it nonstop and just don't see the angle."

"Could have just been a test to see our battle power?" Richard offered his opinion.

"I'm starting to think that's most likely the case," Lucas said.

Jessica came in. "Well there is also that aid. Maybe that secret has something to do with it?"

"Potentially," I said. But we were talking ourselves in circles. There was crucial information we were clearly missing. It was possible, too, that Lazemus was intending to reveal that information to us when the war drums sounded.

When there was just twenty or so minutes till Rhugar returned, everyone went into a quiet contemplation. We were strong, but this dungeon wasn't weak by any means. We had yet to encounter elite gnolls, but surely the commanders and their highest troops could not be push-overs. There was real risk involved here, this wasn't just free loot.

About ten minutes before Rhugar's arrival, I heard a loud horn that vibrated through the entire room we were waiting in. My very body was shaking all the way to my core. "I guess it's time," I said. We quickly went back onto the streets to find General Rhugar atop his own horse. It wasn't some fancy draft horse that towered over men, no. It was a normal riding horse that any civilian might ride.

And yet, Rhugar had such an air about him that it surprised even me. I'd never not been impressed by this seemingly normal human. I didn't know the extent of his abilities, but it was clear even these dungeon people possessed skills, and professions, and potentially even levels.

Our commander was clearly hardened by war, and through the melancholy his eyes held was a fierce will for battle. The scars upon his face proved that, and so did the very way he carried himself. "I will not say much. Today, it is us or them. Us or your children! Your wives! Not all of us will return, but those who don't will not die in vain! Follow me, DIE WITH ME!" he yelled with the will to face death. There was no falsity in his words, just pure bravery.

The men ate up his energy, screaming and yelling as loud as their lungs would let them. "For Rhugar! For Rigar!" they chanted this three times, before rushing off behind his galloping horse. The gates opened as bannermen and guards alike rushed into the open field outside of the walls.

The tar pits had been filled beneath the walls. Wooden stakes had been sharpened or replaced, ready to impale any gnoll with the desire to climb these walls. At least one hundred archers perched atop the wall. Baskets filled with hundreds of arrows poked over the wall every dozen feet.

"Are you all ready?" I looked hard at every face, making sure to never forget.

"Stay close!" Alan started to slam his sword into his shield over and over as if to build momentum.

"The enemy isn't even in sight yet," Maria laughed. She was about to continue when another sword slapped into a shield, and then before we knew it dozens, and then hundreds of men began to shield slam in anticipation.

It was only the forest in front of us now. The shield slamming lasted just a dozen seconds before the area grew quiet. The scouts had reported the gnolls close, we were told that without the trees obscuring our view we would see them now.

The grass waved as a gentle breeze brushed through and the earth thrummed. The heart of the world seemed to shake as a force of death approached. If we hadn't known what was coming, that breeze would have been refreshing, invigorating—I felt it now as the breath of death.

Moments passed and the forest ahead started to shake and move as if alive. Birds shrieked before racing into the sky in panic, they formed clouds and rose together, raptors with their prey, fleeing in panic. The branches of trees cracked before trunks toppled. It sounded like thunder approaching through the woods.

And then the forest became still, presumably because the approaching army had stopped. Then smoke escaped the canopy and raced upwards, dark black smoke from the burning of green wood.

"They're setting up camp?" Anna asked.

"Looks like they are planning for a long period of fighting," I said. "And for that you need a camp."

157

A soldier close enough to hear us spoke up, "Some will setup camp, but the rest will come for us. If the battle lasts until dark, they will get more sleep than us, that's for sure."

"INTO FORMATION!" Rhugar yelled over the random chatter. The earth shook again as a thousand men moved into positions.

# Chapter 22: Battling an Elite Gnoll Brute

Deathly silence. Silence and yet more silence for a dozen seconds until a horn blew in the distant tree line and the earth trembled again.

Gnoll after gnoll came through the forest line. Drums began beating on our side as we prepared for battle. The army in front of us did not cease to emerge from the tree line until a force twice our size had entered the plains and formed up about a mile in front of us.

"That's...a lot of gnolls," Maria said. She pulled the bow from her back, as did Jessica. We all unsheathed our weapons and prepared for what was to come next. The air was vibrating from the sound of horns and drum; the ground began vibrating again as the gnolls started to move forward; everything was coming to a crescendo.

"ARCHERS!" Rhugar yelled from behind me. I couldn't help but look back at the wall, where arrows were pulled from baskets, dipped into torches and lit ablaze, then nocked. "HOLD!" Rhugar yelled again. The gnolls in the distance started to move faster in our direction till they were nearly sprinting. "RELEASE!"

"SOLDIERS, FORWARD WITH ME!" he roared as blazing arrows flew overhead. Rhugar's horse kicked up clumps of dirt as he rode forward with the infantry running behind. They moved a hundred feet forward from the wall before planting down shields like a shield wall, spears stabbing two feet out from the cracks awaiting the approaching gnoll army.

"Let's go!" Lucas said before rushing to the front line. Alan and Richard joined him as the rest of us followed closely behind. There was a wall of shields separating us from the incoming gnoll army, allowing us to pick our targets. "That over there should be a commander." Lucas pointed at a towering gnoll brute with a mace the size of a man in each hand. The brute's body was more green than brown, and one eye had been cut out with a deep gash across its face. It scanned the battlefield in front of it looking for a target.

"If that hits the shield wall, they won't be able to hold up," Thomas said. "It's a good first target for us." It was a valid point, and Rhugar had specifically asked us to support where we could.

"Can you inspect it?" I asked Jessica.

"Level thirty-seven gnoll brute. It's elite," she said before reading off its skills.

"Intimidating Presence: can Fear nearby enemies for up to three seconds, and Warrior's Spirit: increased life regeneration as life decreases."

Both skills were formidable, but Intimidating Presence was the more dangerous by far. A three second crowd control could be the difference between life and death. The other just meant we had to really burst it down, but I didn't think damage would be our problem. "Is it okay to pull?" Lucas asked. "I think we can take it."

"Let's get it out of that encirclement of gnolls," I suggested. Rushing to fight it in the middle of their army wasn't the right decision. I believed we should be able to hold our own against the brute if it was just us and him.

"I'll try to get its attention," Jessica said before turning to Maria, "join me?" And the two of them nocked arrows before sending a Godless Arrow and an Explosive Arrow whistling towards the gnoll brute.

I watched with bated breath as the Godless Arrow struck the right shoulder of the monstrous gnoll. The power of Godless Arrow had been impressive up to now. It had always exploded flesh like bursting a melon. This time, however, there was a smaller than normal burst of blood at the moment of impact. Jessica looked at me with surprise: this was the first time either of us had seen it do so little damage.

Immediately after Godless Arrow connected, Explosive Arrow followed up striking close to the first arrow and seeming to compound its effect. The apple-size wound doubled in extent and black smoke billowed from the shoulder of the brute. The hair there had been singed and the original red bleeding wound was now a disgusting pink from the flames.

The gnoll brute howled loudly in anger before its eyes darted around in every direction. It towered at least ten feet tall and had no obstruction when searching the field too look for a target. Its eyes eventually landed on Jessica and Maria, both standing firm with their bows.

"I think I got its attention," Jessica said. There was no denying that, as the gnoll brute used its massive maces to move aside the gnoll soldiers in front of it, like pushing past children. It took just a few seconds before it was in front of the shield wall and ready to smash down on the soldiers.

Any man hit by those maces, shield up or not, would be turned to a bloody paste. Rhugar understood the strange actions of the brute and could see that we were formed to face it. "OPEN THE WALL!" he yelled.

The men and women in the wall that was about to be battered and sent flying by the gnoll brute quickly moved back, left, and right to create a six-foot opening for the brute to rush through. Its eyes were seeing red, and it didn't even look back as the infantry hurriedly closed ranks again after it had passed. The monster saw only saw Jessica and Maria, the ants that had hurt it.

"Let's go!" Alan said before casting a Charge and ramming directly into the gnoll brute. His shield slammed high into the air, intercepting the arc of the brute's swing at the top and minimized the force it could muster. His jagged sword swiped across the left inner thigh, activating the special effect of Rend and inflicting a bleed.

Richard appeared at Alan's side and used the strength of his entire body to stop the second mace swinging horizontally. The shield Richard wielded bowed in as a mighty clang rang out and he was sent back three or four feet, losing ten percent of his HP from the swing. "Careful!" Richard yelled. "Its strength is insane!" He didn't hesitate to use his instant heal and rush back in.

Lucas used the opportunity provided by our tanks to send out a Wind Slash, leaving a shallow gash on the left arm of the gnoll brute. "Its skin is incredibly tough!" Clearly our melee was not going to be effective in this fight.

The brute tried for a moment to push the two warriors aside and continue chasing Jessica and Maria, but quickly realized the ants in front of it wouldn't move, nor die. It was stuck behind enemy lines, and Richard and Alan wouldn't give it a single foot of progress forward.

My undead troops encircled the brute from behind, and although they weren't able to deal much damage, I could see they were being useful as a distraction. The gnoll brute was surrounded by over fifteen skeletal warriors constantly moving in and out and attacking it. Each of my undead could only take one hit before exploding into a boney mess, but that time was crucial for allowing Richard, Alan, and Lucas some time to pin the elite monster in place.

As soon as our ranged members felt the gnoll brute was well contained, they began pelting it with spells and abilities. Quagmire Trap came out as well as Entangling Arrow, leaving the gnoll brute in a literal marsh. Anna's ice spells began to accumulate on its body, further slowing its movement.

We were all dodging incoming arrows while all of this was happening. The war was still raging around us as gnoll archers rained arrows from above. Men fell all around us, and my bone armor had deflected two arrows so far.

Thomas spent most of his time casting a HoT on our two tanks and then watching the skies to avoid arrows. No one wanted to be impaled unsuspectingly. While arrow damage could be healed, it would hurt like a bitch in the moment and definitely require actual medical attention, which would take one of us out of the fight.

I channeled Decay with my full MP. Pre-summoning my minions allowed me to be in top condition before the fight even began. It was our tried-and-true method, and I didn't even need to tell Jessica to focus on the eyes.

I focused my Decay on the gnoll brute's face, quickly causing it to lighten into a greyish green color. The scars now looked like creases on its drooping face and Jessica didn't wait to send out several Godless Arrows in a row.

The skin of the gnoll brute became soft and vulnerable, and the sturdiness around the eye socket vanished as even the bone decayed. Jessica sent arrow after arrow towards its eye. "I'm spent!" she yelled, but she had successfully blown a hole right through the only remaining eye. Even in this post-apocalyptic world, we could depend on the enemies having glaring weak spots, and these gnolls were no different.

Almost immediately after it lost its vision, the gnoll brute cast Intimidating Presence. A purple wave of what looked like miasma rushed outward from its body for at least twenty feet. Every soldier and enemy in the area immediately cowered in fear. They stopped what they were doing and crouched on the ground holding their head like a crying infant.

The gnoll brute was more than ten levels above us, and we weren't able to resist the effect either. The only exception were my undead warriors. As soon as I saw the Fear cast, I ordered nearly all of them in with no regard for their lives and they dogpiled the boss.

My skeleton general I positioned in front of the defenseless and crouched Richard, just in time as a mace came flying towards him blindly. It hurt my heart to watch the destruction of my general, but I could resummon him. The zweihander he wielded resisted the shock of impact only for a fraction of a second before the mace pushed it back into his bony frame. Then, his boney body exploded into dozens of pieces and speckled the battlefield.

Fortunately, the skeleton general had absorbed enough force to keep Richard from being turned into meat paste. My plus five Fear Resistance wasn't much, but it allowed to me get up a second earlier than the others and manually direct my undead. I focused Decay on the hand holding the second swinging mace and instructed my warriors to pull Alan and Richard back from beneath the boss.

A blind and wild attack from the brute dug a trench into the ground right where Alan and Richard once sat cowering in fear. Dirt and mud was sent soaring a hundred feet through the air before falling in the distance. A moment later Alan and Richard came to and stood up, before rushing back to the boss.

We had passed unscathed through what I hoped was the most difficult trial of the fight. Jessica was out of MP but she continued to pelt arrow after arrow into the decayed spots on the boss. Anna placed a Blizzard directly over top the boss and then sent out pulses repeatedly that cleanly sliced through the thick hide.

The regenerative ability the boss possessed was astonishing: the wound inflicted at the beginning by Jessica and Maria had already fully closed. Even the wound on the thigh and arms and all over its hind legs started to rapidly close. Only the areas burned by Maria's explosive arrow showed resistance towards its regeneration.

"We got this!" I cried. It was merely a tank and spank fight now. The gnoll was still without vision, and all it could do was swing wildly in front and around itself. My undead warriors occasionally died, but my summoned range undead were working well.

Anna began focusing her spells on the wrists, and I compounded her damage with Decay. Lucas expertly Wind Slashed along with her Freezing Pulse and after a minute, the two had bisected both hands clean off.

The gnoll brute had no eyes or weapons anymore. It turned its head back and forth, seeming to feel fear for the first time since the beginning of the battle. The regeneration it had previously demonstrated disappeared. Richard and Alan pushed forward hard while my undead squad attacked from behind.

The earth shook as the gnoll brute toppled onto its back. Explosive Arrow, Blizzard and Freezing Pulse, Wind Slash and Double

Attack came repeatedly. As every skill connected with the now decrepit and soft neck, the head of the brute disconnected from the body and rolled a few feet towards the shield wall.

A solider that felt the bisected head touch his back looked backwards and couldn't help but let out a scream. "DON'T LOSE FOCUS!" Rhugar yelled. "WE HAVE DOWNED A COMMANDER. THIS IS NOT LOST!" And then he rode along behind the shield wall stabbing out a spear at the gnolls trying to break through.

"Is everyone okay?" Thomas asked. He hadn't healed that much during the fight, only Richard and Alan took damage, and most of it was blocked by their shields. They were an impressive duo that even the toughest boss found hard to get through.

The commander had put up more of a fight than I was expecting. It was higher level than I had anticipated. In most games I'd ever played, fighting an enemy a few levels above you solo was usually okay, but maybe not an elite. There was only six of us at the moment, as we'd decided that Mark and Glenn shouldn't come into battle with us this time.

Their potential value was great, and the risk to their lives posed by high-level fights before they fully developed their classes and skills was not something I had wanted to see. Instead, they were atop the wall helping direct archers and standing ready to assist weak spots in the defense.

"Mike!" Rhugar yelled. "Our left flank is starting to fail. I'm going to call for a retreat but I need your assistance! Follow me!" Our whole group rushed after Rhugar, still behind the shield wall, dodging arrows and the occasional spear. Those around us weren't so lucky as I saw several men and women, fall.

My adrenaline was pumping when we arrived to see the scene. Gnolls had already breached the shield wall here and were wreaking havoc on the men trying to hold the frontline. Alan and Richard needed no directing as they rushed forward to meet the enemies.

These were non-elite, and even my undead squad could handle a single gnoll for every two skeleton warriors. Just by myself I could hold off five or six without much difficulty. Jessica stayed by my side and easily picked off the gnolls my minions were locking up. Anna and Lucas assisted both Richard and Alan.

In just twenty seconds, the gnolls that had breached the shield wall were dead, and I got a welcome message.

## Congratulations, you have leveled up!

There was no time to stop or check my stats, we hadn't even looked at the loot from the gnoll brute. Alan swiped it off the corpse and put it away before rushing to assist the others. "RETREAT!" Rhugar yelled. We needed to move closer to the wall, it would allow the archers to assist more accurately, but also use new weapons.

The top of the walls were lined with tar, and humungous rocks that would crush a man when tossed over. The causalities of the gnolls were climbing, and although they were dying faster than their human counterparts, they outnumbered us four of five to one. It was a battle of attrition, and the resource we were losing was people. This was war.

I shook the thought out of my head and quickly resummoned the undead I had lost from the bodies we dispatched. Anna placed a Blizzard in front of the shieldwall in our section, while archers atop the wall laid down heavy fire while we retreated with Rhugar.

The entire army moved back twenty or thirty feet and had reset themselves into preprepared pits. Wooden barricades covered the area all around the pits, and men waited behind them with shield and spear.

I could tell from a glance, even with these preparations, this wasn't a situation we would win. We would be bottled up in the city soon, and without strong reinforcements from the north and west wall, would be kept contained inside.

# Chapter 23: The Waves of Gnoll Soldiers Just Keeps Coming

We found ourselves perched behind a pit towards the left of center of the main battle. Our retreat provided only temporary relief as gnolls pushed forward without a care for their lives, like berserk animals that only knew how to kill.

Rocks launched from overhead sent gnolls and earth flying alike. Yet if only one in three gnolls made it through, that was apparently a sacrifice they were willing to make. The ground in front of the charging gnolls had been lit ablaze by vats of tar, but that didn't stop them. Dark smoke billowed from scorched gnoll bodies that smelled putrid, like burning hair and rot.

"Keep it up!" Lucas yelled. He was waiting just behind a pit, sending Wind Slash after Wind Slash at any gnoll able to make it past that killing zone in front of us. His passive skill, Ruler, was showing its merit right now, as any gnoll hit by Wind Slash died almost instantly: being completely bisected at the chest.

Jessica and Maria were releasing arrows from over a wall of fire, behind the safety of wooden barricades. They had both declared themselves to be fully out of MP, as was Anna. Thomas was nearly out of MP. While Lucas was wreaking the most havoc, he was almost spent as well, and I could see everyone in the group was growing exhausted.

The Fiend had been terrifying, but so was this relentless pressure and threat of being overwhelmed. I had never experienced such a constant battle. My squad were constantly being destroyed and re-summoned, and without them assisting our tanks, we would have been run over long ago. As soon as the nature of the war became clear, I gave up casting Decay. All of my MP went into resummoning undead to keep up our fighting strength.

In fact, our frenzied defense was the only thing keeping Rhugar from calling a full retreat. "We can't hold much longer!" I yelled towards him. He was patrolling twenty feet to the left and right trying to pick up any gnolls fortunate or unfortunate to cross that barrier of death. He couldn't see the MP situation through the party window like I could. "Three minutes at most!" I said again.

Rhugar's horse jerked with the tug of its reins and dirt flew through the hair. "MEN, PREPARE TO RETREAT!" He yelled. This needed to be somewhat organized or the casualties would be unimaginable. He raced to under the wall and yelled at the top of his lungs. "ARCHERS, COVER FIRE!"

The air above was thick with arrows. Preserving supplies for later meant nothing if it could save dozens or hundreds of men's lives now. "SOLDIERS, RETREAT!" Rhugar yelled before rushing to-wards the front line.

"What are we doing?" Maria asked. She had been ready to re-treat ages ago, and as soon as the order was called her body was already turned.

"Hold a moment," Lucas said before sending out another Wind Slash. "Just thirty seconds!"

"Don't push it!" Thomas responded. I could see his MP was al-ready incredibly low. Everyone was nearly out of MP. We were okay now, but a lot could change if a gnoll breakthrough swarmed us.

"We can save so many lives," Lucas pleaded. "Only thirty seconds!"

"Thirty seconds and not one longer," I yelled to everyone. Thirty seconds we could manage as the arrows still rained like hail from above. It was like an obstacle course in front of us for the gnolls. If the wooden barricades and pits weren't enough to slow a rush, half the ground was burning and boulders sprinkled the field. It wouldn't be easy to overrun us.

Maria groaned without retort before turning back and nocking an arrow. Everyone pulled the last bit of MP out of their tanks and fought on. Anna sucked it up and drank a MP potion just to cast another Blizzard. Jessica laid two Quagmire traps to ensure our escape and then assisted others running out.

I was fully prepared to sacrifice my squad, and they filled any gaps discovered by gnolls attempting to reach us. They were enough to block the narrow passes between obstacles. Alan and Richard went into full rescue mode and were hoisting soldiers by the shoulder and rushing them towards the wall.

This was the longest thirty seconds of my life, and it hurt my heart to see some of the soldiers we left behind as we departed. Thirty seconds was all we could muster safely. The thick rain of arrows above thinned until almost no support came from the walls. I noticed the cackling now more than ever, as the gnolls chasing us went into a frenzy.

"Don't stop!" I yelled at everyone before sending my undead squad backwards and into the approaching gnolls. Arrows and the occasional spear whizzed by us, tearing up dirt and grass.

"Please God, please God." Maria was nearly hyperventilating.

"No God's coming to save us," Richard yelled before dropping back a bit to assist Anna. Alan followed his example and raced to

Maria's side. The two turned from side to side, scanning the terrain in all directions. Richard had made the right call as he deflected an arrow about to pierce through Anna's back. "No more shield for anyone, RUN!" he yelled.

We were only a dozen yards out from the gate. Lucas moved beside me and I could see his head wander towards every wounded soldier on the field. Their hands stretched out towards the wall, some screaming for us to help them. "We can't stop!" I reminded him through erratic breaths. "Helping him is hurting yourself."

Stopping now would put us on the chopping block. The gates would close soon, with or without us. The city couldn't afford to allow gnolls to breach the walls. Support had now flocked above the gate, as a new wave of gnolls with battering rams appeared beyond the smoke and flames.

My throat was dry as sandpaper when we reached the gate and passed through safely. I couldn't even let out a good job through the panting, opting to smile and give a thumbs up instead.

"Is anyone hurt?" Jessica asked. Which got a bunch of head shakes. I opened my stats to take a look.

**Name: Mike Reynolds Class: Necromancer**
**Level:** 27 **EXP:** 32%
**HP:** 1172/1290 **MP:** 32/485
**STR:** 5 **Fear Resistance:** 5
**AGI:** 2
**DEX:** 5
**VIT:** 29 +14
**WIS:** 27 +26
**Available:** 18

**Skills:** [A] **Summon Skeleton LV.** 10 | [A] **Summon Skeleton Mage LV.** 4 | [A] **Decay LV.** 3| [A] **Reanimate Dead LV.** 3 | [A] **Bone Armor LV.** 2 | [A] **Vast Shadows** | [A] **Temporary Grave LV.** 1 | [P] **Sixth Sense** | [P] **Bravery LV.** 2 | [P] **Mutated** | [P] **Pain Resistance LV.** 2 | [P] **Skeletal Mastery LV.** 4| [P] **Intimidate Living** | [P] **Inner Calm LV.** 2 | [P] **Necrotic Vision** | [P] **Blood Thirsty LV.** 1 | [P] **Cold Hearted LV.** 1 | [P] **Poison Immunity**

I had leveled and gained another thirty-two percent EXP. We had been absolutely plowing gnolls at the end, well, mostly Lucas was. With Ruler activated and hundreds of nearby enemies, his stats were inhuman. He was a natural leader, and the role fit him perfectly. He would do excellently as a general in an army like this.

My eyes scanned the surroundings and my relieved and happy mood slowly disappeared. While we had made some great gains and came out relatively unscathed, the rest of the army wasn't so well off. This was a horrible and dreary sight.

More than half of the men I saw around me were wounded badly, and another quarter needed some form of medical attention. Triage was badly needed, and there were clearly not enough healers to assist this many wounded men. The losses this day were a horrific blow to the city of Rigar.

General Rhugar was too busy to speak with us as he constantly met different men and women for orders and information. "Reinforcements are coming!" Rhugar yelled. "Rest and heal, the wall will be defended on shifts. The gnolls will not breach!" He yelled. There was no enthusiastic response like before, there was only the groans of wounded men and their broken spirits.

"Let's return to our quarters," I said to everyone. We needed at least a day before our MP would be fully recovered. There was

173

nothing for us to do here. The gnolls couldn't breach the thick walls, but the wooden gate was a worry. I could see the dozens if not hundreds of men perched at the top of the gatehouse. All remaining rocks and oil were being brought up ready to be used in keeping that gate safe.

"Do you think reinforcements are actually coming?" Anna asked. I couldn't say there was no reason for Rhugar to lie—there was a good reason. Morale was at an all time low and being thrown to the wolves without hope might have seen men refusing to fight and instead flee the city.

"We'll ask him when we see him," I said.

We made it back to the barracks without incident and some of us were lying down and trying to relax in order to get MP back as rapidly as possible, when, much sooner than I expected, Rhugar came in.

"Do you have a few moments?" he asked much more politely than I was used to. It was clear his attitude had taken a turn during that battle. Seeing was believing, and we hadn't disappointed in the slightest.

"Can we meet in your office in fifteen minutes or so?" I asked. Not everyone was here at the moment. The women were off bathing, and Alan and Richard and Lucas were waiting for their finish to bathe as well. Those three had been covered in dirt and debris by the time we returned. I was fortunate enough to have bone armor, which only left me sweaty instead.

"That's fine. I'll be in the barracks for the next hour or so," he said before turning and walking down the hall. I wasn't brave enough to go and tell the women to hurry up as Rhugar expected us. I did find the guys and told them about our appointment.

Fortunately or unfortunately, Richard didn't have the same hesitation as I did. His head peeked through the door and yelled out, "HURRY UP, RHUGAR IS EXPECTING US AND I WANT TO SHOWER!"

Almost immediately after his yell came Maria's voice. "GET OUT YOU BUFFOON."

And just a moment later was Jessica. "Sorry, we'll be out soon." We could hear the muffled shouts of Maria, no doubt a joint operation of Jessica and Anna's hands over her mouth was keeping her from spitting more profanities.

"I'll let you handle it," I said to Richard. I didn't want to be in the crossfire. "Meet in my room afterwards." It took about twenty minutes for everyone to arrive. I could see Richard and Maria side-eyeing each other, but decided to not comment on it.

"Let's go see what Rhugar has to say," I said. I felt we had done all we could in that battle and performed without holding back. His room was wide open when we arrived, and Rhugar was inside pacing back and forth. There was no worry on his face, but his actions said otherwise.

"Ah, I'm glad you're here," the commander began, "your performance earlier was excellent."

"Thank you," Lucas replied. "We promised to do our best and did."

"That's good. I wasn't wrong about you all. I felt you would keep your word, from a gut feeling I've honed over many years. It's a skill that's allowed me to keep my place here." I understood that comment after having spoken with Lazemus. Holding a position of power wasn't easy when someone was always looking to take your place.

There was an awkward silence as we waited for him to continue speaking. Eventually Maria couldn't take it anymore. "What did you need from us?" she said. Her mood still wasn't great, probably as a result of Richard demanding she leave the shower early.

"Excuse my rudeness," Rhugar said, "I didn't bring you here just to flatter you." He paused. "The gnolls are acting strangely this time. In previous attacks, even when we were pushed back into the city, they would continue rushing forward endlessly until their numbers were too depleted to continue. So far, they have never managed to breach the walls, and even now we held some confidence they won't be able to."

"Is it true there are reinforcements coming?" I asked the question several of us were wondering.

"That's true," he replied. "The issue is that the gnolls are not attempting to put ladders against the walls or ram down the gate. We are prepared to rotate guards through the night for the foreseeable future, but the gnolls have pulled up just out of arrow range. That's new. Normally, they attack constantly for several days."

"You fear they aren't looking to storm the city but to set up a siege?" Lucas asked.

"Right," Rhugar confirmed. "Even with the arrival of reinforcements, I fear we won't be able to dislodge them." He suddenly unfolded a map and began pointing at a forest to the south east, tracing it with his fingers. "They've infested Delamere forest. The southern gate is being blocked by their numbers, and the east is being watched. Losing half of the trade routes out of Rigar is a catastrophic disaster we can't afford."

"How bad?" Jessica asked. I wasn't as worried as she sounded. There had to be reserves or supplies in the case of something like this happening.

"Bad," Rhugar confirmed, "the city can keep people fed for at most two weeks."

# Chapter 24: Missions that Lead Towards the Dungeon Boss

Rhugar explained the difficulties of the city in event of a siege, "We import a third of our food, the rest is grown on farms that can't be occupied currently, for obvious reasons. I fear that when it reaches that point, the north and west districts will refuse to share their reserves to keep themselves fed."

"Won't that lead to internal strife?" Thomas asked.

"It's very likely, which seems to be the potential outcome the gnolls want."

"How could they have the intelligence and foresight to make such a move?" Glenn asked. "They're intelligent, but not at that level of planning."

"Right, and this is what has myself and my superiors the most concerned. The stark contrast to the wild and barbaric attacks we are used to and the fact that the gnolls seem to now be following a plan leads to an ominous possibility…someone is working with the gnolls from the inside."

"How can anyone work with those things?" Anna asked. "They are disgusting."

Matters were suddenly getting more and more complicated. "Surely this isn't what you called us for? To be bottled up behind the city walls?" I asked. We had the backstory and the problem was clear to see, the question was what Rhugar expected of us.

"Ahem," he coughed, "I don't want to sugar coat it. What I'm going to ask of you is a suicide mission. We need to create a reason for the gnolls to retreat, or at least find out what the reason for this siege is. The gnoll headquarters rest twenty miles south-east of the forest line. Your mission is to go there, learn what you can, and do what you can to disrupt their plans."

"You want us to sneak out, infiltrate, and do what exactly?" Jessica asked a bit sarcastically, "we aren't ninjas."

"Ninjas?" Rhugar seemed confused for a moment. "Right, it is an impossible ask, but I am the messenger and can only follow orders. It is a request and not a demand." He sounded apologetic.

Jessica was about to say something further when I spoke up, "Do we have time to consider?" I asked.

"Yes! Of course." A weight seemed to lift from Rhugar with my question. "You can have two days to consider, by that point food will start to be rationed and things will start to deteriorate from there."

"Alright, we will consider your request. I make no promises though," I said.

"Absolutely, I also understand what it is to do what is best for your men. Their lives are your responsibility. I would expect nothing less: if you had agreed too easily, I'd be suspicious." I shook his hand and gave a nod before ushering everyone out.

"Why would you even humor him?" Maria asked as we left. It wasn't just her that wanted an answer either.

"It's possible this is the main story-line we need to complete to get out of here," I said. "Isn't it possible that the location he wants us to go contains the dungeon boss?" I asked.

"It could…but isn't that suicide?" Lucas replied.

"I don't disagree with you, and we still have time to say no," I said, "I'd rather not close a door we can leave open for a little longer. Saying no also doesn't necessarily mean we won't end up in that situation anyways. This may get us some benefits." It wasn't uncommon for that to be the case in games: being given two choices that lead to the same conclusion, except one path left you worse-for-wear.

"We should collect our gold and go make some purchases," Alan suggested, no doubt under Maria's influence.

"About that…" Mark said. "Most shops are currently closed. A lot of the men on the wall are just family men."

Maria let out an almost wail like groan at his comment. "Where's that prince that owes us gold?" Maria asked. "Surely he can make something happen!"

"You can be the first to reprimand him when we find Lazemus." Richard snorted. Which got Maria staring daggers into Richard again. Alan nudged him from the side as if to tell him he was going to be boiled alive. The fact they were both tanks had Maria throwing them in the same boat, guilty by mere association.

Looking at Maria, Alan formed an expression that screamed 'I'm innocent'. When that didn't seem to work, he unloaded the loot from the gnoll commander. "Look, we have loot!" he said, almost pleading. There were two items, both of rare quality. Alan pulled out a beautiful bow with one hand and the other hand held a hooded cloak.

**Harpy's Wing: DEX +5, STR +2, Perfect Accuracy +10%**

A bow made from the left wing of the mythical harpy. Its frame is lightweight, flexible, and incredibly durable, making it the perfect material for a bow shaft. The tendon has amazing elasticity and provides incredible shooting consistency.

This was an item made specifically for Jessica or Maria. The length of the bow had harpy feathers on the shaft, each feather morphing from red to yellow to gold and giving it a majestic and beautiful look.

Evidently, Maria hadn't forgotten that Jessica had given over her own armor to Maria on account of her near-death experience in their first dungeon. Maria passed the bow to Jessica without much thought, gladly even, which had everyone staring wide eyed at her. "What? I'm sure there will be more loot to buy later…" Her face turning a bit red. In the end, she was still a kid at heart.

The second item was a cloak, and what was cool about it was the pattern draped over the back. It looked like the wing of a beautiful moth. The shapes merged into what appeared like a menacing eye.

**Illusioner's Drape: INT +4, VIT -1, Status resistance +5%, Effect of illusions on you -50% A beautiful garb made from the silk of an illusion moth. The pattern along the back gives a mysterious but ominous feeling, making it harder for others to see through you.**

The choice for who should get this was between Anna and Thomas. I could have used it as well, but was already quite geared comparatively well. In the end, Anna relinquished the item to Thomas. I was curious how the cloak would interact with Anna's headpiece, which already masked her appearance, but it was worn better on Thomas. Having him taken out unexpectedly could leave us in a dire situation. Looking at the cloak on Thomas after he put it on and it felt like my vision was being sucked into a blackhole. Somehow it almost left me feeling dizzy.

Besides that, a few other pieces of gear were removed from inventories, mostly junkier items that Glenn and Mark quickly took and equipped. Any equipment for them was better than none.

With two days to make a decision, we decided to wait to hear from Lazemus. With how noisy things were on the surface, there was no doubt he was having a wild time behind the scenes. It wasn't until midafternoon the next day that Lazemus came see us personally with news.

He informed us that the underlying mood in the castle had taken a dark turn. There was a rumor being spread that seemed credible: the princess's murderer was somehow working with the gnolls to attack Rigar.

Funnily enough, according to Lazemus there was some truth in that situation. The reality was different than rumor, though. According to him, via information obtained through an enemy spy in a not-so-pleasant manner, Edward had somehow found a way to work with the gnolls. Not only that, his good friend and the only person who could implicate Edward in the princesses' murder was being held captive in the main gnoll encampment.

With that in mind, Lazemus had requested us to sneak in and save that person, thereby implicating Edward. That was our only mission on his end, rescue his good friend so as to implicate Edward and allow the Red Prince to ascend to the throne.

"Do we think saving this person will also put a stop to the war?" Lucas asked. "There's no guarantee both missions needed the same clear condition." Lucas said the second part under his breath so as to not allow Lazemus to hear.

"Can't be sure, but aren't you glad I didn't tell Rhugar no?" I asked everyone, almost a bit smugly. Lazemus was basically sending us on the same mission Rhugar had requested, which was leaning highly towards this being the final mission and overall objective of escaping this dungeon.

"Am I missing something? Did Rhugar request something similar?" Lazemus asked, confused at my boasting.

"A day prior, Rhugar asked us on a suicide mission to invade the gnoll encampment."

"For what?" Lazemus asked.

"He didn't specify, only that we need to find the cause for the current predicament," I said.

"Can I ask something?" Jessica looked at Lazemus before he could continue talking. "What is the secret your friend knew that Edward wants? I am refusing to believe you don't know it. No one tells you about the existence of a secret just to tell you. You know what it is, don't you?"

"I do," he said flatly.

"It's important enough that Edward killed the princess to obtain it, which means it's a dangerous secret," she added. "It's something we should know about beforehand."

"It is merely a rumor." He didn't budge.

"A rumor wouldn't be enough to kill a princess and incite a gnoll invasion." Jessica didn't back down either.

Lazemus paused for a few moments before finally cracking. "I assume if I don't tell you, then you won't go?"

"Right," Jessica said. We hadn't discussed this direction of conversation, but it was true that this secret was potentially dangerous, and definitely important for us to know about.

"It happened around twenty years ago now." Lazemus sighed. "It's been a long time. His name is Donivan, my good friend. He was a student alongside myself and Edward. We were trained by our families since youth to become influential in politics. That was our life, study etiquette, how to speak, how to control people, how to run the empire." He paused. "Edward and I, we were naturals. We lived for it—gravitated towards it."

"Donivan though, he was different. He didn't like the deceit, the games, the smoke and mirrors. He didn't have a single bone of desire for power in his body. He didn't care for power. No, Donivan liked adventure, he liked to see the world, be unfettered and free. He would regularly leave the academy for days at a time, hiking here or there and living among nature. Well, one hot summer day he returned after a small trip. A trip that was shorter than average, and he was in a hurry."

"Well, what did he find?" Maria asked impatiently.

"I caught him in the hall running back to his room, his face red as a tomato, a confusion and fear in his eyes. 'What happened to you?' I asked him. He looked frantic, 'There's a portal there, a portal to another world!' that was all he said. I didn't know how to respond as I watched him race away. He changed after that—stopped going out on adventures and traveling. He stayed inside and studied instead."

It was absolute silence. Not even Maria dared to ask another question. Was the portal in question our world? There were countless worlds according to the rulers running this oppressive 'game'.

"I couldn't get it out of him after that," Lazemus started again, "He denied ever saying it even. That was until four or five years ago. It was a cold night; the moon was full and the sky clear. We reminisced about the past over some wine, and for some reason Donivan just wouldn't stop drinking. He drank and drank until he started mumbling. 'You know, I used to think I was such a great adventurer—fearless.' He mumbled through a hiccup and the drunkenness. 'Until that day...that portal. You know what I saw?' He pointed at the sky and didn't even look at me, as if he was talking to himself. I could see the tears starting to form in his eyes, 'A whole world! A world I'd never seen, never knew, ripe for the exploring!' the tears were falling even harder, 'but you know what I felt? I didn't feel the call of adventure...just fear. I realized I was no adventurer, just a coward.' That was all he said before standing up and walking out. In all the years, he never once disclosed the location of that portal, and no one knew where he went that day."

I didn't how to respond. How could you respond to this? We were technically world travelers. The portal could lead to our own world even! Were these people and not NPC's? Was this dungeon just another world we were somehow restricted in?

Even with all the questions, it seemed we were being led in a particular direction. Defeat the gnoll tribe leader? That was probably the dungeon boss. In doing so we could rescue Donivan, implicate Edward and maybe find the location of the portal to go home? It was a plausible theory.

# Chapter 25: Deciding Between a Raid on Supplies or a Boss Encounter

"Edward knows about this portal and is trying to find a way to pry it out of Donivan?" I asked Lazemus.

"Most likely. There's something else going on too. Something to do with the gnolls. They are attacking again and again at great cost because Edward has something they want. I've no idea what though."

Jessica was frowning. "You're the one who wanted gnoll shamans."

"Right, why do you need them?" Lucas asked. This was one of the loose ends we had constantly discussed without having any answers.

"Actually, I only sought out gnoll shamans because I found out that Edward had been collecting them secretly for years. I joined in to muddy the waters, as well as see if I could figure out why he wanted them."

"You have no idea what Edward needs them for?" Jessica asked. I could tell she was suspicious.

"None. Whatever use are gnoll shamans is his best kept secret."

"So, all we have to go on is that we need to rescue Donivan?" Lucas asked.

"That would be ideal. Not only would it save my friend from mortal danger but what he's learned from his captivity might answer our questions." Lazemus looked around hopefully.

"I see," I said before anyone jumped in to agree to the mission on the spot, "we'll talk over whether we accept your quest and have an answer for you tomorrow morning." It was likely we were going to accept, but Rhugar had given us two-days to consider his request to raid the gnoll camp. No reason to not accept both quests at once.

Lazemus had no time for pleasantries and raced away upon the conclusion of our talk. "What does everyone think?" I asked. "I have a feeling that whether we accept or refuse his mission, we'll end up facing the dungeon boss: most likely the gnoll tribe's leader."

"We have no idea what we're getting ourselves into," Lucas said. "I'm not against accepting, but what we're dealing with right now is a thick fog of war."

"While true, it isn't much different than usual," Jessica pointed out, "we've never had good information ahead of our quests."

"I think that's by design," Thomas said rather unhappily.

"Heading into the unknown and depending on Jessica would be nothing out of the ordinary for us," I said. "I have full confidence in her ability." No one disagreed with that, to go into the unknown was to be filled with anxiety but we had always found a safe way forward thanks to Jessica's scouting skills.

"What about our loot? Our professions?" Maria moaned. "That was supposed to be the goal since the beginning! I don't see a new earring on my or Anna's ear." She hmphed.

"I'd like to know the answer to that too," I said, "we have a lot of gold coming our way, but as of right now it doesn't seem like shops are open." I started to question whether shopping for gear upgrades was always the intention of this 'scenario.' This felt less like a dungeon compared to the first place we had unlocked.

"It seems like we'll have to resolve this situation before being able to spend any of our gold," Anna complained, 'let's just get it over with. I want some reimbursement from Lazemus though." I agreed, although there was now a real chance that we wouldn't get to spend anything in the shops; I didn't say that out loud.

Instead, I said, "Mark and Glenn will have to come with us. There's a chance we go to the gnoll camp and have to leave this dungeon for some reason. If that portal is real, it's possible there won't be any other time to use it, leaving you two stuck if you're not with us."

"Right," said Mark, and Glenn gave me a thumbs-up.

"How long till we're all fully recovered?" I changed the subject. Apparently one day wasn't enough for everyone to get back to full MP.

"I think I'll be good by the morning," Jessica answered. I looked at Thomas who just nodded as if to say he was already good to go. Anna was also okay. Even Alan and Richard were good. It seemed Jessica's built might have benefited from increased WIS: it was my belief that she had pumped everything into STR, DEX, and AGI.

"So, we're good to say yes to Rhugar and Lazemus tomorrow then?" I asked. "I think we'll listen to what Rhugar has planned for us and go that route. I believe the outcome of both should be the same. Lucas, we'll leave the decision-making on the fly to you." I then looked at Jessica. "You'll be the one calling shots as we move, how do you feel about taking the quests?"

Jessica had been very skeptical and suspicious of almost every-one in the city. It was a warranted suspicion, and I respected her intuition. If she didn't want to take the quests sensing a trap, I'd back her. We hadn't had much alone time as of late and I hadn't been able to pick her brain.

"I'm confident we can take this on," she replied, "I still don't trust them, though."

"That's settled then. Tomorrow morning I'll inform both Rhugar and Lazemus. We go with Rhugar's plan, but only if it isn't complete suicide. In the end, we aren't going to take on a major risk for anyone in the city," I reminded everyone, "the people in this room are our priority and no one else."

With our course of action agreed, the group drifted apart and I spent the remainder of the day with Jessica. She had grown quieter the past few days. "What's on your mind?" I asked her.

"Nothing, I just have an ominous feeling. There's something not right about this entire situation." I wasn't feeling the ill foreboding she was. My Sixth Sense wasn't giving me anything.

"About our mission? Or this entire dungeon?"

"The dungeon," she said. "It feels like we've made our own choices, but everything we've done has almost been scripted since the beginning."

"I was thinking that about the gold earlier," I confessed, "it dictated our entire path—meeting Lazemus and being sucked into this feud."

She laid her head against my shoulder. "It's exhausting. I don't think I've gotten a good night's rest since we came here."

I wrapped my arm around her and pulled her closer, "If all goes well, we should be leaving soon." These were the only moments of peace I still had in this world.

The following morning came faster than expected. I started to feel a foreboding as the time to meet Rhugar approached. It wasn't

Sixth Sense, but just a malaise that stemmed from Jessica's comment. Was I really in control of my own actions?

Fortunately, Inner Calm seemed to kick in and extinguished the slowly burning unease. If I was under control without realizing it, well what was happening was going to happen regardless of if I worried or not.

"You have made up your minds?" Rhugar asked. His anticipation was clear to see across his face.

I said, "We'll take you up on your offer. Do you have a plan in mind?"

"That's a relief." The smile he gave me made it look like he had gained ten years of youth back. "Come over here." He beckoned towards his desk as he unrolled a map. "This here is where we believe the gnoll tribe's main camp to be." He pointed to a small mountain range dotted with crude drawings of huts. There was at least a dozen of them spread over several miles, but the one his finger rested on was most central, and largest. "This should be their main base, and where the gnoll tribe leader should be."

"He's not with the army?"

"No. In the past, he only made an appearance towards the end of drawn-out battles. So early in this campaign, I consider it unlikely he will appear, especially given the current situation."

"The siege?" I asked.

"Right, there have been no further attempts to storm the walls Rigar. However, the gnolls are still out there in full force. We can see the trails of campfire smoke from the forest. Your main problem is that they have scouts along the edge. If we so much as step outside the city they know and will probably attack. Fortunately, that's where you come in," he said, "there are two possible solutions to this problem that we see. The first would be the killing the gnoll

190

tribe leader. If that was accomplished their hierarchy would crumble and need restructuring, forcing a retreat."

"And the second?"

"The second would be cutting off their supply line. There isn't enough in that forest to feed ten-thousand hungry gnolls. They're constantly bringing food in. You may not know this, but as barbaric as they are, gnolls can farm. They keep cows and goats, even work the fields for crops. They just aren't as efficient as us."

"Do you have any information about the gnoll leader?" I asked. It was likely we would have to face against it regardless, but with the gnoll commanders being level 37, it was hard to imagine what level the boss might be.

"Not detailed enough, no. The few times we've seen him he has been an unstoppable force on the field. I saw him rip a man and horse in half at the same time, like breaking twigs," Rhugar shuddered at the memory.

"It doesn't sound feasible for us to kill him," I said. "While our group can set up as a dangerous threat to any gnoll; I'm not going to die trying." I told Rhugar the truth. This place was not my home. "Do you have a detailed map of their supply routes?" I asked.

He nodded and pointed on the map on his desk. "These are what our scouts have gathered over the years. There may have been more added, and some may not be used currently, but it should be eighty or ninety percent accurate." He then reached into his desk and pulled an exact replica of the map on his desk and handed it to me.

"As easy as it is to say 'just go do it,' how are we getting to that point?" I asked. He still hadn't explained a single step in his plan.

"Tonight, just past midnight you all will escape through the west gate. I've been told it's a cloudy night, and the moon will be barely visible. It will be the darkest night in the coming months. My men will escort you to the forest edge here." He pointed at the map. "From there you will travel east to the opposite end and about two or three miles out." He pointed again, "From there, you will be clear of the army in the forest and should be in view of the mountain range here. Once among the foothills, you can travel south through the fields along the cliffs and pick off supply wagons moving through here, here, here and here." Rhugar pointed at each route as he crossed them with his finger. "They will send most shipments midday, none at night and none early morning."

Following his plan, we would literally be behind enemy lines. It seemed there would be four or five routes ahead of us before we were in line with the main encampment. "How long of a walk do you think that would take us on foot?" I asked, my finger tracing the five routes and pointing a path to the main encampment of the gnolls.

"You wouldn't reach it till night fall of next day. That is if you want to be quiet about it and not have a thousand gnolls on yer ass. This area should be low traffic, and I'd suspect you'll make it to the mountains with very little action."

"And how can you be sure they won't travel at night and early morning?" I asked.

"The gnolls aren't exactly the disciplined type. You can hear them off the walls all through the night, partying or fighting or who knows what—in turn, they sleep in quite late. That doesn't mean they won't wake up on a dime if being attacked though, but it should be to your advantage."

"Understood. What time are we leaving exactly?"

Rhugar looked out the window and at the sun high in the sky. "Fourteen hours or so. My men will come and get you, just be reasonably ready. There's a little wiggle room."

"Can you supply us at all?" I asked. "MP potions, HP potions?" I asked, without being quite sure if he even knew what they were.

"You can take the map. Other than that, I'll find out what we can get for you," he replied, "there should be some of what you call 'rations' but I'm not sure about the potions you want."

"I'll inform the others," I said before leaving.

My friends were still waiting on breakfast when I returned and I gave them a quick rundown on the very rough plan, holding down the corners of the map on the table with cutlery. "I'll consider this a success if we can somehow rescue Donivan," I said, "defeating the gnoll tribe leader might be the work of another day. According to Rhugar, we can reach the encampment by tomorrow night, which might allow us to go on a night-time raid."

"We'll be able to make it there unscathed?" Lucas seemed skeptical.

"Rhugar thinks we can make it here without much trouble," I pointed, "most of the battle took place here, and the army should be situated mostly here." I then pointed out the encampments, supply routes, and where Rhugar believed we would find the gnoll tribe leader, as well as the likely place Donivan would be.

"How likely do you think we'll be able to interrupt these three supply routes undetected?" I pointed to the middle of the map and looked at Lucas for his opinion. It was the region I thought would best serve both requests best.

"I think it's possible, but only depending on how organized they are," Lucas was thoughtful, "if they are on high alert, we may end up only making it to those hills before encountering heavy resistance in the form of reinforcements. If that happens, we would probably have to retreat."

"So don't get caught is the rule?" Jessica asked. "We should be able to avoid any trouble, I'm confident in my ability to do that."

"That won't be enough unfortunately," Lucas said. "We don't have very many places to hide, and allowing ourselves to be surrounded could be the end." The scenario Lucas was describing reminded me of what happened on the way into this dungeon. "We could probably take out three of the five routes before the first route realizes their supplies are late, but going further than that would be putting our head on the chopping block. If we decided to skip the interruption of supplies and go straight for the gnoll headquarters it would be another story."

"Well, is disrupting the war or rescuing Donivan the most pertinent to ending this war and getting our reward?" Mark asked. "It doesn't seem like doing both at the same time is possible with our current strength."

"What about avoiding the supplies and just killing the leader and rescuing Donivan?" Anna made the suggestion.

"While it might be possible, we don't know anything about the boss. Not only that, if it's a situation we can't run from, we would be doomed," Lucas said.

"Rhugar claims the gnoll boss is quite formidable," I said, "considering he's seen what we have to offer in a fight, I don't think we could accomplish it easily on enemy territory at night."

Lucas had another thought. "Ending the war would allow the shops to reopen, which would probably give us a big boost of power ahead of a boss encounter. If we can disrupt their supplies even for a single day, that might prove to be enough to see results."

"Hungry gnolls will probably be angry gnolls, and I could see them taking it out on each other," Thomas added.

"Okay, that sounds like a solid plan then. We'll move tonight with Rhugar's escort. By sunrise we should be through the forest and under cliff on the edge of these farm fields, here," I pointed to the map, "from there we'll move between these two supply routes and intercept all traffic on them. Mark and Glenn you two will be responsible for keeping an eye on the roads here and here. You'll keep an eye for incoming traffic and move back to us here with any information."

# Chapter 26: Out of the Besieged City

Our planning for the forthcoming mission turned to the question of intercepting gnoll supplies. It was possible that all the gnolls' convoys were sent at the same time. We could only on one of the roads, and in that scenario, rushing the attack and then trying to hurry after the others wouldn't be safe nor feasible. We had to hope that the convoys set off at different times and move to set up in advantageous ambush locations rather than run along the roads looking for them. I pointed to the map, indicating one of the two central paths, where it entered a forest.

"If we safely dispatch any caravans here, we will be able to dispose of the bodies and evidence and wait to see the gnolls' reaction. If the hornets' nest isn't stirred, we could move to here," I indicated another path, "and make another attempt. From there we can play it by ear as to whether to try for a third."

My suggestion was well received and not one made an alternative proposal.

"How long until we leave?" Anna asked.

"Rhugar said around fourteen hours, which I estimate to be one or two in the morning. Everyone should sleep as much as they can during the day. I've also requested supplies so hopefully there will be more rations and some MP potions for those who need it." MP potions were rarer than the other elixirs and it would be a real assistance to us if the city could provide some.

Lazemus came around two hours after our strategy meeting to hear what we planned to do. I gave him the basic rundown, and left out the part where we didn't plan to rescue Donivan, not first thing at least. "We were hoping to buy consumables and gear, to increase our chance of success," I told him, "but the shops have all closed."

"I can have something arranged, but not at such short notice," Lazemus replied, "when you return with Donivan, the prince will surely reward you handsomely."

All I could say was, "Sounds good." It wasn't that I didn't trust him, but I felt that as of now we wouldn't be able to defeat the gnoll tribe leader in his own territory. Something would have to change, and for that we needed further development on our part.

The day crawled along. After meeting Lazemus and Rhugar, there was nothing else for us to do. The entire army was patiently waiting for a gnoll attack that probably wasn't coming. Besides that, an undertone of unease was slowly seeping through the ranks. Meals were now being rationed for the soldiers. Very soon, when the civilians ran out of food at home, their purchases would need to be rationed too.

"This place might be very different when we return," I said to everyone. A lot could change in a few days. I secretly feared it might come to bloodshed inside Rigar.

Only after taking to my bunk and reviewing our tactics for the upcoming battles did I start to feel drowsy.

Sleeping during the day actually wasn't as difficult as I had been expecting. Now that I knew what we needed to do and when, it was like a weight had been lifted off my shoulders. I was the last to join the group at the mess around supper time.

Rhugar came and found us while we were eating full portions: the staff had been told to feed us ahead of our mission. "I've managed to acquire some rations and a few of the potions you asked for." He handed over two sacks. One had twenty rations inside of it, the item that we could consume as players for food. The second sack had seven or eight HP potions, and then just three MP potions. The HP potions were distributed one each. Of the MP potions, Thomas took two and Anna took the third.

"Thank you," said Jessica and I nodded my appreciation. I hadn't really been expecting much when I asked, and this was definitely useful. The rations were distributed equally in case we got separated at any point. No one would be without the supplies they needed to survive.

It was a humid night; after Rhugar left Jessica and I sat side-by-side on a bench outside the dining hall. The air seemed to sit still and weigh you down. With no wind it was silent, eerily quiet. The moon had already vanished behind the clouds above, and only the twinkling stars occasionally shined through a gap in the clouds.

"Mike?" A whisper came through the door behind us, just barely loud enough to hear. "Orders from Rhugar; I've to escort you and your men." I nudged Jessica awake and put my finger over my lips. She knew to check without my asking and scanned the surroundings with her tracking ability before holding up a single finger. Could never be too careful.

"Coming," I said, before meeting messenger in the room. He waited for me to gather the others and when everyone was present he took us to into the streets.

"We leave immediately. We need to get as far from their lines as we can before dawn and we can't use a carriage outside the walls."

"Can't we ride at least?" asked Maria.

"Best if we go on foot. A few people in the dark of night shouldn't have any issues."

Maria, Richard, and Alan all seemed to have been sleeping like rocks as they rubbed the crust from their eyes. Yawns were constantly going off as if contagious. "I miss caffeine," Mark groaned.

A carriage was waiting outside the barracks and we jumped in immediately. The entire city was on curfew so besides the sound of the horses' hooves trotting on cobblestone and the wooden wheels bouncing along there wasn't a peep of noise. The driver made quick work of the empty path, despite only having a single lit torch; our escort rode alongside us on horseback.

"From here we have to go on foot. I'll escort you through one of the gaps between gnoll camps as far as the forest, from there you'll be on your own."

I didn't even take ten steps after leaving the carriage and I was already sweating. The humidity was insane and there wasn't the slightest breeze. If there weren't other people beside me, I'd think the world had stopped with how unbearably still everything felt. There would be a lot of clothes removed and plenty of complaining before this trip ended.

"Last chance to call it off," I said to everyone. Although I was sure this was the right way forward, I wanted this to be a group decision. I gave it ten seconds of silence. "Alright, let's go." And we walked through the gate and onto the dirt road. Our guide moved in front of us like a shadow, his footsteps made no noise as he jogged, but the rest of us couldn't be any louder.

"Won't they hear us?" Lucas asked. We weren't exactly very stealthy.

"It will be fine; they have camps all around the city but don't stretch themselves by posting lines outside the walls of their stockades. Am I going too fast?" he asked.

"Not at all," Jessica answered. Even without our stat increases, we were all superhuman now. Our stamina and endurance were better than even someone who trained as an Olympic athlete. "Go as fast as you want. The sooner we can get there the safer we will be." She was right; there was a considerable amount of risk being here—but gnolls wouldn't be looking for us on the farmlands near the mountainside, not until we made a move at least. We would be safer there for the time being.

We set a good pace, and after thirty minutes we reached the place aimed for by our guide without encountering any gnolls. The escort held up some sort of glowing object and showed us a map. "You're here. If you pass straight through to the other side of the forest, cross about a mile, you will see a statue of an angel along the road pointing north. That statue is right here," he pointed again. "From there you can travel east ten minutes and you should see the mountain range." This was close to the first supply route.

"Thank you," I whispered, "we can take it from here." Our escort nodded and then took off without a word or sound.

"Must be one of their spies," I said. "Surprisingly efficient."

"Agreed," Lucas spoke quietly, even though we were a good distance from the nearest gnoll stockade. "Jessica take the front, Alan and Richard shadow her." He started to give out instructions, "Maria, Thomas, Anna in that order behind them. Maria you watch left, Anna you right. Mark and Glenn you're in front of me and Mike." Everyone move promptly into a proper formation.

"I can't summon my undead at the moment. Keep that in mind everyone." The sky was so dark and moonless that I didn't even have a shadow at the moment. Vast Shadows wouldn't cast even if I tried.

"We avoid fights for now. Stealth is the name of the game—if we alert enemies they will know something is up and our cover will be blown," Lucas warned. "Let's go." And off we went. We stuck close, as everyone but Jessica and I were almost blind. My vision wasn't obstructed in the slightest at night, and I didn't see any life signatures ahead of us.

"It shouldn't be long through the forest. Just a few hours," Lucas said again. The speed at which we could move was greatly hindered here. The paths that had once been here were overgrown, as random gnoll attacks kept people from venturing in the forest for wood.

It took over an hour of nonstop walking to come out the other side of the trees. Lucas made a rough estimate on my map of where we were, and how much further we needed to go to find the angel statue, "Looking at the distance we traveled from the forest and there, at most we'll see it in ten minutes."

I trusted him without complaint. Everyone had gotten good rest during the day, we were good for several more hours—and in the case of emergency, all of us could go more than a day without sleeping if need be.

"Do you all smell that?" Jessica asked from the front. We were downwind, and a terrible stench wafted over us. It was the smell of death and decay at its absolute peek.

"Smells like roadkill baking in the sun." Richard gagged before covering his nose and mouth. Everyone quickly followed suit as we kept moving. A little stink couldn't stop us.

"I see the statue ahead," Jessica said. The sky was still dark, and I estimated it sometime around 4 A.M. No one else could see the angel but her, but we followed her closely until it was only a few feet away, and even in the darkness we could all make it out.

"There's a road, too." Jessica said. It was an actual road, and the angel statue was at the cross section, it pointed northward, as we had been told, and we confirmed our position on the map. There were four paths, and we were taking none of them. From here we would cut across farmland and head for the mountains south east. It was still too dark to see the mountain range, but we had a direction to walk at least.

"The smell is getting worse!" Maria groaned from the back. "This is awful." I could only pinch my nose harder as we entered what looked to be farmland. The cause of the stench became clear as soon as we passed a large hedgerow. Goat, sheep, cow and chicken corpses were strewn about. Most of them had been pointlessly slaughtered it seemed, and some had been half-eaten and left to rot there on the ground.

The air wasn't so quiet anymore as we moved, flies could be heard buzzing and swarms of gnats occasionally surrounded my face. "Should we check the farmhouses?" Anna asked. The chance there were survivors was very low.

"I think its best we not," Jessica said. "There's no one alive in them." She had already cleared the area, and I wasn't interested in seeing what the gnolls might do to human bodies—a grim look into our own potential fate.

"Keep it moving, it's not much further," Lucas said.

It seemed what Rhugar had said was proving to be true. We hadn't encountered any gnoll patrols or scouts, and now it was likely we were outside of their main base and operations. None should be appearing here. It was good news, but the plan had only just begun, things would get much more dangerous.

We moved carefully for another ten minutes towards the mountains, eventually leaving the farmland and stink behind us. "According to the map there should be gnoll settlements a few miles further ahead. We need to turn and move towards the roads," I said. We stayed in formation and spent even more time traveling.

As we moved in a more south-easterly direction, we were coming closer to the area gnolls would potentially be traveling along, maybe not at this time of morning, but campers could be near. While humanoid, they also resembled a hyena, and I wasn't sure how good their smell was. We were upwind, too.

"Stop, there are tracks here," Jessica announced. The grass at her feet was patchy and torn asunder; dirt had been scattered awkwardly around the area.

"Looks like a thousand people moved through here, at least." Alan squatted down to take a better look.

"Like you'd know if it was ten or a thousand," Maria joked.

"Do we keep going?" Anna asked. Things were getting real now.

"We have to keep going," I replied. "Or we've wasted our time coming in the first place." I looked at Jessica and gave a nod. Everyone got back into formation and we kept moving.

We made it barely three minutes before Jessica stopped us again, "Enemies. Three of them." She pointed down the road to where it dipped out of sight. "They aren't moving," she added.

"Asleep?" Lucas asked.

"Hopefully. Slow and steady and we'll be fine."

I still couldn't pull out my undead squad yet, but only three gnolls were no threat, we just needed to be quiet. Jessica walked in a path towards them that perfectly zigzagged around any debris that could make noise. Somehow or another, even with the gear our tanks were wearing, we moved within a few feet from their camp undetected.

It helped that Jessica could see them move if they woke. Lucas and Jessica were the best candidates for the job once we got close enough, both crept forward until they could use Wind Slash from pointblank range to de-head one, and then two quick arrows to dispatch the other two.

# Chapter 27: This Gnoll Elite is too Intelligent, and too Insane

Despite facing no further encounters with gnolls, it still took over an hour of steady travel to reach our destination. We were just west and slightly south of the main gnoll camp and carefully embedded in a small meadow between the two roads caravans would most likely travel.

I was well aware there were probably going to be multiple caravans passing us at different times throughout the morning and early day, but without insider knowledge all we could do was wait, and wait we did.

We waited for what felt like an eternity before the sun began to rise. My undead soldiers were summonable now, but due to their size and glaring lack of stealth, I could only wait for battle. Jessica patrolled back and forth between the roads and was able to scout any incoming enemies. While Alan and Richard waited, one on each side of the meadow just in case she needed immediate assistance.

The temperature quickly rose and I found myself sweating from the heat and perhaps too from anticipation of the ambush to come. The hours dragged past though and just as I began to feel impatient, and to wonder whether there would even be any cargo moving through here, Jessica rushed back to us with Alan and Richard in row. "A group of enemies incoming." She pointed to the northern road. "At least twenty. They are so tightly knit it is hard to get an exact reading."

"Follow them and we'll make a move when they are in the open, half-way across the field," Lucas said. "Can you get a better look?"

Jessica nodded and then ran along a hedge row, ducked down, looking for the best place to watch while the rest of us moved into the long grass nearer the northern road. Not only did we need to win the fight, we would have to do it in a timely manner, and then dispose of any evidence in time to move to the next ambush. Intercepting one caravan would hinder the enemy, but not enough to put a halt to the siege due to lack of supplies.

We had only moved about fifty yards when Jessica came racing back towards us. "They're coming! They have a tracker as well!" she yelled.

Alan and Richard didn't wait for orders as they rushed to Jessica. A moment later, the sounds of incoming troops entered my ears and one towering gnoll came into view, no doubt the elite of the bunch.

"Looks like you were right," Alan yelled back. We had been wagering whether the caravans would be well protected or not. The twenty gnolls weren't an issue at all, it was the gnoll elite that could bring us trouble: he was 'elite' but honestly felt more like a mini-boss.

"Shouldn't be any harder than the first!" Lucas yelled. Alan and Richard changed directions to meet the gnoll group. Jessica had already laid two Quagmire traps as she ran, and Maria shot Entangling Arrow before the fight even started. Everyone knew what to do without being told.

My undead troops came out in a rush from behind me and charged forward with reckless abandon, crashing into the wave of melee gnolls attempting to swarm us. Alan and Richard expertly tied down the gnoll elite while the remainder of us picked off the weaker gnolls. We had ample experience fighting them now, and twenty gnolls wasn't going to be enough to hinder us for long.

Lucas moved like a phantom through to the back of the group, arriving upon the two shamans who were casting from behind their melee. With every swing a head, arm, or leg flew off. Maria was careful to assist him, sending several gnolls surrounding Lucas flying with a single explosive arrow.

Anna had cast a Blizzard on the elite and then sent pulses of ice out at any gnoll unlucky enough to make it past the wall of my undead and towards Thomas and our casters. "Careful!" Jessica yelled towards Anna, and this alerted me to move in front of her and hold out my arm. An arrow deflected off my bone armor and the ricochet sliced across my calf, drawing a line of blood.

I groaned and regretted not using Bone Armor to its full potential. I could choose at will what to cover, and had assumed my upper body was enough. Fortunately, there was no second shot from that gnoll archer, as its head flew off immediately after releasing. "Back is clear!" Lucas yelled towards us. The teamwork of him and Maria had dispatched the three archers and two shamans in under thirty seconds; the shamans hadn't even had the chance to cast a spell.

"Three or four more left!" I yelled. With no healing and no ranged support, the melee gnolls crumbled fast. My skeleton general rammed his zweihander through the back of a mace-wielding gnoll before raising him in the air and ripping the torso in half.

Blood rained down over his white frame giving him a gruesome but ferocious look.

The remaining two gnolls were swiftly surrounded and devoured by my horde of summoned undead, leaving just the elite there on his lonesome. There was no fear on its face, though. Just a rabid desire to rip us to shreds.

The monster wielded a gigantic two-handed sword as long as a man is tall. A human skull was inlayed into the hilt with the blade coming out the top of the skull. It wasn't leather, but instead human flesh that made up the grip. The sword itself was more like a paddle than a conventional weapon, as the tip was not sharp, and neither was the blade.

An unlucky gnoll warrior that came too close to his own leader had been hit by a full powered swing aimed at Richard. There was no cut, just a bone-crunching sound before the gnoll body was folded like paper around the dull blade and then went flying in a bloody mist.

Bangs rang out constantly as Alan and Richard took turns deflecting the frenzy of attacks. Every missed swing sent dirt flying through the air. Alan and Richard were covered in grit and sweat from each blocked or dodged attack. Their legs bent at the knee to disperse as much force from each swing as possible.

"This one is very strong!" Alan yelled between the clangs of metal on metal. It was good news he had the ability to speak. The elite wasn't so overbearing that the two couldn't retaliate or handle it, and both Richard and Alan backed off momentarily to regain their footing and regroup with us. The gnoll elite was already isolated, and running would not be an option for it any longer.

There were clear differences between this gnoll and the first elite we had battled, mainly the age. It was clear to see a much more youthful appearance for this one. The fur was lighter, the eyes brighter, even the muscles of its arm and shoulders were more defined. It cackled with excitement before dragging the paddle-like blade through the ground towards our two tanks.

There was no honor in war, and Jessica didn't wait for the fight to start up again before sending Godless Arrow through the air. Maria joined her with an Explosive Arrow while Alan cast Charge and Richard assisted.

The cheekbone of the gnoll exploded in gore and the eye almost fell out of its socket. Surprisingly though, this wasn't enough to blind the gnoll elite. It howled in agony and jumped back a dozen feet, evading Alans and Richard's forward charge while grasping at its face. The eye that was moments from dangling out was held firmly in place between an open hand, the eye fiercely gazing through its fingers.

"Humans, you die." The gnoll elite grasped the sword more firmly and then rushed forward with a sweeping motion. Alan and Richard both raised their shields to their chest and planted their legs, but that alone wasn't enough. The two couldn't block the full sprint momentum and were sent flying back onto their asses six or seven feet in front of us.

My undead soldiers rushed forward with reckless abandon, trying to buy time for the two to regain their footing and keep the elite off our vulnerable members. Jessica aided with another Godless Arrow, this time dispatching the right eye completely.

Even with its hand firmly covering his wounded eye, there was no stopping the Godless Arrow, which left the gnoll elite perplexed. It howled again; this time louder. Loud enough to hear half a mile at the very least, which left us potentially exposed.

"Human will die here," it said again, "your skull will be new weapon." It pointed at Jessica and hoisted the blade over its shoulder, caressing the skull that acted as a decoration piece. Red blood from its missing eye poured down its face. All around me I saw frowns and concern. This gnoll was too intelligent, and too insane.

"It might've called for backup," Lucas said. Which I was thinking too. The problem was, the elite was faster than us. While we could easily keep it here if it wanted to run, we couldn't just run away from it. It would slow us just enough to bring us to our graves.

"Let's go all out," I said. It was our only option, and there was no hesitation from anyone. Jessica and Anna both popped an MP potion immediately, as did Thomas. Blizzard came down and another Godless Arrow exploded on the face of the gnoll elite. It only cackled, not seeming to care about the wound that was inflicted, or if it would die here or not.

Instead, it came forward like a storm, the paddle-like sword sending a wave of air that blew our hair back. Alan met it head on and didn't take a step back this time. He drank a strength potion and seemed to let go of some of the reserve he was feeling, his muscles bulged behind the shield as his face turned red. He was boiling for battle and blood—he wanted to fight.

Lucas was the same. His reserve had disappeared completely as there was no time to wait. He rushed from behind during Alan and Richard's onslaught and stabbed his blade directly through the back of the gnoll elite, so deep he couldn't even pull it out with all his strength.

Like lightning a huge hand flew back and smacked into him, sending him flying through the air and hurdling into a tree a dozen feet away. His HP plummeted from 90 percent down to just twenty with one attack. Thomas threw him a heal-over-time and Lucas chugged a HP potion before waddling forward.

The gnoll elite was essentially blind, but that fact didn't matter at all. It only needed to swing its blade in a circle to hear the clash of a shield being smacked. No one but the ranged could attack, and Lucas couldn't recover his blade. Eventually, Richard made a bold move and rolled forward during one of its attacks, narrowly dodging the blade and causing the gnoll elite to trip face first over his body.

Alan jumped onto the gnoll elite's back and plunged his blade into the spine several inches deep. The serrated edge left blood gushing, but similar to Lucas, he couldn't remove the weapon when he pulled back. "More enemies coming!" Jessica said suddenly. "No, it's the second caravan!" she added.

The gnoll elite below was on death's door but building one last burst of strength. Just before it could fling Alan and Lucas off its back, Mark came forward and jammed his spear straight through the neck and into the other side. Blood poured out like a faucet and the elite collapsed to its knees, scrabbling at the weapon before falling over. Mark was a big guy like Richard and clearly gifted in strength, "The neck is the weak spot," he said confidently.

# Chapter 28: Battling Two Gnoll Elites

Before anyone could loot the corpse of the gnoll elite, a boulder three-feet wide came smashing down like a bomb. Dirt flew through the air twenty feet high. The scattering of debris could be heard shaking tree leaves around us. Eventually, the boulder rolled into a tree trunk and made it crack like thunder. Another twenty gnolls came running at us.

"Hold them back, for just a minute!" Alan yelled at Richard. Both Lucas and himself needed to retrieve their weapons still.

"Got it," Richard spoke confidently. His sword began smacking into his shield, which started to grow hot like molten iron. Thomas threw a heal-over-time on Richard who started running forward to meet the incoming enemies.

My undead soldiers joined in just behind Richard, with instructions to intercept any stragglers who tried to run past our tank. I pulled two MP potions from my inventory and tossed one each to Jessica and Anna. Decay wasn't nearly as useful in these large-scale fights as the area-of-effect dot that Anna could cast.

The power of a mage class was marvelous, not only did Anna drastically slow the incoming enemies, powerful and sharp shards of ice punctured every portion of their body. It was if their hide was nothing in front of the power of mother nature. I suspected even bone armor would be torn like paper under her spells.

Lucas managed regain his weapon out first, just in time to bisect a gnoll that was barely five feet from Thomas. Another gnoll had gotten past Richard and my undead soldiers. I cast a full body Bone Armor and had no choice but to tackle it to the ground so as to save Maria from being battered into meat paste. The side of my arm acted as a hammer as I pounded it into the gnoll's head, only stopping when it ceased biting at me.

It was havoc all around, and I could only shift my attention away from our group for just a moment, long enough to see one gnoll elite swinging a rock trapped inside a net of rope. Every time it hit Richard's shield, our tank buckled another inch, and even though his blocking was successful his HP was dropping steadily.

"Hurry up Alan!" Richard yelled between blows, and then swiftly retreated back towards us. More than half the gnolls had been dispatched, although my undead squad had started to dwindle. I constantly picked out corpses from which to spawn new skeletons and keep fighting.

Between Lucas, Richard, and my undead soldiers, we kept Anna, Thomas, Jessica and Maria well protected. The melee skeletons I summoned fell quickly, but all my MP went into resummoning. Further off, two gnoll shamans and three archers were dispatched with well-placed releases of Explosive Arrow by Maria. Two of them lucky or unlucky enough to survive the blast were struck through the neck by Jessica.

Only after the regular gnolls died could we focus our attention on the elite. As I did so, I realised we weren't facing just one, but two elites. It seemed like the battle had been ongoing for a long time, but since the gnolls had arrived and the twenty common types were dispatched, a mere fifteen or twenty seconds had passed. We had become that efficient at killing the fodder.

The first gnoll elite was several heads taller than the second. There was a striking red mohawk coming from the top of his head, and this wasn't because it had red fur. I assumed it was blood, but it could have been from berries or some other coloring dye. The tall elite wielded a rock as its weapon, strapped by thick ropes that let it swing it around with incredible deadly force.

The second gnoll was smaller, and didn't look much like an elite at all. It wasn't easy to tell at a glance, but on closer examination it was clearly different from the yard trash we had fought. There weren't any weapons in its hands, instead there were metal claws attached to its arms, almost like Wolverine.

"That one might be fast," I called out. Its body was too sleek, too compact.

We had finally regrouped; Alan had barely managed to retrieve his blade from the first gnoll elite's back, the corpse of which was a dozen feet to my right.

"Human, you did?" The smaller gnoll elite looked at the corpse and back at us while asking in broken English, almost in disbelief, whether we had killed one of their generals.

"You're next." Alan said with a bloodthirsty smile. Jessica and Maria both nocked an arrow at the same time, promptly taking aim. As soon as they let loose, Alan rushed forward with Richard behind him. I moved half of my undead soldiers to assist and kept the other half back as a reserve against any unexpected development. Lucas shadowed both of the elites while priming a Wind Slash.

The smaller gnoll gave me a bad feeling from the get go. It moved at the same time as Alan, and it was clearly twice as fast, or faster. It avoided Alan, who faced off against the tall, mohawk elite. Fortunately, I had half my squad in hand and I sent my skeleton general rushing to block the fast elite, only for it to be sidestepped. I was next and I put myself in the path of the swift elite: it was after our ranged, and was smart enough not to have calculated this was how to defeat us.

"RICHARD COME BACK!" I yelled. A moment later, a claw came grazing past my shoulder. Bone armor caused the metal to spark and my Sixth Sense was screaming bad news. I could see the second attack coming for my gut, and was certain it would tear right through bone armor and all the way out my backside.

Just before that happened, a bolt of ice came flying at incredible speed and smashed into the gnoll elite's side, sending him off balance. Richard arrived a moment later and cast his instant heal on me, topping me off before blocking its path. "Sorry," he mumbled.

Having failed to cut down our ranged members, the fast elite backed off with Richard taking serval steps after it.

"Nice save," Jessica yelled. She hadn't expected the speed of the elite either. She had focused her attention and her archery on the bulkier enemy. But the sooner we could isolate the fast one, the easier it would be on us. I recalled all my undead troops and I surrounded us in a wall where each skeleton stood shoulder-to-shoulder with the next. Unable to close on the fast elite, Richard also came back, waiting to intercept any further attempts.

And there were. The fast elite tried several times to break through to our less well protected members, and even though it could slice my skeletons into pieces in half a second, that brief pause allowed Richard to fill the gap and keep us safe, and for me to resummon my undead soldier. After about ten attempts, the gnoll elite grew frustrated and listless.

When I was able to check on the battle with the large elite, I could see it was missing an eye and one arm. The weapon it once had no longer worked, as Lucas had Wind Slashed through the thick rope and sent the boulder hurdling away. There were more rocks in the caravan, but it couldn't move to grab them. Blood dripped down from a dozen slashes and several parts of its body were frozen solid in ice. The confusion in its eyes grew each passing second, all it could do was flail its arms and legs in a desperate struggle.

Victory looked to be in sight, but then the gnoll that seemed to want to assassinate our squishiest members did something unexpected. It faked a frenzy of attacks, killing several of my undead soldiers, before shifting direction and sprinting towards Alan from behind.

"ALAN CAREFUL," Maria yelled, but it was too late.

The blades on the arms of the elite went straight through his Alan's back and then tore out in one swift motion sending blood squirting through the air. Richard could only see red and rushed out with reckless abandon, Lucas did as well. Lucas didn't even use Wind Slash and instead decapitated the bulky elite with a jumping swing before landing to try to guard Alan's fallen body.

We all went forward to Alan in response. Thomas sent three heals in quick succession, but our tank's health was rapidly plummeting still. My undead quickly surrounded him to keep any further attacks from happening, but the Wolverine gnoll elite kept his distance, without making a second attempt on Alan. He was smart enough to realize that we were powerful enough to hold him off. Suddenly, it raced into the distance, likely for reinforcements.

Maria supported Alan from underneath, while I removed his shirt in haste. The wound was terrible, and I couldn't be sure if it was poisoned. I pulled out several bandages from my bag and an HP potion.

I uncapped the potion and poured it into the wound—I wasn't sure if it would have any affect as for now his HP total was back in the safe zone, I just hoped it would have some form of healing effect to slow the rate at which Alan's HP kept dropping. Jessica helped me wrap bandages around Alan tight five or six times, sparing no expense on supplies.

I could hear Glenn mumbling under his breath, "Please let it have missed." Adrenaline was high and I could only assume he meant important organs. As soon as we bandaged him up, the rapid falling health slowed, but it was still going down.

"He has internal bleeding," Thomas said. I was certain that was true, but didn't know how bad this was and if it would stop on its own.

"We have to go," Lucas said. "More gnolls are surely coming."

I nodded. "Destroy the carts." I looked at Maria. "Use Explosive Arrow." No response. It was as if she couldn't hear me, she was in complete shock.

Jessica reached down and patted Maria's shoulder, "We did all we could, we have to finish what we started." She helped Maria let go of Alan and then started off towards the far cart. There were two explosions within fifteen seconds and the two raced back. "It's time to go," Jessica said.

# Chapter 29: The Yellow Prince

Mark and Richard supported Alan on each arm as we raced towards the farm fields. We had been a lot less stealthy than we wanted, and no doubt the fast gnoll elite from our battle would be back shortly with more enemies.

We had been running for about ten minutes, and a less-than-ideal distance, when a horn blew from behind us. Pursuers had arrived sooner than I expected, and anxiety started to set in among us all. Alan was mumbling under his breath, almost delirious. "It's gonna be okay," Maria gripped his hand tight as we rushed along.

"What do we do?" Richard asked as we moved. The issue was whether to stop and fight or try to outrun the chase. Thinking about how dangerous the surviving elite was made my decision easy.

"Don't stop running," I called out. "If we stop, we are gambling with all our lives." Alan was also still steadily losing HP. It was hard to tell if it was poison or internal bleeding, but his condition was not good.

We had left in such a hurry that not a single piece of loot had been collected. It was clear now, though, that we were not strong relative to the gnolls as I had imagined we would be.

As we ran, I saw Jessica launching Quagmire traps behind us. So long as she had mana it was a good idea but the size of the trap was so small I doubted they would help much.

The seconds and minutes passed to the pounding of my legs and my increasingly heavy breathing. By the time we made it to the farmland, there was still no sign of gnolls on our trail. Whether they had given up or through sheer luck, it seemed we had lost them. Knowing the difficulty of the terrain of the forest ahead and considering our speed, I had no doubt we would have had to make an impossible decision if the gnolls had been close enough to see us. We would not be able to outrun them.

The angel statue was a welcome sight in the early afternoon. Sunlight hit it so that I felt a sense of piety. The silliest thought came over me, that maybe it had protected us in some way.

Alan slowly stabilized as we moved. His face lost its sickly red hue and his eyebrows un-scrunched. He was still losing HP, but the rate of decline had decreased substantially. Even without potions or healing, it would take a day or two for him to perish. Earlier, his HP were falling so rapidly, he wouldn't have lasted two hours without Thomas' heals.

I'd never have thought I'd be so happy to see the open plain just west of Rigar. It was quiet at the gate, only one guard there on duty to let us in. He was in the know, and wasn't surprised to see us. "Where's everyone else?" Lucas asked.

"The gnolls breached the forest again and look to be mounting an imminent attack. Everyone is on the southern wall preparing for the worst." I gave a nod and followed the guard to the road where a cart had been waiting. We loaded up Alan and made our way back to the barracks as fast as possible.

General Rhugar was there waiting for us, and on seeing Alan's condition, wasted no time. "Get a medic immediately!" He barked an order at a subordinate who rushed away. "Tell me everything." He ushered us to a side room with full privacy.

Thomas stayed with Alan as did Maria, ensuring he was stable in the moments we waited for an actual medic to look at his wound. None of us were doctors and knew exactly how bad the situation was.

Lucas took the reins with Rhugar and explained the situation as clearly as possible. "So two Caravans?" Rhugar asked after some clarification. "It's not the best case, but it should help." He sighed. "It's only been twelve hours but things change fast. Since daybreak they've steadily exited the forest and seem prepared for a charge."

"The guard mentioned imminent attack," I said.

"That's the consensus right now, and it's stirring the pot in a bad way," Rhugar confirmed.

"Sowing discourse and causing chaos or a genuine attempt to storm the city?" Lucas asked.

"I can't say for certain." Rhugar wasn't going to be drawn on Lucas' speculations.

"Where is Lazemus?" I asked. There were things he needed to know as well.

"He shouldn't be long," Rhugar said. "The man at the gate was one of his men, he knew as soon as you were back. If there's nothing else, you all should rest. It will be many hours before we know if your efforts have borne any fruit."

I gave a nod and led the others out and into the hall. They all chose to get a warm meal despite such meals not really doing much to satiate hunger anymore. I wasn't in the mood for tasting, so opted to get nothing for myself.

An actual medic came and took Alan before we even finished meeting with Rhugar. Our tank seemed to be in safe hands and Maria had gone with him. There was relief on the medic's face on first look at Alan's wounds, which gave me some confidence things would be fine. To be sure though, Thomas was monitoring Alan's HP in the party window.

I had underestimated the gnoll's intelligence and readiness. The caravans of supplies were not as easy to pick apart as I had expected them to be. Their intelligence also put us in a precarious situation with Alan. Encountering gnolls with the foresight to deflect and then sneak attack Alan wasn't something I was familiar with. The world seemed to be growing yet more dangerous, worrying me further about returning to the outside world.

It only took some thirty minutes before a messenger arrived to get the news from us. To my surprise, I went to give my report and found that I wasn't meeting with Lazemus, nor one of his servants. In front of me was the Red Prince in person. "Lazemus couldn't be here," the prince said. "I will hear your news and assist however I may."

Lucas took the time to explain the situation, which seemed to get a rollercoaster of facial expressions out of the Red Prince. "I don't think we're strong enough quite yet to rescue Donivan. We wanted to get new equipment and learn some professions, but the city has been basically locked down."

"Very well," the prince announced. "In that case, I will take you to the royal armory as soon as possible. However, even I have to make an appointment with father and that may take some time."

"Alright, in any case one of ours is injured so we may need a few days," Lucas said.

"Badly injured? I'll have one of my men send remedy. We have some miraculous medicine in Rigar." He smiled with pride. "I'll also gather a few craftsmen and profession masters. I need to inform Lazemus, but expect word soon."

The Red Prince appeared to be a man of few words but this made him seem all the more dependable when he did make a promise. Even better was that I felt completely normal around him. My sixth sense usually gave me the vibe of anyone I encountered, and almost always it felt like I needed to be slightly cautious around people we didn't quite know.

Even more surprising was our next visitor, and someone I hadn't expected to meet in the slightest. The Red Prince's opponent for the crown, and someone we hadn't really heard much about—the Yellow Prince.

Edward was thrust to the fore as an enemy by Lazemus, but he didn't much talk about the Yellow Prince whom Edward worked for. Reality was though, that Edward served only two people, the current king and his second son, the Yellow Prince. It was hard for me to separate their connection.

The prince was dressed in full military attire minus a hat. A sunflower-yellow trench coat covered from neck to shin. The buttons were made from what appeared to be white ivory and the tassels sparkled gold. Every military emblem he had, while not many, was embroidered with sparkling topaz that shined like the sun.

The Yellow prince had a striking resemblance to the Red Prince, and I'd almost suspect they could be twins of some kind if they weren't born years apart. My sixth sense though, it made my hair tingle at the nape of my neck. While it wasn't a guarantee, I knew despite his outward appearance this man was a crafty individual and someone to be wary of.

"Are you Mike?" He approached with steady and measured steps, the result of diligent training no doubt. His facial expression was stoic and didn't give off any inclination of disgust or excitement in meeting us.

"That's me." I stood up to show my respect and offered him a seat. "You must be the Yellow Prince?" No one else could afford to adorn themselves with so many brilliant gems on their clothes besides those two.

"Indeed, I am he," He replied. The Yellow Prince sounded nothing like the Red Prince. There was almost a suave sort of charm to his voice that made me feel a bit icky. "I came to find out if I can help with anything you may need." It was too measured.

I was actually at a loss for words. I was expecting the leader of our opponents in the city to maybe mention our negative relationship and try to smooth it over. Alternatively, perhaps use force to threaten me to discontinue assisting the Red Prince. Or, the Yellow Prince could simply put on a friendly face and stab us in the back— there were many numbers of things he could have done or said to intimidate me.

Instead, he spoke in the most pacifying and appeasing tone. As if his only purpose to exist was to ensure things went as smoothly as possible for us. I almost believed that to be true; it probably could be if we agreed loyalty to the Yellow Prince, but that was already out of the question.

Lucas spoke up swiftly in my place to avoid an awkward situation, "We appreciate the offer but are currently on standby while a member recovers. I can fill you in on the details if you would like." His offer got a few odd looks from the group, but I agreed with his appearing to be in favor of peace. There was no need to blow the factional rivalry of the princes out of proportion right now. And in any case, the Yellow Prince would discover the information he wanted with or without us.

Lucas moved him several tables away and started to give him the rundown.

"I don't like this," Jessica said as the two got out of ear shot.

# Chapter 30: The Patronage of the Red Prince

While Lucas talked with the Yellow Prince, Thomas was getting fired up. "We know what side we are on and so does he. This is a trick of some sort."

"It's fine." Richard put a hand on our healer's shoulder and I was glad to see it. Normally, Alan kept Thomas in check, but with him recovering from his wounds, it seemed that Richard was willing to play the role of peacemaker. "There's no point in starting a fight right now. We might be able to get out of a confrontation down the line, but right now we would starting something that must suit the Yellow Prince or he wouldn't be here."

"Right, we need to keep out of the crosshairs for now and wait for our moment," I agreed wholeheartedly. "It's frustrating, but we aren't able to go wild until we get what's available to us here: the new gear and professions we badly need." I had no doubt we could fight our way out of here at full power, but then the gear and skills and future professions would be out the window. "Let's endure the politics for a bit longer," I said to everyone.

Lucas continued with the Yellow Prince for a dozen minutes before the rival faction leader stood up and left. The entire time I watched him his facial expression didn't change, but the feeling I got from him did. It was clear the initial friendly greeting was only because we weren't yet closed off. It seemed Lucas thoroughly rejected him, and the Yellow Prince when he left ¾ without any farewells ¾ his face was stern.

"Hopefully that's the first and only meeting we have with that guy." Lucas wiped the sweat from his brow and let his actual feelings show through. "He's dangerous, much more so than the Red Prince. He nearly trapped me with his words a dozen times."

"He is a politician after all." Glenn laughed. "You made it out without starting a civil war."

"Barely. It felt like I was talking to a snake ready to strike."

"If there's nothing else I'm going to get a shower and nap," Mark said, and Richard suggested the same shortly after.

"Go; we aren't doing anything without Alan." I said. Alan was still losing HP slowly over time, which meant his wound was still bleeding internally. Our main tank being fully functional was our biggest concern.

The next day we received news back from the Red Prince. He had gotten the go ahead to allow us access to the armory, as well as recruited over a dozen crafters to assist us in any profession we wanted to learn. I didn't know how that process worked, but Lucas was convinced it was possible to do so. The Red Prince had also sent the miracle medicine, which to my surprise worked as he had promised it would. I couldn't help but wonder if the Red Prince had made more of an effort to keep us sweet after learning of the visit of his rival, the Yellow Prince. In any case, this help was what we needed and I appreciated that.

The internal wound that Alan seemed to not be able to heal disappeared just a few hours after we gave him the medicine. His HP finally stopped dropping and a rosy complexion covered his cheeks.

We let the Red Prince know we would be prepared to set out again the following morning, giving Alan ample time to rest. I had an early night in the hopes of removing the fatigue in my bones—the next mission was all or nothing.

I didn't wake normally the following morning, but instead to rabid commotion. We didn't even make it out of the garrison before the news reached us. The gnolls had temporarily retreated into the forest and showed signs of leaving. When we met him, Rhugar was all smiles. "It seems whatever you accomplished has put them on pause temporarily. The gnoll warrior you fought first was someone of importance. Rumors say he was the son of the current gnoll chief, and others just say he was a nephew or distant relative. Regardless, good work." He didn't come empty handed either, passing a pouch that had a dozen MP potions at the very least as well as thirty or forty rations. "It was all I could get on such short notice, but it's not enough to repay you."

"What's going to happen now?" Anna asked him.

"We are sending for food supplies from a nearby kingdom immediately. It's risky, but if we can bring in some grain, we may buy ourselves valuable time."

A guard approached just as he finished speaking. "The Red Prince is here." He addressed Rhugar, which got a chuckle out of him.

"He's not here for me. I suppose you all have some business?" He was clearly curious but didn't push for an answer. I had been cautious of Rhugar at first, as was he to us, but slowly he had become someone that left me feeling comfortable. He was a straightforward and honest man, and I realized that I trusted him whole heartedly.

"We are going to the palace today," Maria said, barely holding back her excitement. She had returned in the night after Alan's turnaround. She had needed a good night's rest, too.

"We're being supplied," I could see that Lucas had cut her off before she spoke too much. "Then we'll make another attempt to ambush the gnolls."

"Well, you've bought valuable time for yourselves and all the citizens of Rigar. I truly respect you." Rhugar's eyes scanned each and every one of us. "I won't keep you any longer. If there is more that I can assist you with, don't hesitate." He disappeared around the garrison wall and headed for the southern gate with haste.

"Shall we?" I looked at everyone while beckoning with my arms. We had to stop and pickup Alan, and then we would take a carriage to the palace. I was bubbling with excitement, not only for the loot and possible professions, but the experience.

We shadowed Rhugar for two blocks before he fully disappeared, leaving us in a medical area. Tents were strewn about that housed the majority of those injured; Alan had been put in his own room on the far side and had a full-time nurse watching over him.

The guard outside his room gave a nod as we approached. "Visitors!" He yelled towards the opening of the tent before moving aside and allowing us entry. Alan was awake and sitting up in bed already waiting for us. "Took you long enough." He laughed before gripping at his lower abdomen.

We crowded around him. "How're you doing?"

"Never better." He joked while holding up his clothes. There were now several holes the size of quarters where he was pierced by the gnoll elite's claws. "Came to take me away?"

"We're taking you shopping," Richard joked. "We have a hot date at the capital."

"The Red Prince has gotten us access to the royal armory, we're going to gear up and see what benefits we can get."

"Finally," Alan said while leaning up, letting out a slight groan.

"Careful," Maria supported him as he stood up, showing a rare affectionate side.

"When do we leave?" Alan asked after finding his footing. He slipped on his tattered clothes and followed us out with Maria and Richard hovering closely. "I'm fine guys," he said. "It just aches, I can walk on my own."

"We leave now," I said. "The carriage is here already. Make sure you thank the Red Prince thoroughly; he provided the medicine that took care of your wound." Alan nodded in understanding.

The carriage in question was clearly a show of goodwill, and I questioned whether it might even be the prince's own personal transportation. The body of the cart was made entirely out of metal and not wood, perfectly polished and shining in the early light. The encasement was a beautiful wood embroidered with red intricate engravings that screamed wealth.

Even the horses were extravagant. The two draft horses were tall and wore body armor. A metal spike extended from their skulls that would clearly impale a man if needed. They alone were weapons of war and gave off an intimidating presence.

"Thank God," Alan let out a sigh, "if I had to bounce up and down in a cart I might die." He groaned while holding his wounds.

Both chauffeurs stepped down and elegantly opened the side doors, carefully assisting the women in first before allowing the rest of us to enter. I was honestly blown away. I'd have considered myself hard to surprise after all I'd seen, but I couldn't distinguish the inside of the carriage from what a beautiful car would look like.

The seats were covered in a blood-red silk material. Fluffy pillows, lightly embroidered with gold and red, covered every seat. There were even windows that could open, albeit with a handle. Overall, though, it was more luxurious than I could image, and it was much cooler than the outside.

"Where has this been the past week? I'll have a word for Lazemus when I see him..." Maria moaned while the rest of us marveled.

"Feel this material," Anna said while running her hands along the seat cushion. "I'd like to sleep in this just once." I couldn't tell if it was silk or not, but it was incredibly similar and insanely comfortable to rest on.

"I feel like I'm going to slip off," Richard joked while melting into the floor like a puddle. This action inadvertently helped him discover a compartment full of casks of liquor. He gave one look at everyone and decided to not even bother asking, popping the top and chugging several gulps. "It's safe to drink," he said. Only Glenn decided to join him.

"Excuse me, whose cart is this?" Lucas called out towards the front.

"This is the prince's personal carriage." That was a nice sign of goodwill, and I felt a little bit less nervous about the consequences of Richard and Glenn cleaning out his alcohol. Money wasn't something he lacked.

"Maybe we should just ask him for it," Anna joked.

I felt even more amazed when the carriage started moving. It wasn't perfectly smooth, but the softness of the cushions absorbed any bumpiness we would normally be feeling. Alan was the most grateful of us all for that.

The royal palace was located dead center of Rigar. We were in for a luxurious trip to say the least, and both Richard and Glenn fell asleep with a soft red pillow scrunched in their chest. They had emptied two bottles of an amber liquid together, and were now lightly mumbling in their sleep.

As we moved more towards the palace, the signs of closed businesses and empty streets I had experienced in the southern part of the city dwindled. Shops were open and people bustled through the streets. It was clear most of them were wealthy individuals shielded from the problems of the poor.

Nearly two hours passed before we spotted our destination. Towering was an apt term to describe the dome-shaped palace when it came into view. It was hard to believe such a medieval looking city could have structures that looked so magnificent. Lazemus's palace could not compare in size or grandiose nature to the tower.

"It has to be constructed with magic," Lucas said. "I refuse to believe this is manmade." If it had just been a question of size, I'd have disagreed with him, but the entire palace sparkled like a gemstone under the sun.

It appeared to be made out of glass, but not interconnected pieces. It appeared as one continuous structure, as if a giant took up glass blowing and formed and molded the dome himself.

The surrounding garden was vibrant with hundreds of flowering plants and majestically carved bushes shaped like any number of animals. The entire aesthetic screamed rich beyond belief, and any guilt I may have had over taking gear from the royal family vanished at that moment.

# Chapter 31: Inside the Vault of the Royal Palace

"Clean 'em out," Anna whispered under her breath, loud enough for all of us to hear but not the nearby chauffeurs. Maria gained a dangerous glint in her eye which almost had me laughing, like a dog that had spotted a steak and was waiting for their owner to give the go ahead.

"Don't be shy," I said to everyone, giving tacit approval for the idea of gaining a share of some of the wealth on display.

There were two butlers waiting for us when we arrived. The chauffeurs stayed to tend the horses while we made our way deeper into the palace. Despite its beauty, it was a lonely place, and it seemed that almost no one but workers resided here.

"Where is everyone?" Jessica asked and I realized she wasn't just talking about the rooms we could see: her tracking meant she could also tell how many people moved about the grounds.

"The king likes his privacy." That seemed to be all the butler would say, even though Lucas encourage him to say more. I'd never heard mention of a queen, and perhaps with his beloved daughter passing recently, the king was retreating into total privacy.

"Will we meet the king?" Maria asked next and again got the same response about privacy. Perhaps the king was on a path to becoming a recluse. He certainly couldn't run a large city while mourning. If so, the fact that the fight for the throne was becoming so intense made more sense to us now.

"Right this way," one of the butlers said, clearly rushing us along and trying to avoid any more questions. "Please be polite, the king likes his quiet."

I nodded to show my understanding and we raced through the hallways at a brisk pace. The floors were marbled; the twenty-foot walls were decorated with golden and red and blue and purple drapes; there was stained glass in every other window and doors carved of hard wood three inches thick depicted battles won and lost to history. The building was huge and all of the interesting art-works we hurried past meshed together as if one. Very quickly, I was completely lost.

The guide turned left and right, and eventually we happened upon the Red Prince. "I'll take them from here," he said to the but-ler, "Please continue to take good care of my father." He clapped his hand on the guide's shoulder and gave a smile. I could tell at once that it was genuine.

"It's good to have you all here." The prince turned to us. "It's just this way." I liked how few formalities he needed, there was no pride or ego. He was down to earth, and I could imagine he would serve the empire well. Better, it felt, than the Yellow Prince. Some-how, we had ended up on what was probably the good-side. "Are you liking the palace?"

"Very much so," Anna said, "it's beautiful."

"It's been standing for three-hundred years now." The prince gestured vaguely towards a large hall. "It was constructed as a gift by the elves. To them it will still seem like a new construction, but the royal palace has been our family residence for several genera-tions."

"We're here." The prince had brought us to a large, complex double door, with metal strips over a wooden frame. He turned a key in the huge lock and pushed it wide, steeping aside to look at how we responded. "This is our store of precious items. Take what you need to defeat the gnolls, but please, nothing more."

"We'll only take what we can immediately use," I assured him.

"That's all I can ask." He gave a bow and gestured us inside. "I have urgent business to attend. A butler will remain outside for you all and fetch you in an hour. One hour is all you have before trainers arrive for you, so don't waste it." At that, he briskly rushed away.

None of us could wait a second longer, pressing together to get through the open doorway. The royal vault was a lot different how in my mind I had believed it might look like. Somehow, I figured it would be like a dragon's den: unorganized with gold and goods strewn about randomly.

Instead, everything was arranged efficiently. That the entire room was well maintained could not be doubted. Racks held all the weapons along the wall, neatly organized to their specific sections. Stands held up metal armors, while the leather and animal-based armors hang upon the wall.

Everything was sparkling clean, from the greaves made of steel, to the arm guards made of leather. Someone took meticulous care to keep this place well maintained. Probably the butler waiting outside for us to finish up.

"I'll help myself," Maria said obnoxiously loud, making it abundantly clear she would not be holding back.

I couldn't resist either and respectfully walked over to a pair of leggings made of scales linked together to form a chainmail.

### Basilisk Scale Leggings: VIT + 5, Damage Taken -10%

Leggings made from the scales of a mythical basilisk. Their extreme resilience absorbs substantial amounts of damage.

The leggings didn't quite fit me, but this item would be an upgrade for Richard or Alan either of whom would love to have them. "Nice tank pants over here," I yelled to the both of them and then moved for the next piece of loot.

I made my way around the room inspecting gear as I gazed.

### Loath Beads Turquoise Amulet: INT +5, Effect of Curses +25%

An amulet made from the bones of some evil creature. The beautiful turquoise doesn't take away from its menacing nature.

Not for me, unfortunately.

### Blight Torch Medallion: INT +3, VIT +1, Fire Skills +15% damage.

A crystal of unknown nature holds remarkable power. The ghastly swirl resting inside the stone leaves you feeling uneasy.

I kept looking through as I was fascinated by the gear I was seeing. The others were the same, shopping through every piece of gear of the hundreds upon hundreds in the room. Eventually one of the necklaces caught my eye.

### Corpse Beads Bone Amulet: INT + 5, Summoned undead damage and movement speed +25%

An amulet of unremarkable construction. A single fiend's finger bone seeps ghoulish miasma that aids in the control of the undead.

I was absolutely ecstatic with my find and this prompted me to search through every slot of gear until I was putting on an entire new set.

### Grim Knot Band: INT +4, VIT +2, +1 to maximum number of summoned undead.

This simple band contains an unimaginable amount of resentment. You feel closer to death wearing it.

With that, I now had two rings because I didn't see myself getting rid of my other ring. Temporary Grave was incredibly useful and it also gave me skills. For now, it didn't seem I could equip more than two rings, but I hoped that would eventually change as we leveled more. I could have taken more, but reminded myself of my promise to the Red Prince.

### Cadaver Hide: WIS +5, VIT +5, All Resistances +5, Summoned undead have +15% cast speed.

The hide of an undead abomination. It provides wonderful protection and resistance.

This chest piece was above rare and instead glowed purple. For now I would call it 'Epic' as the tier of loot. I couldn't turn it down despite it looking so bad, stats didn't care about my aesthetic.

### Sin Step Boots: WIS +3, DEX +1, Fire Resistance +10, Movement speed +15%

Crafted from the leather of a demonic beast, these boots have a hellish feeling to them.

My pair of corpse runners had been with me since nearly the beginning, but the measly +1 VIT couldn't compare to the stats this was boasting.

"How's it going for you all?" I asked curiously. It wasn't difficult for me to find incredible gear and my requirements were probably much more stringent than the others. Stats alone weren't enough, I also wanted special effects, especially those beneficial for my summoned undead squad.

Only Anna had the ability to respond as the others furiously rummaged through piles of rings and amulets, "Amazing! Ha ha." She spoke like a programmed robot. The abundance of loot was frying her brain.

"Mike, this bracelet is for you." It was Jessica calling me over.

"Let me see." I reached out to take the steel band.

### Bloodied Shackle: VIT +5, DEF +2, Allows the user to contract a demon.

The dried blood on this shackle of unknown material holds tremendous power over demons.

While not having WIS, this was still hard to pass up. The defensive stats were impressive and the idea of contracting a demon was too enticing. I started to feel my excitement bubbling imaging what kind of new abilities I may have after fully equipping myself.

"I'll keep my eye out for you." I told her, but from the looks of her new attire she was having no issues finding suitable gear for herself.

I still wanted to get a new headgear, gloves, and leggings at the very least. Finding a new weapon and shield would be ideal, but I had no guarantee I'd be able to do so. We only had one hour to search through hundreds upon hundreds of (often heavy) pieces of gear.

After thirty minutes, I had satisfied my requirements:

### Skull Head Bone Helmet: WIS +2, VIT +5, DEF +2, Summoned Undead Maximum HP +20%

This sturdy skull provides magnificent protection from physical attacks to you and your undead.

### Demon Nails Scaled Gloves: WIS +4, VIT +2, Casting speed +15%

A pair of gloves made from the weaving of nails from demonic creatures. Every movement makes an eerie sound.

### Parasite Clutch Leggings: STR +2, VIT +7, Disease Resistance +25

Leggings made of a sturdy but malleable material. They wiggle and bulge as if parasites push and maneuver through them.

I almost couldn't bring myself to take these due to the pants looking as if maggots crawled beneath the surface, but they really were incredible. There were other pairs that had INT, but the stats didn't match up, and these were also Epic.

Amazingly, I had also found a new wand.

### Lich's Bone Wand: WIS +8, Minion Damage, Attack, and Cast Speed +15%

The wand of a powerful Lich. It glows and radiates a beautiful but dangerous miasma. Holding it too long may cause rot!

The wand perfectly balanced with the Parasite Clutch Leggings. My previous Survivor's Rod only gave 50 HP and 3 WIS, so the upgrade was substantial to me and my minions.

I opened my gear to take a look at my new stats in the light of all these items.

**Name:** **Mike Reynolds Class:** **Necromancer**
**Level:** 27 **EXP:** 88%
**HP:** 1290/1565 **MP:** 595/595
**STR:** 5 + 2 **Fear Resistance:** 5
**AGI:** 2 **Shadow Resistance:** 5
**DEX:** 5 + 1 **Disease Resistance:** 30
**VIT:** 29 + 39 **Cold Resistance:** 5
**WIS:** 27 + 48 **Lightning Resistance:** 5
**Available:** 18 **Fire Resistance:** 15

**Skills:** [A] **Summon Skeleton LV.** 10 | [A]
**Summon Skeleton Mage LV.** 4 | [A] **Decay LV.** 3|
[A] **Reanimate Dead LV.** 3 | [A] **Bone Armor LV.**
2 | [A] **Vast Shadows** | [A] **Temporary Grave LV.**
1 | [P] **Sixth Sense** | [P] **Bravery LV.** 2 | [P]
**Mutated** | [P] **Pain Resistance LV.** 2 | [P] **Skeletal
Mastery LV.** 4| [P] **Intimidate Living LV.** 2 | [P]
**Inner Calm LV.** 2 | [P] **Necrotic Vision** | [P] **Blood
Thirsty LV.** 1 | [P] **Cold Hearted LV.** 1 | [P] **Poison
Immunity**

I couldn't stop myself from ogling at my stats. My HP had
jumped up nearly three hundred, which was an incredible percent
increase. I had also gained 110 more MP and an unknown amount
of MP regeneration, but it would no doubt help in the fights to
come. I still kept 18 stats in reserve just in case. If I needed to add
WIS during a fight, it would provide me with the MP immediately
and could make the difference between life or death.

Besides that, the +5 All resistance on Cadaver Hide seemed to
allow me to see all the elemental status currently in the 'game'. The
three main elements: Cold, Lightning, and Fire and then three
darker elements, Fear, Shadow and Disease.

My summoned undead squad had also undergone a drastic
change, maybe even more so than me. Between the new equipment
and old, I had gained +1 to my maximum number of undead, 40%
to their damage, 15% to their attack speed, 30% cast speed and

25% movement speed. I imagined they would move around like a swarm and truly over-run anything in their path. This was my ideal for being a true necromancer.

Between my Skull Helm and the Skull Mask, there seemed to also be a special effect added as Intimidate Living was now level two instead of one.

"You look like a Hollow straight out of the Bleach anime," Glenn said. I understood that reference, and it gave me a slight boost in confidence until Maria spoke.

"Don't look at me please, it's gross and gives me the ick."

Jessica came over and wrapped an arm around me. "Just be sure to take these off when we go to sleep." She pointed at my head and new Parasite Clutch leggings. I didn't blame her in the slightest.

"How did everyone do?" I asked. There was merely ten minutes or so left before we had to meet the profession trainers.

"Out of this world," Alan said, "I think I'll take an elite gnoll one-on-one when we go back." He was burning with excitement. Anna did a twirl that showed off sparkling gems imbued with magic and I couldn't help but wonder if she went for aesthetic over stats.

Everyone had done remarkably to increase our strength, and there was more to come. I had no doubt we would be powerhouses once we returned to Earth. This boon was not something easy to come by and would keep us alive and thriving.

# Chapter 32: Choosing Crafting Professions

"I found a piece for every slot," Maria said proudly. "I even had time to spare to help Anna." I could tell the two of them had been up to no good, but decided against poking that hornet's nest.

"We probably have a few minutes remaining," I said. "Does anyone want to keep looking or should we finish up?" There were a few unsure faces but in the end no one decided to take another trawl through the gear.

Alan rushed to the door and knocked hard. "We're done in here!" he yelled. The sound of a lock unlatching echoed through the room and the door swung open slowly. Only when I looked at the edge as I passed it could I tell just how sturdy the door was. The door was made of solid metal at least three inches thick, which went to show just how much the city valued this storeroom. I hadn't noticed it coming in, because I couldn't look at anything but the potential gear we could obtain.

"I hope none of you have any regrets," a guard said. "There will be no coming back once you leave." He pulled a time-keeping device from his pocket. "You have six minutes remaining before you are due to meet your crafting mentors, do you still wish to leave?"

I suddenly had the impression that this was a person who took great care in maintaining the room. It almost felt as if he was offended that we weren't looking through the gear up until the final moment.

"I appreciate your concern," Jessica spoke up before anyone else could. "We've found all we can use. It will help us tremendously."

"Very well. I'll take you to the showing room now then." The guard turned and led us out of the armory.

"What's the showing room?" Lucas asked.

"It's a place for entertainment. It doesn't see much use these days, and the prince has decided it will be perfect for speaking with you." That reply left me all curious, but the guard didn't expand on it any further. We followed in silence for a few minutes before arriving at a place that was much grander than I had expected for a 'showing room'. There was a massive wooden stage at one end, no less in size than one a modern play would be held on. The seats extended out and up, with balconies sitting in four spots around the room, providing perfect vantage points.

In fact there was nothing plain in the room, the cushions of each seat were vibrant with colors, and the way the light glistened atop their surface told me they were silky smooth and no doubt comfortable. The entire area screamed of wealth, and yet the butler only referred to it as a 'showing room.'

"Are you sure you have brought us to the right place? Isn't this a theatre or grand hall?" Glenn muttered, obviously thinking along the same lines as me.

"The grand hall burned down twenty years ago," the guard said, "This was the replacement they put up on short notice." Maria looked like she wanted to bop him upside the head for not realizing how extravagant a room this was. "Come wait upon the stage, I have placed chairs for you behind a table. The professionals you will meet will walk along the other side." He ushered us up the stage and onto some expensive-looking chairs, then rushed swiftly into the wings.

"What crafts do you think we can learn?" Mark asked. "I don't suppose there will be many options."

"I wouldn't be so sure," Lucas said. "The leatherworker I spoke with definitely alluded to having many friends interested in gaining our business."

"I can't wait to find out," said Maria. "I'm going to get some overpowered profession."

I leaned forward to look at her. "Patience. It might be a while until they are organized to come in to us. And it might all be a waste of time."

"Let her daydream." Jessica gave me a playful nudge. Had I become the fun-killing uncle of the bunch? Funny enough though, we didn't have to wait long as I said. The steward came back huffing and puffing as if he had run the entire way.

"Sorry to keep you all waiting," he said hoarsely, "I will bring them in."

My anticipation was overwhelming. After five people came through the door without stop, Lucas had a smug look on his face. Eventually, a dozen people stood in front of us, each representing a different profession.

It wasn't guaranteed that every profession was something we could obtain and learn, but the more opportunities, the merrier. Men, women, old and young stood in front of us. Some were elegant and aesthetically pleasing—the tailors, the jewelers—others not so much, such as the blacksmiths and manual laborers.

They introduced themselves one at a time, and the list of possible professions we could learn started to roll in, a long list. Not all of them seemed useful, but most did. It seemed the Red Prince had grabbed someone from every useful job he could think of, as even a banker was included in the lineup.

Starting from what Lucas already knew, there were craftworkers for: Leatherworking, Blacksmithing, Tailoring, and Jewel Crafting. These encompassed the three basic armor types of leather, plate/mail, and cloth as well as accessories. These were extremely straight-forward and self-fulfilling professions. Eventually you would be able to improve your gear with it, which was the allure.

Magical and crafting professions like Alchemy, Enchanting, Rune Smithing, Gem Cutting, and Jewel Crafting caught the eye of Anna and Maria. I suspected mostly because of their fancy hand movements and beautiful emblems. These professions were best suited for gear augmentation and while it could improve your own gear, seemed to have a much broader implication.

There were gathering professions too, which included Herbalism, Farming, Mining, Skinning and Witchcraft. Witchcraft was the only one I had not been familiar with, but after a very basic explanation it seemed to revolve around harvesting even the bones and organs of creatures you killed, which may have come in handy for some demonic class types, of which we had none.

All the gathering professions paired well with another profession except witchcraft. Mining with Blacksmithing and Jewelers, Skinning with Leatherworking, Herbalism with Alchemy, and Farming with Cooking. Cloth for Tailoring seemed to be a random drop from monsters according to what the instructor said.

There were also professions that went well together on their own. Gem Cutting and Enchanting were two such professions. Gem Cutting was just the base form of Jewel Crafting, which was the act of enchanting a gemstone to be embedded into gear. Jewel Crafting was not, however, related to the practice of jewelers

244

making equipable accessories. It was slightly confusing, but still understandable. You could be a Gem Cutter and sell raw gems to enchanters for them to enchant and sell as Jewels. While those Jewels could potentially be put into rings and amulets, the actual crafting of those accessories was not related.

This pairing made it much easier to decide what route one should take after picking a main profession. Alan didn't have to think much at all, instantly requesting to learn Blacksmithing, and in turn also Mining. Everyone else took a bit longer, and carefully watched Alan's experience play out.

Each of our crafting mentors in front of us had brought several books with them, which were clearly notes they had taken over the years. If we were in the mode of old Earth, Alan would have needed to study hard under the tutelage of his mentor. Instead, he took the book of notes and information in his hand, and said, "Yes."

"What was that?" asked Maria.

"I was prompted by a message: Do you wish to learn Blacksmithing?"

"And did you get the skill?" Lucas was eager.

"It's not like I'm suddenly an expert by any means, but I now have a profession tab showing my level in Blacksmithing. The book has become an inventory item which outlines the different types of ores I will need. as well as how to compose them in crafting: How to smelt and wield a hammer, those types of things. They are all gated by my Blacksmithing level.

"The mining profession works the same. I learned it as simply as placing my hand on the booklet. Information filled the profession tab: where certain ores are best found; how to mine them efficiently; even what materials were best to use in recipes; when to upgrade my mining pick; and how to forge tools like that as a Blacksmith.

"I have a third profession slot as well," Alan added. This was an amazing surprise for me and, to judge by their expressions, everyone else. With the professions working so well in pairs, I was expecting there to be only two slots. This welcome news meant I could take two main professions plus one gathering profession. Meanwhile, Alan announced that he had learned to be a Jeweler as his third. His brief overview showed that Mining paired well with Jewelry Making as often bands and chains were made from gold, silver or some other rare metal material.

Anna went next, and her choices were also not very surprising. She was our only caster, and her mentor had urged her to choose Enchanting and Jewel Crafting. According to her mentor, those apt in magic were much more adept at these two professions, as they were mostly caster-based. Runic circles and magical hand signs were required, which she was familiar with already. Her third profession ended up being Tailoring, as none of the gathering professions interested her. I suspected she might not want to get her hands dirty.

Jessica went next, choosing Leatherworking and Skinning, she chose Cooking as her third profession.

Richard followed and chose a similar combination to Alan, except he selected Rune Smithing as his third profession instead of Gem Cutting. We were quickly covering all the bases of available professions. While I didn't think this was every possible profession learnable in this new world we found ourselves in, it was a great start.

Everyone put a good amount of thought into their decisions, which was nice to see. Eventually I was the only one left.

Do you wish to learn Alchemy?

After talking to the appropriate mentor, I was given a prompt and swiftly said 'yes'. My character sheet now had a new tab to access, my professions. Clicking on the Alchemy tab allowed me to see my level, which was 1, and a few basic potions I could make, which all turned out to be some grinded herb and water mixed in a bottle— as basic as it could get.

After that, I selected Herbalism. Maria had also taken Herbalism, but I didn't want to depend on anyone to obtain the things I needed for my main profession. Maria hadn't selected Alchemy, only I had done so.

My third profession was what had me brooding for so long. "Is it possible that materials obtained from Witchcraft would be usable in Alchemy?" I turned to the instructor for Witchcraft.

He was a decrepit old man late in his years. His back hunched and a can held him upright. His grey eyebrows were long and twirling and his entire demeanor was somewhat menacing. "It's not uncommon, but they are mostly used as substitutes to bring out different Alchemical affects."

I didn't need to hear anymore, swiftly learning Witchcraft.

# Chapter 33: Leaving the Palace of the Red Prince

"A good choice." The decrepit old man who I had gone to patted me on the arm. "Come here, I have something extra for you." He took a book from a brass box and held it out for me to touch.

I walked over excitedly and placed my hand firmly on the book cover. A swathe of information flowed through the rugged, aged leather and filled my profession tab. With a thought, I browsed the new tab under Witchcraft to see what the book contained.

It was full of Witchcraft Alchemy recipes: long lists of how adding certain materials to traditional Alchemy concoctions would produce variations instead. The names of the items and mixtures were completely foreign to me, but it was enough to know they were there to be confident I could eventually learn to make these alternative potions and pastes.

"If everyone has gotten their professions, it's time to meet the Red Prince," the steward stood anxiously at the door.

"Thank you all," Lucas said to the staff who had brought us these important new powers. "We'll do our best to quell the gnoll invaders."

"Try to not get eaten alive." The decrepit old man laughed. He was clearly a bit eccentric and not afraid to mince words. That made him more agreeable to me than those who tiptoed around their words.

"No one will be getting eaten," Maria replied proudly. I could see that everyone was feeling a lot stronger than when we walked in. "We are…" Maria was about to continue boasting when she was cut off.

"The Red Prince should be here any moment now," the steward raised his voice, clearly trying to move everything along. "Can our mentors and guardians of the professions follow me now please," he was almost shouting as he herded the crafters and artisans out the door.

"We all appreciate it," Lucas called after them, but the steward had already disappeared out the doorway and most of those following him were out of earshot.

"I had so much more to say," Maria harrumphed.

Conversation quickly turned into a fiesta of profession talk that Jessica and I excused ourselves from.

"How do you feel about our chances?" I asked her. I trusted her judgement more than anyone else's, even more than that of Lucas.

"I think we'll be okay," she replied. "If everyone else upgraded themselves as much as they seem to have, then I think we will prance our way out of here."

"Prance?" I chuckled. "Honestly, I think that even though you and I are better geared than the others, they have probably upgraded even more than we did." I paused. "I do hope we can prance out of here though." Now that we had professions, a quick return to Earth would be ideal. In my daydream we had an easy boss fight and then we unentangled ourselves from the throne feud. "I'm interested to see if we can now do more for the people surviving on Earth."

"Agreed. We've achieved as much as we could have hoped for here."

"Except perhaps help the Red Prince to power and get another reward for that." And as I said that the door creaked open and the Red Prince walked in.

"I hope you've not been waiting long?" he asked. His eyes stayed for a longer than normal time on Anna and Maria, who were decked out in their splendid new items. I wondered if the Steward had found something else to do so as not to be reprimanded. We were supposed to be modest…I was going to speak up and say something apologetic when Anna rushed forward instead.

"Not at all," Anna spoke sweetly. She was wearing enough jewelry to be considered royalty now. "You're just in time. We really appreciate what you've done for us." I'd seen this move before from her, and it usually worked. I was optimistic.

"Good…" He paused. "I'm sure your new capabilities will take a bit of getting used to. Let's get you all back and well rested for your mission."

No one complained as we followed him out and I didn't feel like talking or trying to justify our choices. It was a relief to leave the palace. While beautiful, the atmosphere of the palace demanded a certain level of respect that was oppressive and tiring. The buildup to seeing what was on offer had been so suspenseful that now it was hard to believe it was over.

There was already a carriage waiting for us when we stepped outside. I turned to the Red Prince for a moment. "What mission is planned for us when we return to our barracks?" I asked. While he was considerate, the idea of giving us extra rest was a bit far-fetched to believe.

He gave me a long look and then said, "It's true, you're expected to leave tonight to tackle the gnoll general." This made more sense to me and was probably also why he didn't make a comment on Anna and Maria's extravagant 'shopping spree'.

"I suspected as much," I replied. "All is good. Thank you for the help. The gear we've obtained will make us that much more likely to succeed." The entire interaction was mutually beneficial. I didn't feel so bad about looting his treasure when I thought about it that way. Some items for the throne? I was sure he would take that deal any day.

For us, the sooner we dispatched the gnoll boss, the sooner we could get back to Earth. The risk we were undertaking compared to him wasn't quite equal, but we had no choice. "We'll do our best." I waved to him as I raced towards the carriage and then stepped in.

"What a lonely place," Jessica said as we pulled out, leaving the view of the palace far behind.

"You mean the whole sub-world or the prince's place?"

"All of it. The city surrounded by a gnoll army."

"I really wanted to get out of here originally," Mark said, "but it's grown on me."

"If we go back to Earth, I'm gonna miss it," Maria confessed, "sleeping under the stars with no security is not my idea of a good time."

"Treat this like a vacation then," Jessica said, not just for Maria to hear, but for everyone. "This might be the most relaxation we get for a while."

Jessica had given me the perfect opportunity to speak up. "Relaxation isn't on the menu currently. We will be heading out tonight." I told them what the Red Prince had said. "Which means our nights of sleeping in a bed are gone."

"Do we have a new plan?" Thomas asked.

"I think we use the same route, but this time head straight for the main gnoll encampment," Lucas said. "Before, we weren't confident in a direct confrontation so we avoided it and opted to be sneaky instead."

"We can discuss it now," I said to everyone. "I'm on the side of direct confrontation."

"That leaves us open for counter-attacks though," Glenn said. "No sneak attack means the full force of the gnoll invasion could very well loop back on us, or even be waiting for our arrival."

"Just have the city deal with that problem," Richard suggested, "have them send out their men and force the issue on the open field."

Jessica spoke next, "Ideally this is going to be in the middle of the night. But we can't rule out they will be prepared for us."

"I'll talk to Rhugar when we return," Lucas said, "if he can have a sizeable force ready in the early morning, the threat of their attack will impede any retreat and reinforcement attempt."

The idea for the plan was starting to come together quite smoothly. "So we take the same route, approach as undetected as we possibly can, but we aren't shying away from a fight. If Rhugar can mount a force that will keep the front lines busy, we can make a play against the gnoll leader and potentially end this entire incursion in one night." After I paused, I added, "as of right now, this should be our game plan."

"What about the Yellow Prince?" Alan asked.

"We can't influence that situation anyway. The Red Prince and Lazemus are surely hard at work keeping him in check. If he is assisting the gnolls in some way, it will be hard for him to make a move openly when our mission is public knowledge," Lucas said.

"We should expect them to be fully prepared for our arrival, even having traps ready for us." I looked at Jessica. "You'll be our eyes as usual, and the final call can be made by you whether we advance or retreat." I looked around the carriage at everyone. "Does anyone have any questions or concerns?"

No one did, and the trauma from our last battle seemed to have disappeared with the acquisition of our new gear. Even Alan was fully confident and roaring for a fight. I only hoped he didn't have some underlying issues from his past brush with death. Only time would tell.

"Let's get some rest when we return, it's going to be a long night." I leaned back on a comfortable pillow and closed my eyes. The excitement of the palace, our new gear, the professions, it all faded away into some obscure feeling of unease. It wasn't even Sixth Sense giving me that feeling.

I guessed that was just the human psyche at work. We were walking into the unknown and it was scary, regardless of how well we were prepared. All we could do now was push forward and hope for the best. Cracking my eye allowed me to see Anna, Glenn, and Thomas with glazed looks watching the passing streets. I couldn't be the only one feeling this pressure.

The entire carriage hummed through the streets, and before long the rhythm helped me push all concerns out of mind and bring me to a deep sleep.

"Mike." I heard Jessica's voice and felt her nudging me awake. "We're here." I hadn't slept so deeply in a long time. It was surely a feeling I was going to miss once we returned to Earth. "Lucas is taking care of the preparations with Rhugar. He said everyone should rest up if they wanted to."

"Alright." I nodded as I wobbled off the carriage. I was starting to feel the hunger of having not slain any enemies. It wasn't possible for me to eat rations and sustain myself anymore. "Let's take it easy until tonight," I suggested. I was still drowsy from sleeping on the carriage.

Lucas returned around an hour and a half after I got off the carriage. "I've talked to Rhugar and we are good to go," he said, "sunrise tomorrow morning he will sound the horn and all available troops will enter formation outside the walls.

"So we strike then?" Alan asked.

"We strike shortly after we hear the horn of battle. That should focus the gnolls on the city, and give us crucial time."

"Anything else?" I asked him.

"I spoke with Lazemus as well. We haven't seen him, but he's been busy. He's almost certain there is cooperation between the Yellow Prince's side and the gnolls. He's been applying heavy pressure with the nobility, and spreading rumors about the deceased princess and a gnoll conspiracy. There are too many eyes for the Yellow prince to act without being discovered."

"That should give us an earnest fight then," Richard said, "I hate playing these pissing games anyway." There was some battle spirit in his words, and I could tell Alan was firing up as well.

"That's the hope." Lucas looked at Jessica. "You'll still be the determining factor on if we go for it or not." She gave a stern nod in response. "We'll be leaving in around six hours. If all goes well we'll be coming back here at least one more time. If not, this may be our last time in Rigar."

While fond, I hadn't grown overly attached to Rigar. The Red Prince and Rhugar were the only two people I truly felt indebted to. While Lazemus had helped us greatly, he had also embroiled us in this mess in the first place. I had said my goodbyes to the Red Prince, and tonight I'd see Rhugar before leaving. There wasn't any other attachment I needed to consider.

# Chapter 34: When the Hawk Flies, Armies March

When we left, the moon was just a slim crescent in the night sky. The air was thick and humid. I felt weighed down just walking in the night-time air, and in only a few minutes of travel, my clothes stuck to my skin as if glued on.

Cicadas, or maybe crickets, sang without stop. It was an orchestra in the dark, the sound encompassing us from every direction. An occasional gust of wind moved the short grass like a wave and provided a moment of reprieve from the humidity. Somehow, I felt for a few moments I was back home on Earth. The feeling of nostalgia was only interrupted by the occasional rattle of Richard's shield and mace.

We didn't have a guide to bring us this time, and that was fine as we knew the proper path to avoid early detection. No one knew what we would encounter this time though. Were the gnolls going to be extra cautious because we had just attacked? Or would they remain lax and not expect a second attack so soon? We could also be walking into a trap, too.

The extent of the strength of the gnolls had probably never been tested as much as it had been by our involvement in the war. And it made me worry that they had powerful reserves that would now be deployed, especially since they had the courage to assault the city. It was this mission or nothing, though. Our ticket home.

We moved in our normal formation, and Jessica was scouting the front. The more we experienced this post-apocalyptic world together, the more I realized just how insanely lucky we were that Jessica had chosen the class she had. Her tracking was invaluable to our survival.

"Nothing besides scouts," Jessica said as she surveyed the surroundings.

Maria stuck close behind Alan. "Nothing is good," she said.

We made quick work of the forest. If there was one thing I noticed about our increasing power, besides the glaringly obvious skills, was our ability to adapt. I hadn't gained any skill like 'Forest Running' or anything, but moving through the undergrowth felt only slightly different from walking on a clear road now. This terrain couldn't easily hinder us anymore.

The statue that acted as our guide, and quite possibly our guardian angel, was in multiple pieces. It had been broken at the waist by a blunt object and part of the upper torso shattered a second time when it impacted the cobble stone. The hands and arms were in multiple pieces in the nearby grass, and the beautiful and pious face had been dug out. Like an animal had savagely bitten the flesh off in rage.

"Savages…" Richard whispered.

"It looks like they eventually made it here when they chased us," Lucas added, "Careful." It was clear they had tracked us back to the spot. Even though we had escaped to Rigar by then, traps and ambushes were now a possibility. I looked around with a bit more focus.

"Nothing," Jessica said after a few moments. "Stay close to me." We were hand-to-back in the dim night sky. Jessica moved swiftly while not losing us, expertly guiding us through the farmland. I thought she might have neglected to take into account the possibility of traps with how quick we were moving, but I soon realized that even at that speed we were going, she was scanning a route ahead for us as well as checking for enemies further off.

I could only imagine how fast Jessica could move if she didn't need to lead us. Despite the fact our path of escape had been discovered by the gnolls, there were no traps waiting for us. We made it through the farmland and into open prairie.

"The map says to go three miles that way." I pointed while Lucas and Jessica leaned over my shoulder. The moon barely illuminated a dozen feet ahead of us. We could see the mountain tops in the distance though, pitch-black silhouettes only visible while looking up at a backdrop of a starry night sky.

"It's so peaceful here," Anna said. And I agreed, without any light to interfere with the view, the clear night sky was a beautiful sight to behold.

We kept our steady pace as we traversed the open prairie. It was the middle of the night now, and with a few hours till sunrise, we had plenty of time to cover the three miles. The wind here came more frequently, and it howled now instead of whistled through the trees. I felt a chill up my back for the first time since we had left.

Every step forward might be a step closer to death, and yet I couldn't stop from advancing. It wasn't by choice though. It was by design. I had originally believed I was making the hard decisions; the reality was more that these decisions were forced upon us. To remain in the city would not only risk being there if the gnolls were able to storm it, but we would be caught up in the civil strife that unfortunately seemed to be heading towards open conflict.

"We should stop just ahead," Jessica announced after we had walked up rising ground for some time. "There's about two hours till sunrise."

The humidity that tormented me had seemingly disappeared. Now I was cold from the sweat that dried on me. Maria started to shiver and I could make out goosebumps on Glenn's forearm. We were just a hundred yards away from where the dark horizon marked a pass between two mountains that rose to left and right.

There was nothing to keep us out of the wind that seemed to blow stronger and stronger from the direction of the pass with every passing minute. It was amplified even more by a steep cliff face to our left that seemed to capture the wind and send it back at us for round two. I suddenly missed the warm forest.

Our only option was to keep moving along the cliff face and towards the pass that the map showed as leading to the main gnoll encampment, about a mile out further down the far side. Despite the uphill march, we moved faster and faster as we crested the hill, wanting to get out of the cold wind. Once down the far side, it eased off and so did my pace. Even better, Jessica found a small cliffside cave with room enough for us all to hide inside. The moon had mostly disappeared on the horizon, only the top of the crescent still remaining there. In around an hour things would start to get busy when it was light enough for us to see the camp properly. From here, I could only make out a few deep red, smoldering fires.

The plan was simple: once the horn was blown back at the city, there should be some reaction from the gnoll camp ahead. Ideally, they would send reinforcements to their forest fortification and leave this place under-defended. We'd wait long enough to see if that was a possibility, and if it did happen, what were our options for tackling their commanders.

As Lucas ran over the plan again, Mark interrupted: "If they don't reinforce, what then?"

"Jessica determines how likely it is we can succeed in finding their general and eliminating them," Lucas answered.

I looked at Jessica. It was a tough responsibility to make that call, knowing that we might not have another chance at this again. This could potentially be the only time we could strike without them taking precautions. And I still didn't trust the Yellow Prince's agenda. It might be that once he learned of our mission, he'd prefer to tip off the gnolls in the hope of wiping us out than have the gnoll threat removed.

"Should we make a rule to help Jessica?" I asked everyone. "What is the maximum number of elite enemies we can deal with while fighting the boss?"

"Two," Maria said.

"Three," Anna followed right after her.

I sighed. "Assume that if we don't succeed now, we never have a chance at the boss again." It wasn't entirely impossible that we could be trapped in this dungeon. As soon as I thought that I suddenly felt it wouldn't be entirely bad. That idea passed as quickly as it came, though. The creators of this 'game' were sadistic, and I was sure that they'd never let something like living in a dungeon give anyone a free pass.

Being trapped in this dungeon likely meant death for us. How that would happen, I couldn't be entirely sure, but it was a plausible idea that failing to kill the gnoll boss would somehow lead to the city being taken. Or a scenario where the Yellow Prince ascended the throne, and our heads descending to the floor.

"There's maybe thirty minutes till sunrise, if that," Lucas said, looking out the cave at the brightening sky, "we should all have our consumables good to go." Everyone who needed MP potions had them, and everyone else had HP potions already. Besides that, we each had some miscellaneous stat potions available to us.

I only kept a VIT potion for myself, and the rest had been distributed to others. WIS was useful to me as well, but my undead troops didn't expend constant MP, so I didn't go out of MP as fast as say Anna or Thomas.

My skeleton warriors were summed for the first time in days, and definitely the first time since I'd gotten new equipment. The number of upgrades they had received was considerable, and to my surprise they even looked slightly different.

The bones of their frames were thicker and less brittle, and they were each a head taller at the very least. My skeleton general towered over the others, and little bone spurs had started to pop out here and there on his frame.

With a command I sent them moving, and damn they were fast. Before, I was most useful at blocking enemy attacks and playing the perimeter of our little attack squad, but now that could be changed. The skeletons were quick enough that I could run down enemies with them, and maneuver them through the battlefield to attack and defend, especially when the fight was spread thin. I was missing a single undead soldier since I had gained +1 to my summons, but that would be summoned after dispatching the first of the gnoll fodder.

An orange hue grew on the horizon until the top of the sun could be seen through the distant trees. The cold air still made me shiver, but in moments the warmth of the sun basked me from head to toe. We were tucked away and waiting just a few minutes from the gnoll encampment.

The air vibrated as a massive horn echoed in the distance. It was Rhugar's battle call. "Be ready," Jessica said. We waited patiently for several minutes, and then a hawk flew into the valley from the distant mountain top.

The sky was bright enough that I could see the raptor clearly; it swooped in with great speed and then a moment later, a horn blew from the gnoll encampment. Hundreds of gnoll reinforcements, and even elite generals, rushed out and tramped past us and over the rise, heading for the city.

"It seems our plan is working," Lucas whispered.

Jessica waited patiently, closest to the cave entrance but safely out of sight, detailing the enemies leaving and how many. After twenty or so minutes, the commotion of march stopped, and in a few minutes more there was nothing but the sound of the howling wind once again.

"Let's go." Jessica stepped out of the darkness. It was time for battle.

# Chapter 35: Face to Face With the Dungeon Boss

We raced up the crest and through the massive gate that led into the encampment. Gnolls were few and far between at this early morning hour. The few we did see looked to be elderly or extremely young, and their surprised and then scared faces told us they were no threat. They did let out little yelps but these did not seem to be loud enough to draw a response towards us from more dangerous mobs. "Ignore the yard trash," I told everyone.

"High level enemy just ahead," Jessica announced. She was pointing to where the boss must be. There was one particularly large building just forty yards in the distance. It towered over the little mud-and-straw huts in the area and it was clearly significant. Not only that, Jessica continued, "There's five or six people in close proximity inside."

We raced through scattered abodes and eventually stopped under the animal skin tarp that acted as an overhang to the entrance of the large structure. "Gross." Maria groaned. The walls just a foot away were a reddish-brown clay, but that wasn't the cause of her dismay. The problem was the human skulls that had been embedded inside and covered every inch of clay between the pillars that towered twenty or thirty feet high.

"Richard wait, Alan in first," Lucas whispered. "Mike's undead after them. Everyone else, you know your role."

"How many mobs inside?" Alan looked at Jessica.

"Five, elites," she answered while tossing out a Quagmire Trap at the entrance. "Just in case, but they don't seem aware of us just yet. They aren't moving."

"Strike fast." I looked at Alan. The longer we waited, the more likely we would be discovered. He nodded and then walked with steady steps through the entrance with Richard directly behind. My skeleton troops trailed them, and had no difficulty entering as the doorway could fit a giant.

The entrance didn't open up into one big room, as I had expected. Instead, there was a ten-foot wall in front of us. It didn't go to the ceiling, so its only use was to obstruct direct vision into the main room beyond. Alan glanced over everyone and then nodded to the right to indicate our direction. A moment later we could hear talking, which caused Alan to pause.

"Did you hear something?" Were the muffled words that came through the wall. Something was placed down onto a table and then footsteps began approaching. Whatever way languages and translations worked in this game-world, my comprehension of the words was perfect, and yet there was an accent that sounded quite feral. I knew that gnolls could communicate through speech, but that they could do so at the same level as a human was a surprise to me.

The footsteps came closer and closer, until a shadow was visible on the wall and clearly just a few feet away. Alan didn't wait any longer, and cast Charge with his sword pointed straight ahead. Richard was on his tail and my undead soldiers flooded the room a moment later. A loud yelp sounded out, and by the time I had

264

turned the wall and could see our foes, a gnoll general had already been felled.

Alan had stabbed his blade directly through the heart of his opponent, whom still had a face of utter surprise and confusion. Beyond that were four more gnolls sitting around a large table. My first impression was that of a war room, and they were clearly strategizing based on the contents upon the table: layer after layer of animal skin maps.

"Impossible!" the gnoll sitting at the head of the table yelled. He stood up, towering over everyone, including my largest skeleton warriors. His face was speckled with brown and black spots in a healthy brown fur. His black eyes were crystal clear and contained an intelligence that it shouldn't have if it were simply playing a role in game. My initial thought was that this person was a human in a gnoll costume.

The other gnolls raced around the table to face us, and we stood just a few feet from them. Alan kicked the corpse attached to his blade and sent it tumbling to the ground. The blood of the dead gnoll spread out on the rug.

"Who are you?" the boss asked. He moved slowly to the side of the table and grasped a weapon off the wall: a hammer, the head as big as a man's torso and the shaft as thick as a thigh. No one spoke in response. "No matter." He twirled the mace in his hands like it was a toy. "I'll find out soon enough."

"Go," Lucas said just one word and both Alan and Richard rushed forward. The other gnoll generals raced to grab whatever weapon they could muster. It was clear though, they had not expected any attack on their home turf. Other than the main boss's mace, the other weapons on the walls looked to be mostly for show.

Alan charged directly for the boss, and Richard picked two elites as his own targets: one wielding a sword he ripped off a wall rack and the other just one dagger, embezzled with fancy jewels and definitely for decoration. The third opponent, who was my target, held a spear. As my skeletons rushed him, he flipped a table and propped it up as a makeshift shield.

There was a snarl and then a smirk on his face as if he held the upper hand. Spells exploded into the wooden table and bit off chunks as my warriors did their best to attack him. Unfortunately, in such a closed space they couldn't show their full strength, many of them struggling to move around each other or striking empty air.

I cast Decay, not on the gnoll, but on the table that hindered our advance. It took only a moment before it decayed into a rotted wood that fell apart in chunks of dust, unable to support its own weight. My skeleton general kicked the scattered debris into the gnoll elite's face, allowing a fireball from my mage to hit the elite a moment later. "Shitty human! Weak!" He hissed out through the dissipating flames.

Before another word could come from his mouth, before my undead troops could rush over him like a wave, Lucas appeared to his side and sent his head toppling with a single wind slash. "The squeaky wheel gets the grease," Lucas said, which I assumed was him shit talking in his own weird way.

Gnoll elites now were pushovers for us. Some of us had literally doubled our stats since our last battles with them. But the boss, the boss was a different story. Its hammer came down on Alan and sent our tank buckling to the floor. If Alan wasn't so STR heavy, he would have been flattened or buried three feet into the rug. I felt bad, as it seemed like his role had become that of a punching bag.

"A little help!" Alan yelled. All his boasts of taking the boss solo went out the window. Maria and Anna both sent out supporting spells and attacks, as did Jessica. The next time the boss went to swing his mallet, an arrow pierced his underarm and a freezing pulse trimmed the hair around the nape of his neck. He lost balance from an explosive arrow at his feet and was forced to step back, not daring to swing again.

Richard remained fine in the two-on-one, but he didn't excel in doing damage. He was just a sustain tank, and the two gnoll generals watching their leader being barraged with spells let out loud yelps of frustration. Richard was an unbreachable wall, they could neither attack nor defend and were at the mercy of our attacks. "Don't worry it'll be your turn soon." Richard yelled at them while deflecting the dagger and sword in unison.

The two elites grew more frantic and eventually, after losing their cool, fell to a Godless Arrow from Jessica and the frenzied and suicidal attacks of six of my skeletal warriors. It was now just the boss and us remaining. We were stronger than ever before, but I felt that this would be our most difficult challenge yet. A dungeon boss was a different beast altogether.

"Careful," I said, "let's take our time." I assessed everyone. We were all in good health, and now completely in control of the situation. Alan and Richard backed away and the boss stood uneasily at his war table.

"You are his men," the commander of the gnolls spoke with some confidence. His eyes looked around the room and rested on a piece of paper. He grabbed it with care and tucked it into his palm. The mace couldn't be swung with one hand, but he pointed it out at us. "He will pay for his betrayal." There was a low growl to the words that made him sound even more bestial.

There was suddenly a low rumble, and the ground beneath Richard exploded upwards. The earth had formed a jutting rock that aimed to impale him from below. "Careful, Earth magic! Richard was struck on the thigh and then sent hurdling into the wall. Everyone else rushed towards the sides of the room to avoid an eruption.

In the brief moment I had taken my eyes off the boss, he had turned around and attached the piece of parchment to a hawk's leg, and then sent it hurdling up towards the rafters. The roof was merely a tarp, and it wasn't sealed at the top. There was a large gap between the walls and the tarp roof, which the hawk flew directly out of.

"Jessica!" I yelled. She had seen it already too. Whether it was a message to the city or a signal for reinforcements we had to stop the bird. I saw her close her eyes and pull her bow string. The sound rang out even in the rumbling, and the hawk suddenly screeched. There was relief in her eyes when she opened them again.

"Got it," she said.

"Outside!" I yelled at everyone. The room was too cramped, between my undead and party members, there wasn't much room to maneuver. On top of that, we couldn't even see the ground through the rugs on the floor.

"How are you?" Alan raced to Richard and helped him up. The boss was still by his table, and had no ability to obstruct our leaving.

"Fine, just a scratch," Richard said and then cast his instant heal on himself. They were the last out, and the commotion had drawn a crowd now.

# Chapter 36: The Giant Gnoll Boss Fight

I looked around at the children and elderly gnolls, there were obviously former warriors in the bunch, too. They walked on stump legs or were missing arms and eyes. A few of them were brazen enough to carry weapons and stare menacingly at us. The crowd looked like it would close around us. They weren't all helpless.

It was Jessica who turned to face a rather menacing-looking gnoll. His single hand held a serrated dirk, the other arm had no hand, but a claw had been embedded into the flesh there to replace his fingers. One eye was completely grey and a bit disfigured and one leg below the knee was gone, replaced by a stump of wood. It was clear he was a veteran warrior. "Just try it," Jessica threatened.

Instead of being deterred, he started to walk a bit closer, and the crowd with him. Jessica had shown enough restraint, and then loosed her arrow. The ground beneath the gnoll exploded, and even in this situation she had shown mercy. It was clear he would attack when the situation provided him an opportunity, but Jessica had shot his wooden leg to bits and he could no longer stand, toppling to the side. An elderly gnoll helped drag him away and the crowd inched back a few steps. "Last warning," she said while swinging around.

I was growing impatient now. Dozens of seconds passed and the boss hadn't emerged from the hut. "Fighting the boss inside isn't an option for us. We need to get him out."

"I'll take care of it!" Maria boasted before sending a fiery arrow towards the roof of the building. It landed with an explosion and the dry animal hide lit from the extreme heat, a few skulls exploded out of the clay where the arrow landed.

In just a few moments, the fire spread from the tarp to the supporting beams, even the clay interior was mixed with straw that lit up at the smallest crack. The structure was burning rapidly and a deep smoke billowed into the sky.

"Uh oh," Maria said. I hadn't thought about it in advance, probably none of us had really considered the consequence of starting a major fire, but we had created our own beacon of smoke. For now it wasn't a problem, but it would turn into one soon enough. We were on a timer.

"It's okay. Without the message from the hawk I don't think they will suspect anything out of the ordinary for a while." Lucas steadied my rising nerves. He was the calmest of all of us, and for good reason. He didn't say so, but his passive Ruler was working at an insane capacity right now. While they weren't actively attacking us, every onlooker was an enemy and therefore giving him stat bonuses.

"He's coming," Jessica warned everyone. Richard and Alan grouped at the front. Alan was so hyped he started to chomp at the gnolls that inched too close, it looked like he was going to randomly go berserk any moment.

"Don't lose control." I touched his shoulder. "Redeem yourself." I knew already he was feeling disappointed in his previous display. Any sane person knew taking a dungeon boss one-on-one wasn't something he should be shooting for, but I didn't damper his enthusiasm.

The boss walked through the hut entrance and into the open air. His eyes scanned the gnolls around, and the fervor and admiration they showed in response to his gaze was honestly scary. "Retreat, this isn't a place for all of you!" he yelled at them. "Don't needlessly throw your lives away." The second line could have been for us, too.

Our spectators immediately retreated a good thirty or forty feet. Some even went into their houses and ceased spectating, but most stayed within view. Lucas frowned, perhaps because of the losses from his passive, but perhaps too at level of the respect and control the gnoll boss had. He received the kind of fervor that was given to a good ruler, and not a tyrant. "Did he think we would take hostages?" Lucas muttered under his breath.

"You humans are a despicable bunch, so I never put it past you to do anything, including making cubs hostages." The boss responded with amazing hearing. "I ordered them away because otherwise they would risk their lives in a helpless attack." I suddenly had a bad feeling at his response. He had spoken with more moral authority than either of the princes.

The boss's muscles became taut and his expression ferocious. It was zero to one-hundred in a second as he exploded forward towards us. Alan and Richard rushed to meet him, as did my undead soldiers. The two opposing sides moving for a head on collision.

I knew the inside of that hut was a massive disadvantage for us, but I had not considered how that was also true for the boss. He was large and wielded a heavy weapon; I never expected his agility to be so high.

Alan was the first to reach the boss, or it would be better to say the boss reached Alan first because of his charge. There was no deflection or stabbing or tanking of any kind happening, instead the boss's massive right hand grabbed Alan from behind his shield, spun him with one swift motion to the right, sending Alan hurdling into Richard like a bowling ball and pin.

The two collided with a metal thud and rolled ten feet together while the boss continued to spin in one motion. His now free second hand grasped the massive mallet he raised high during his spin and slammed it down with both hands. It hit the ground with a deep thud that I felt twenty feet away.

"Dodge!" I yelled at everyone. That was his earth magic, and the effect it would have was uncertain. Not many of us could dodge in time, but Anna and Thomas were the most immobile of the bunch and most susceptible to surprise attacks.

A second hadn't even passed but my heart was in my throat. I was ready to rush to help anyone injured as my eyes scanned my party members in what felt like slow motion. Suddenly, a thunder like sound exploded from the earth as it sheered apart from his magic. A fissure appeared beneath Jessica's feet that she couldn't quite dodge on account of priming a shot a moment prior. Still, her reaction wasn't bad.

As the fissure rose beneath her, she jumped at the same time and rode the momentum to its peak, launching twenty or thirty feet in the air. The jutting rock hadn't impaled her, but the fall alone would be enough to break bones.

My skeletons were only now just halfway to the boss, but they provided a decent barrier to our party. I wasn't worried about the boss coming for us in this brief moment. Alan and Richard were fumbling to their feet and would intercept him soon.

Knowing that, I immediately sent both skeleton generals rushing for Jessica as she fell. I wasn't confident in any of us catching her, but their strength would manage it. Their physical prowess might not be as much as that of Alan or Richard, but their overall balance and agility was impressive. I was confident they could catch her without hurting her.

Jessica was in free fall for what felt like three or four seconds, a testament to just how high she had been flung. The two generals, one wielding a zweihander and the other a butcher's cleaver, dropped their weapons and braced for impact. I could hear their bones rattle as she crashed down upon them. She rolled away and groaned, but was in one piece.

"Nice going spikey!" Maria suddenly yelled at my minions. Spikey eh...I kind of liked it.

The boss was clearly surprised at our quick reaction to his attack. No doubt he had imagined that Jessica would have been impaled from below and instantly killed. I could understand why he had focused his attack on her: Jessica's Quagmire traps and accurate shooting posed a big threat to his mobility.

"Stay focused," Lucas said to everyone. While it felt like a long time had passed since the start of the duel and Jessica landing, only a few seconds had expired. Richard and Alan managed to regain their balance, and instead of charging blindly, moved in side by side.

"Sorry everyone!" Alan yelled and then smacked his shield with his sword. "I won't let you down again!" Richard's shield started to glow white hot beside him. Even the holy power in his mace glowed brightly.

My undead encircles the boss and Spikey Number One and Number Two ran to either side of him. We now had a proper setup in place. The boss was more contained, and we held the advantage. "Shall we try this again?" I asked everyone.

Every face was filled with a new intensity. Alan had learned this lesson multiple times already, and it seemed to have finally stuck in his brain—he was part of a two-man tanking team. This time, with Richard at his side, they crept in slowly. They created a constant pressure on the boss while Anna, Maria, and Jessica prepared to assault it from range.

My undead were also there in the periphery, ready to react with attack or defense when needed. Bosses always had a multitude of skills, and battles with them were never as easy as just hitting the boss until it ran out of HP: possible tactics and responses were at the forefront of my mind.

"Careful of the ground attack," I warned everyone. After seeing it once, I was more confident we wouldn't be caught unaware again. My summoned soldiers started to close in slowly as did Richard and Alan. We were slowly constricting the boss and the fight was going to erupt at any moment.

Thomas casted a HoT on both Alan and Richard, which seemed to be the right spell to start the encounter once again. This time there was proper support in place for Alan and Richard. Blizzard appeared above the boss followed by both Jessica and Maria's frenzied arrow assault. Lucas blended in with my warriors from behind and repeatedly dashed in with flanking blows before retreating as quickly as he appeared.

With Lucas and my undead attacking from the back, Maria, Jessica, Anna and myself attacking from the front, and Richard and Alan acting as immovable objects, the boss lost its upper hand. There were too many attacks to deflect and defend. The healthy sheen on its brown coat dulled grey and red from the dust and blood. The wounds were only superficial in nature so far though.

The boss grew more flustered. His two gigantic hands grasped the mallet and slammed down at our tanks with as much force as he could muster. "Help me!" Alan yelled. Richard didn't hesitate, and the two nearly connected at the hip to raise their shields. There came the sound of an explosion when blow of the mallet collided with the iron of the shields. Our tanks had managed to hold on, and gave not an inch to the strike.

Instead, they pushed back hard and sent the mallet lunging into the air and the boss fumbling several steps back, being truly over-powered for the first time. Lucas took a piece of flesh from the bosses' thigh as it retreated, which infuriated it even more. The boss swung the mallet in a half circle trying to catch Lucas, but instead exploding three of my skeletal warriors in the process.

The boss started to growl from his gut. It was such a visceral thrumming that slowly built until it was all I could hear. By the time I realized it, my hair was standing and I had goosebumps. He started to look more feral by the second. His calm and intelligent-looking eyes grew belligerent, the whites slowly turning red. Even his hands, albeit large before, morphed into something bestial.

"Jessica..." I muttered. "What's happening?"

"I don't know," she said plainly. Her inspect ability wasn't high enough level to discern anything other than that this was a boss. Its abilities were completely unknown to us, but I could tell the current boss was completely enraged.

# Chapter 37: A New Boss Ability

Alan and Richard were taut and ready to attack, but battle after battle had slowly honed them into experienced warriors. We all watched carefully, curious what was about to unfold. No one wanted to recklessly charge in without knowing what was happening.

Time seemed to pause for ten seconds, as both sides were stuck in a stalemate. The boss very well could be powering up, but without assurance, who could rush in blindly to check? What if the red aura was an ability that would make him explode? Richard and Alan would be history if that was the case.

A dozen more seconds passed before the boss finally moved. He held his giant mallet in one hand and extended it in front of him, holding it perfectly vertical. His next action was completely unexpected. He dropped the mace, handle facing towards the floor. The thud I expected in such an odd situation didn't appear.

The mallet just disappeared into the earth, and a ripple spread out from its location. Dust raised just a few inches off the floor as the invisible wave passed below us, but did no damage. I had no idea what was happening. Attack or defend? My thoughts raced.

Stone creatures started to spawn all around us a moment later, and then the boss didn't give us a choice. He rushed Alan and Richard with newfound fury. "Thomas, focus your attention on Richard and Alan! Everyone else assist in taking down the adds as soon as possible! Lucas use your best judgement!" I barked a quick series of orders.

My undead that had been surrounding the boss rushed away like insects and towards the earthen golems that had spawned. A quick glance showed six of them had appeared, one for every party member that wasn't one of the two main tanks. I wasn't sure if this was a coincidence or just the typical result of the weapon's triggered effect.

The earth golems didn't hold any weapon, but they didn't need to, as they towered over two meters tall, each with fists raised. They were a head taller than my skeleton generals, and I could tell their defense was nothing to scoff at. "Thomas' golem first!" I yelled. Everyone else could defend themselves somewhat, but Thomas was a healer with no physical or attacking abilities.

An earth golem had spawned dangerously close to him and was moving with conviction. While large, they weren't slow or clumsy looking. Their joints, made of jagged rocks, were just for show and clearly had no restraining effect on their movement. A few seconds longer and Thomas would be badly mangled at the very least.

Anna was the fastest to react, shooting into the golem's raised arm with an Ice Spear and freezing its attack for a brief moment. By the time the ice shattered, Lucas seemed to appear out of no-where and kicked the back legs with so much force the golem toppled backwards. An Explosive Arrow struck the golem's head just as it hit the floor.

The situation seemed to unfold perfectly; the golem's head rested directly over a hole created by the explosion, as if waiting for the guillotine to fall from above. Fortunately, Spikey Number One and Number Two were on both sides and swung directly down as hard as they could, cleaving the head clean off, which was only possible because there was no ground below to stop their falling weapons.

"Careful!" Jessica yelled out. "These aren't alive." She was reminding us that creatures like this might not die from having their head cut off.

Fortunately, the golem didn't rise again. "It seems the core is in their head," Lucas said, "aim for it." He rushed to assist Richard and Alan for a moment, determining he wasn't as much use for anyone else. I couldn't help but gaze over to the boss fight, where the sound of scraping metal and the sparks that flew constantly gave me an ominous feeling. Still, our two tanks held up as best as they could. Lucas would be a big help to them.

The boss attacked with his hands and feet like a trained martial artist. Sharp claws extended from both, and looking at the scraping metal, they were as good as steel claws. Alan's HP constantly bounced in the party window, even when blocking most attacks.

Thomas had been fully focused, keeping Alan's HP in that sweet spot to abuse his passive as a knight which gave him damage reduction below a certain HP threshold. Richard was also in on it, and if Alan ever got too low in that window between heals, he had his instant cast as well as the ability to take blows.

Now with Lucas weaving blows on the boss when he could, the biggest worry – the safety of our two tanks – disappeared. My undead troops had also entangled the remaining golems. While strong, the golems weren't intelligent at all, and definitely not being controlled. Once my soldiers blocked the paths they were taking to a party member, my summoned troops became the target of the golem's aggro. With that, our ranged damage dealers quickly began dispatching them, all focusing on one at a time.

Our second target was the golem fighting Mark and Glenn. Even though they weren't combat classes, and Mark didn't even have a class, I believed that their combat ability was good enough for this situation if they focused purely on defense.

Our strategy appeared quickly and spontaneously. Anna using Freezing Pulse or an Ice Bolt would freeze up the golem's chest, and a hard, blunt attack from one of my warriors staggered it. Then Jessica's arrow severed the head clean off. We quickly moved on to the next with the same tactics, Jessica and Maria competing for who would land the kill shot. In under a minute, we managed to dispatch the six golems.

Now though, with how dangerous the boss was in melee, Mark and Glenn's ability to contribute disappeared completely. "Focus on our surroundings, watch the boss carefully for further tricks," I said to them. It was important to not be complacent.

I cast Shallow Grave after issuing my orders and re-summoned skeletons to fill up a squad that had been badly depleted. While in theory I could control each summoned undead soldier individually, the difficulty was immense. Think about rubbing your belly and patting your head at the same time, but then extend that control to a dozen troops. The most I could control at once was three, although it seemed as my WIS grew, that challenge became easier.

Because of the difficulty of managing each warrior, the golems had done a number on my melee types, on top of the three the boss had dispatched. I only had my two skeleton generals, my ranged caster skeletons, and one gnoll reincarnation. I attempted to reincarnate the earth golems, but as they were never living creatures, I simply received a message:

## Skill has Failed

279

Tsk. It was expected, but nothing could be done about it.

With all our firepower now focused on the boss, and Glenn and Mark carefully assessing the boss and surrounding arena, we developed a sort of 'flow' of battle. Events moved smoothly as we whittled down the boss one blow at a time.

Alan shifted his shield at just the right angle to avoid the claws piercing his shield and severing his arm. Lucas retreated just a second faster than the boss could retaliate after his attacks. Jessica and Maria only took shots at the boss when he was mid-attack which provided those openings for Lucas, and reduced the chance their arrows were deflected. Even Anna, dressed head to toe in something only a royal would wear, sent her ice spells at the perfect timing, never allowing the boss any gaps to take advantage of.

Boss fights could never get too comfortable, though. "Thomas dodge!" Glenn suddenly yelled. Thomas hesitated for a moment, as Alan was under fifty-percent HP and needed a heal. That split second of hesitation sent Thomas flying six feet in the air sideways. The ground beneath his right foot exploded upwards.

Alan, feeling the pressure now, chugged a potion. Even at thirty-percent HP, a direct attack might have been enough to end his life. Richard could feel it too, casting an instant heal on Alan and slamming his mace and shield with even more fervor at the boss. The situation suddenly took a disastrous turn.

I sent six undead against the boss on a suicide mission as Jessica rushed to Thomas. The six skeletons jumped at the boss's back like monkey's and clung to its fur. If you looked at their thin frames and made a judgment, you'd be underestimating their strength. Their boney bodies latched around its arms and thighs from behind. Their vice-like grip stopped the bosses frenzied attacks and gave a moment of reprieve.

Jessica used that moment to pull a potion from her inventory and poured it into Thomas's mouth. He wasn't moving and didn't seem conscious, but a moment later we heard a cackling and loud coughing. His HP was somewhere around forty-percent and steadily climbing from the potion. Jessica helped lean him up and then he cast a heal on Alan from a sitting position.

The six skeletons on the boss had been ripped off one at a time in quick succession. Their grip was so strong that their hands still held patches of fur from the boss. They had been tossed away, exploding like glass on the face of a nearby cliff. Still, they had done their job well.

But, as if things couldn't get worse, the ground pulsed again and six more earth golems appeared. Jessica was the first to react, fully taking Thomas in her embrace and dashing away from the two golems that spawned near here.

"Follow Jessica! Everyone except Alan and Richard!"

The moment the golems appeared I had a new idea. With everyone rushing to where Jessica had put Thomas down, the six golems were chasing in one big group. Anna didn't even need to be prompted, casting Blizzard above them and engulfing them in swirling icy death. The sound was a constant pattering that grated on my ears, like hail hitting concrete repeatedly. Chunks of stone and ice flew through the air.

Maria and Jessica both used their respective CC: Quagmire Trap and Entangling arrow. The golems, with no intelligence, fell into an impossible situation. The ice whittled away at them one chunk at a time, and when the golems were nearly approaching the end of Anna's AoE spell, Lucas was waiting with Wind Slash. The six had become brittle enough to lose their heads in one strike.

While this had seemed to be the best way to deal with them, there had also been great risks involved. I hadn't paused to dwell on what might have gone wrong, as the situation was developing into something we were losing control of. With great risks came great rewards and I had taken a chance. Our grouping the spawns together had paid off: the golems were gone, and the boss hadn't cast a ground AoE effect under our feet.

After that small victory, the fight fell into a rhythm like before. The boss was now as exhausted as we were. His attacks no longer as frenzied, which allowed Alan and Richard to gain the upper hand.

# Chapter 38: The Mystery of the Gnoll Commander Revealed

Thomas had managed to heal Alan through his fatigue and injury with the help of Mark and Glenn supporting him. With that, we had won the battle of attrition. The boss didn't have HP and MP potions, but we did. Thomas had chugged three MP potions, as well as rationed his healing about as skillfully as he could, which showed just how much damage the boss was putting out.

The gnoll commander was now wobbling with every attack. His chest heaved up and down like it was his last breath. His bruised and bloodied body was patchy with missing fur, and deep red blood mixed with what little remained. The red glow surrounding him had slowly disappeared until there was nothing left of it. Even the claws on his hands and feet receded, and his mallet that disappeared into the earth, it didn't seem he had the power to retrieve it anymore.

It was obvious this was the end of the fight. I didn't know what final card it might have to play, but no one was going to slow up. As if he'd practiced the attack, Lucas came in from behind and cast Wind Slash across both thighs. From the front, Alan and Richard both shoved their shields with as much force as they could muster. Anna had frozen both shoulders of the boss, and with it not being able to use its arms, nor its legs to defend and maintain stability, it toppled backwards with a deep thud, like a giant flat stone had smashed into the earth.

Instinctively, everyone moved back a dozen feet and gave ample room to the boss. We watched with bated breath as the boss's chest heaved up and down with great effort. Blood splattered from coughs that escaped his throat. The redness in his eyes disappeared as his rationality returned.

"Why?" was all the boss could ask. "It was a simple promise, so why go back?" he asked. "I don't understand?" There was a silence, no one really knew how to respond.

"It's because you trusted the Yellow Prince," Maria spat out.

The effect of these words was as if a veil had been lifted for the boss. "You aren't his men then?" he asked, almost sighing. "Then the Red Prince?" He knew a lot, apparently.

"How do you know so much?" I asked him.

"It would be weird if I didn't. I used to be a human." Which was like a bomb going off in my minds.

"You…used to be human?" I asked.

It didn't seem the boss had any reservations left now he was at the end. "I was once a human, yes. You could even say Edward and Lazemus were once my good friends."

I had an epiphany in that moment. "…Donivan?" I asked.

"…you know of me then?"

"We were sent to rescue you from the gnoll boss," I admitted.

"Haha, fate is quite cruel then," he groaned. "I thought that being framed for the princess's murder was the worst it could get."

"Do you mind explaining what happened to you?" I asked. Things had taken such an odd turn that I was confused on what we should do right now.

Lucas approached me from the side and whispered to me, "Should we try and heal him?" he asked.

I looked at the others who seemed to be unsure of what to do, and then I looked at Thomas, "Heal him just a bit." Although the boss was much stronger than us and dangerous, a single heal wouldn't be enough to give him his fighting strength back. Some pain relief and maybe a chance at living might prove enough to get his co-operation in explaining to us the story of his life and to get insight into the nature of this dungeon.

The heal came through and his ragged breathing slowed down just a bit. "Ah…that's much better." He lifted his head. "You came to save me, so you must be Lazemus's men."

"We are." I didn't deny it. "Can you explain what's happening right now?" I was worried he would be reserved in his explanation, but that wasn't the case. I didn't know if we were friends or enemies in this moment.

Donivan started to laugh before coughing hard. "I'm grateful, honestly. I can finally tell someone what happened." He started, "As you may have heard, I was the suspect for the princess's murder, but in reality, it was Edward's doing." I nodded at his words. "I was kidnapped, but the location of my prison was actually not here. In fact, I wasn't held for long and I wasn't 'forced' to come here."

"Edward tortured me for three days, he was trying to find the location of a portal I had discovered many years ago. All of it was to force me into revealing that information." His eyes scanned us from the ground, as if searching to see if we knew what he was talking about: there was a deep fury in his gaze.

"We've heard of the portal," I said.

"I never revealed that information to Edward, and his torture was unsuccessful." Donivan's head fell back flat on the ground. "I was badly mangled and scarred, though. My body was ruined, my reputation was ruined, I was a criminal that would be killed on sight." He paused. "Did you know Edward was gathering gnoll shamans for research?" he asked. It was a weird tangent that didn't quite make sense.

"Lazemus told us," Lucas said, "he even had us catch some."

"Right, Lazemus probably found out and looked into it. He obviously never found out the reason why." He paused. "I am the reason why. That research allowed Edward to do something unheard of—he turned me into a gnoll."

"After I became a gnoll, I was let loose outside the city. It was interesting though; I was no regular gnoll. I had the intelligence of a human, the thought, the rationality—but my fighting strength too, I was more powerful than any gnoll I encountered." I nodded, to show him I could appreciate what this must have been like.

"Edward didn't know this at first, but when he found out, his men approached me. He dangled a carrot in front of me when he said, 'I can turn you back into a human.' It was a hard to resist that carrot.

"I believed it at first. Why not? He had turned me into this monster, surely, he could turn me back and for that I agreed to cooperate. Where his torture had failed, his entrapment of me in this body succeeded. Every now and then a letter would be sent to me. Plans, or some instruction to follow. I created this settlement, I united the gnolls into a force that could threaten the city. He never asked about the portal, which he knew was my bottom-line."

Pieces started to fall into place as Donivan spoke. Everything was beginning to make sense. "His goal became clear to me, but what did it matter to me if he succeeded in putting the Yellow

Prince on the throne? I only wanted to be human again, to be able to journey and travel again like before."

"Did you ever confirm he could turn you back?" Lucas asked.

"That...I dreamed about it, constantly. But over the years, I grew to know that he could never turn me back—even though that reality was too terrifying to face. Still, my hope had turned to hatred. Not just for Edward, but for everyone who had abandoned me. Many knew I didn't kill the princess, so many knew Edward kidnapped me. Why did no one come to save me?" He paused as if waiting for an answer, "Politics. Because of politics this is my fate...and because of that I truly hope the city falls." He had been warped through his years of living as a gnoll.

"I have lost my humanity, and seeing the treatment the gnolls received over the years, started to resent humans, even though I was once human. We are despicable creatures, even more so than a gnoll. Gnolls stab you in the front, look you in the eyes. But humans? They sneak in the shadows, betray your trust, destroy the very fabric of your being."

It was the darkest explanation he could give, but no one standing here could disagree. We had seen what human nature could do when pushed to the limit, when tempted by greed.

"What will you do?" I asked him. In the end, whether this entire situation ended in our favor was up to him.

"I know that I'm wrong..." he said. "But I also know who brought me to this point. I have not sat idly by over the years. There is enough evidence to have Edwards head on a spike by sunrise tomorrow." He said, "I'd like to see Lazemus and confess my sins, and take any punishment I receive. The princess shouldn't have to be alone." He seemed to be suggesting that even if the ruling was execution he would face it bravely.

287

After looking around and getting everyone's approval, Thomas healed Donivan as many times as his MP allowed him. Maybe it wasn't the right decision, but given the story so far in the dungeon, it seemed this was the correct course of action.

As the heals poured in, Donivan recovered some of his depleted stamina and managed to stand with a groan. "Inside my war room, under the rug the table is resting on, there is a chest buried in the ground. That has all you need in it."

I nodded at Alan and Richard, whom quickly disappeared inside. The building had collapsed somewhat, but the fire didn't burn endlessly. After removing two half burnt pillars and uncovering the rug, Richard returned with Alan in tow, a small chest in his bosom.

The chest was stacked with documents, and about midway down was a book. I took it in my hands curiously. The Basics of Gnoll Language was written in clean English on the cover. I flipped the page and was prompted:

**Do you wish to learn the basics of gnoll language?**
**Yes/No**

This was a surprisingly unique find. I selected 'no', because this was something we should discuss as a group first.

Besides the single booklet were just piles and piles of letters accumulated over many years. The letters never mentioned anyone by name or incriminated the Yellow Prince or Edward. The lettering was all created by ink stamps, so no handwriting could be discerned, but the contents made it clear what Donivan said earlier was true. With his testimony and some good detective work, I was sure this would be enough to put Edward on the chopping block.

The crowd that had disappeared before had reappeared and were staring at us with fear and trepidation. "Just a moment, please." Donivan approached a gnoll shaman, a female that was well on in her later years. He started to yip and growl and communicate in the gnoll language before returning. "I had to pass leadership to her or things would become problematic here. These are still my people." As if he needed to explain himself. "I need to send a hawk as well. To call off the attacks on the city."

When I glanced at Jessica, she shrugged. Then said to him, "Go ahead."

After everything we taken care of, we slowly departed the encampment. It was silent and peaceful. Even Donivan, whom had an angry look on his face even from the moment we met him, was relaxed and carefree, seemingly taking in the environment.

"It feels good," he said, "to finally face my fears. To let go and accept."

"I wish I could say the same." I laughed, but doing so would end with my death and all of my party members. We had to keep fighting to survive. "Can I tell you a story?" I looked at Donivan.

He nodded peacefully as I began to narrate our journey here. The portal was his dying secret, and I feared even now he would never let go of its location. "So you're from a different world?" He asked. He took the explanation better than expected, but the fact that he was turned into a gnoll from a human, and even found that portal in the first place. "I guess I've seen it before."

"Speak with Lazemus," I urged him. "After you confirm, you can make a decision."

# Chapter 39: Return of the Lost Gnoll Leader

A singular horn shattered the peaceful silence. Trees shook in the distance as perching birds flew into the sky. "That's the signal for retreat," Donivan said, "we must not run into them, though. Gnolls value strength over everything. If the warriors see me like this, they will kill you first, and then me."

"Don't fret," replied Jessica, "we have a route."

Lucas approached us. "I have a question," he asked Donivan. "How did you learn to speak the gnoll language? Was it possible once you became a gnoll?"

"No," Donivan responded flatly. "Actually, I couldn't speak it at all, but Edward gave me this so that I could carry out his plans." He held out a necklace.

"Can I see?" I asked. He didn't show any hesitation and handed the necklace to me. It wasn't beautiful, or covered in gems, in fact I'd have thought it was a piece of junk metal if I spotted it on a store shelf.

**Polyglot's Teaching**
**Allows the wearer to more easily grasp new languages**

There were no stats, only that description.

"With that, I slowly learned how to converse with gnolls while keeping my distance, as they usually traveled in groups. Eventually I could speak enough to take control and lead them. I've left my notes in the chest."

I glanced over to where Richard was still carrying the chest, but the book had already been stored in my inventory for now.

"How effective is it?" Lucas asked.

"Honestly, extremely. The issue was how little I had to converse with the gnolls. They are extremely territorial and aggressive. Until I took over the tribe, it was survival of the fittest. My inability to speak was enough of a reason to be killed. Only my strength and careful nature allowed me to develop to this point. Try it on." He passed the necklace to Lucas whom donned it around his neck.

Donivan started to yip and even growl for a moment towards Lucas. To myself and everyone else it seemed like a mindless act of aggression, but Lucas had a thoughtful look on his face.

"Did you tell me your name?" he asked, unsure.

"Yes! I told you my name, the one the gnolls use to refer to me, and while you might not have understood the details, you quickly picked up the gist of what I was trying to say." Lucas nodded and started to take off the necklace. "I have no use for it anymore." Donivan held his furry paw towards Lucas as to tell him to keep it.

"I could definitely understand that you weren't an enemy, at the very least." Lucas said. Which in and of itself was extremely useful.

"Are you sure?" I asked Donivan.

"Absolutely, you're my benefactors." He spoke with complete sincerity. It made me feel happy about our actions that he should see us this way. What an insane turn of events: the enemy boss I had so dreaded was grateful to me.

The conversation of our whole group was cheerful as we returned to the city. While killing Donivan may have seen us get some powerful items among the loot, I felt that we had gotten the best scenario outcome. We had cleared the camp; stopped the coordination of the gnoll attacks; and we'd gained a useful magic item. One of us had the potential to learn the gnoll language, and Lucas now had a necklace that would assist in future translating situations such as this one.

"Hold your hands behind your back," I said to Donivan as we approached the castle walls. "I don't know if they'll open the door if they think you aren't restrained."

He nodded in understanding and held his hands behind his back. Alan and Richard stood on either side of him with their right and left hands behind Donavan's back. From someone standing on the wall, it would look as if he was shackled and they were holding the chains to do keep him in check.

"Halt!" guard man atop yelled. His eyes were glued to Donivan and he seemed at a loss for words.

"We are Lazemus's men!" I yelled back. "Please bring him immediately, we have captured the gnoll leader."

"...wait here!" he yelled down and then disappeared off the top of the wall for several minutes before returning. "Please wait for Rhugar to arrive! Lazemus is coming as well."

The wait was about twenty minutes. Eventually the door creaked open and Rhugar walked out, his face full of surprise at the sight of the gnoll boss, whom was acting incredibly passively.

"He's under the effects of magic," Anna said, a quick little lie wouldn't hurt anyone.

"Good...good!" Rhugar laughed cheerfully. "I was wondering why they retreated so abruptly" He was basically yelling with delight. I could understand why, every moment below that wall was someone's last, and often was someone he knew. "Come in." He ushered us.

All of us surrounding Donivan, we walked together until we passed through the barrier and inside. The guards looked at Donivan with a murderous yet fearful gaze. "He's under the effects of magic. Please lower your weapons," Lucas said. These words were effective enough: while the guards didn't lower their weapons, they backed away fifteen feet and allowed space.

Their actions made me think they would rush Donivan at any moment, and the fact he wasn't restrained wasn't known yet. "Can we go to a room?" I asked. I wasn't sure what would happen if they realized the gnoll leader was completely unrestrained.

Rhugar nodded without a word and rushed us into the waiting room we had been in previously. His eyes went wide as saucers though when he saw Donivan sitting in a chair, with no sign of any restraint on him.

"It's fine," I told him before he could even open his mouth.

"It seems I've underestimated you," he replied, "I'd be glad to hear the story but Lazemus will be here shortly."

"You'll understand everything then," I said. He nodded without a word and stood in the corner of the room. He couldn't take his eyes off Donivan though. I couldn't blame him.

"Lazemus has arrived!" We heard a shout from a guard outside barely ten minutes later. The door opened abruptly and Lazemus walked inside. As with Rhugar, his expression was severe as he spotted Donivan. It was like a Mexican standoff as Lazemus and Donivan stared at each other.

This hadn't been planned, but Donivan spoke for himself. "Hi Lazemus," he bared his canines in what might have been a grin, "it has been a long time."

"Yo-you, who?" Lazemus could barely find the words. His eyes darted around the room at each and every one of us, anyone who could give him the slightest idea what was going on. No one said anything though.

"I guess I look a bit different than how you would remember me." Donivan chuckled, which came out as a growl unintentionally.

Lazemus at the gnoll chief with amazement. "...Donivan? Is that you? Can it even be you?"

"It's me," Donivan said then fell silent. I could see the tears start to well in his eyes. It seemed as though if he tried to speak some more, instead he would explode into a fit of tears.

"How...? Huh?" It looked like Lazemus was losing his bearing on reality. "What is happening right now?"

"We should leave you two to catch up," I said to Lazemus. He still hadn't quite understood exactly what was happening. "I'm sure Donivan will be able to make you understand."

Rhugar quickly approached me from the side. "Is this okay?" he whispered. I understood his meaning, but this had to happen. Lazemus needed to know the story before Edward could make any move against him.

"Lock this place down." Lazemus seemed to come to his senses. "No guard can leave." He spoke to a man at the doorway who disappeared.

"As resourceful as always." Donivan chuckled. We all quickly left the room and allowed the two to talk.

"Can you explain what's going on?" Rhugar finally asked me. "Donivan? The man who killed the princess? And he's a gnoll?"

"He didn't kill the princess," Maria corrected. "He is a gnoll though."

"The war is over." I patted Rhugar on the shoulder. "The gnoll army won't return, and that's all that matters. You spread the good news," I said.

"But don't mention him?"

"Right." Deliver the news that the gnoll leader has been felled and the war is over. It's time for Rigar to prosper again.

All the other guards were locked down, those rules didn't apply to Rhugar. He was therefore able to ride off on his horse and we were left to our own devices.

The following two days were extremely busy. Once Lazemus heard the story, we were all taken to the royal palace and testified in front of the king. I expected him to be of bad health, but he wasn't even middle-aged. It seemed the death of his late wife, and then daughter, had put him so deep into depression his will to take care of himself vanished.

Edward was called as well, and once everything was brought to light, threw himself to the ground and begged the king. "Forgive me. I did it for the Yellow Prince. Your son. It was all an act of loyalty sire."

But the king had no mercy and in a frail but audible voice pronounced his verdict: death.

Edward was immediately dragged away, pleading for amnesty, for the Yellow Prince. But he was executed in the central plaza outside their adventure hall the same day. The Yellow Prince was not executed, but instead disowned and excommunicated to a neighboring empire. He would live out his life as a normal person, with no hope of ever ascending the Rigar throne.

Donivan received a lighter sentence than I expected. Even though Edward had committed the majority of crimes and initiated it all, Donivan was still an accomplice. He still had waged war against the city, and many lives were lost over the years from those feuds. Despite that, he was put under 'house arrest'; his new job was aiding the empire as an ambassador to the gnolls, and potentially bringing some good out of the entire situation.

Unfortunately, there was no magical potion to restore his humanity. While Edward had managed to have him transformed, his subsequent catching of shamans had never borne fruit on undoing the transformation. It even came to light that Edward had been snatching orphaned children for experiments, and those missing children had risen into the hundreds over the years.

"You have done a magnificent service to this empire." At the end of a long day, the king addressed our group. "I was originally going to reward you a fief and noble titles, but Lazemus has informed me that you are not from here, and have no plans to stay?"

"Yes, your highness," Lucas said, "we are merely passing by."

He was right. While for Rigar this was an historical moment, in the grand scheme of things, I felt this experience would only be a minor section of our journey.

"That is unfortunate, as great warriors such as yourselves are hard to come by. In that case, I only have this to offer as a reward." The king held up a red and sparkling gem. "It was my late wives, but I no longer can bear to hold it anymore." He paused and turned to Lazems. "Lazemus, I am sorry. I have let this kingdom nearly fall to ruin."

A royal guard walked carefully towards the king and bent to one knee. His hand carefully pulled a box from somewhere within his wardrobe and presented it to the king. From a side glance I could see the beautiful silky fabric that fluffed over the edge like an overflowing cloud when he opened it.

With a moment of hesitation, the king placed the gem carefully inside and gave a nod. The guard stood and then presented Lucas with the box, except not with nearly as much care, "Please cherish it well, as the king did." Lucas passed it to me.

"Nonsense!" The king laughed. "It is merely a rock, use it as you see fit." He then turned to Lazemus, "We will be returning to a regular meeting schedule. For now, I will take my leave."

"I will arrange it your highness." Lazemus bowed as the king walked out. His royal guards scurried away behind him leaving only Lazemus and us in the room. "Donivan wishes to speak with you." Lazemus put a hand on my shoulder, "You will always have a home here." It might have been the only true sign of emotion Lazemus had shown during this entire fiasco.

"I hope you'll honor that." I said half-jokingly. I didn't know if returning to this dungeon would put us in this same timeline, or something else entirely. If Earth was ever that bad, any refuge we could find to survive might be a consolation.

He smiled in response. "My guard will see you to Donivan."

"This is goodbye then," I said. "May we never see each other again." Earth would never get to that point? Right? I almost couldn't convince myself of it. He nodded in understanding and took his leave, his step a bit more energetic than before.

Donivan met us in his 'cell' which turned out to be a regular room in a secluded part of the castle. His punishment was merely a lack of maid service, as the discovery that the king housed a gnoll wouldn't be well received. "It's good to see you again," he said.

"I'm a bit conflicted on that one," I confessed. "Lazemus said you wished to see us?" I asked before he could retort.

"Yes, I've talked to him and confirmed pretty much everything you said." He pulled a pamphlet that had been tied with a string from a top his desk. "Take it."

I didn't hesitate, as if it was what I suspected it was there was no need for modesty. Feeling the old parchment in my hands made me excited, and without any decorum I ripped the string and opened it wide.

It was a map: a map of the mountain range past the gnoll encampment, and on it was a single marker. "There is your portal," he said. "I feel this makes things even."

We had spared his life and escorted him safely back to the kingdom, making sure he met Lazemus, and even putting us between him and potentially dangerous guards. Still, we truly were even now. "Absolutely!" I exclaimed happily.

He nodded. "I understand the desire to want to be home."

With the route to the portal in our hands, we could walk out and off into the sunset right now if we wanted to.

I opened the door to the hall and hid my excitement from my companions as long as I could. "I...have a map to a portal out of here!" I yelled. The little hallway exploded as everyone hugged the nearest person they could find in celebration. Jessica embraced me with a deep kiss and when we separated I could see the excitement in her eyes. Something that I hadn't seen in some time.

"We can go home," I said to everyone. "Let's leave tomorrow morning." It wasn't a good idea to take the trip and arrive on Earth at night. We didn't know where the dungeon would spit us out.

I had wondered if Maria or Anna might object to leaving. This pocket dungeon offered more safety now than Earth did. But it seemed both were just happy to be getting out of here. "We will room at the barracks tonight. It's closer to our exit."

"The barracks?" Maria groaned out loud. Jessica smiled at me, as if to comment, *Here we go...*

# Chapter 40: Undead Skim Boards

Continuing in her spirit of acceptance that it was right to leave, Anna somehow managed to take the side of peace and calm Maria down as we walked the halls. The ride back was maybe the most peaceful moment we had experienced in this dungeon. I had no words, or thoughts, just a feeling of bliss.

The cumulation of all our efforts in this pocket world, everything we hoped and strived to accomplish, had come to an end. Tomorrow we would venture to the distant mountain range and then depart from this place.

This expedition had been a fruitful trip. While the EXP had not been the biggest gain for Jessica and I, Mark and Glenn had caught up quite a bit. Three levels for each of them in fact, bringing them up to level 24. Jessica and I were both on the cusp of reaching 28. Killing Donivan would surely have given us a large boost in EXP, but not only did it turn out to be a moral choice to let him live, would there have been another quest option to find the portal and escape? We couldn't be sure of that.

With that thought in mind I didn't regret our mercy towards the gnoll boss, and in any case, it was the gear we acquired and our new skills that was our biggest reward and boon. We now had another facet of character progression that would work alongside our levels to increase our power, and significantly, too.

Leveling had drastically slowed down, and I suspected the strength of our enemies back on Earth would probably not remain low. The system would never afford that luxury towards us, which meant we needed new ways to grow stronger. Individual powers were the safest and most surefire way to survive, but I suspected doing it alone was not smart nor a good way to live long in the post-apocalypse world.

Half the party was asleep by the time we reached the barracks, and waking them seemed near impossible. I carried Jessica back to my room without the slightest guilt, leaving Richard and Alex stumbling to carry both Mark, Maria, and Anna. Lucas was there too to help. It should be fine...

Jessica looked as peaceful and beautiful as an angel descended on Earth. I had never felt like I could see her face so clearly as I did right now: here with just the two of us, the moonlight shining through the barracks lightly illuminating her face. It was a serenity and peace that I hoped to never lose. I knew it though, that it would never last, and that terrified me more than the monsters.

I did my best to ensure the memory was etched into my mind, and would eventually become nostalgia down the road if I managed to survive. If the time spent in the dungeon and real world worked at the same speed, then nearly a month had passed in the real world, any number of things could have happened.

We had left during a tumultuous shift in the world, and I was sure that it was ongoing as we arrived here, too. What would we return to? That was why I felt my current peace and bliss would never last...we had to return and face whatever confronted us, or die. I slept in the chair along side the bed that night, not bearing to disturb her peaceful dreaming. I took one last look at her face and closed my eyes.

The journey the following morning was uneventful to say the least. There was no grand precession or goodbyes. Rhugar waited by the gate for us and said his farewells, even the Yellow Prince came. Besides that, though, there was no one. We were no heroes here, and in fact most didn't know our name. It was better this way. No lingering attachments.

A carriage was prepared for us, though. Which was nice of the empire to do, as we weren't going to be returning it. It would rot in the wilderness for all eternity where we left it I suspected, or at least until some lucky or unlucky soul stumbled upon it.

"Mike," Rhugar put a light hand on my shoulder, "it was a pleasure."

"I feel the same," I said honestly, "you are a good man."

"I am nothing of the sort," he replied. As we talked, Anna and Maria surrounded the Yellow Prince, trying to pull any other benefits out of him as they could. Alex and Richard stood to the side, Alex's face a bit annoyed by Maria's fawning.

"She's just trying to get you some more loot," Richard nudged him with a devious smile.

Glenn and Mark and Jessica had already boarded the carriage. Lucas was still with me near Rhugar. "I guess we won't be seeing each other again," Rhugar said a bit wistfully.

"We won't." I left no room for doubt. Today we would leave, and nothing would stop us.

"That's too bad." He scratched his head a bit awkwardly. I could tell there had been a request coming before I had shut down that avenue. "I wish you good travels Mike," was all he said, "you too, Lucas."

"Ditto!" I yelled before boarding the carriage. "Anna, Maria!" I yelled at the two, my tone urging them to cut the shenanigans and join us.

"Rhugar, you may be a valiant warrior, but before that you are a man of the people," Lucas yelled to him as we left, "consider government!" The expression of pleasure on Rhugar's face was priceless, from jubilance to shock and then stone-faced, his eyes glanced at the Yellow Prince who eyed him back with a devious smile.

"I'll take good care of this one." The Yellow Prince laughed as he walked towards Rhugar and wrapped an arm around his shoulder. "A king must know how to value his men."

"Make sure you do!" I yelled at the both of them with a laugh. "We'll be going!" On my words the carriage took off through the massive towering gate and onto the dirt road and into the prairie. My two skeleton generals sat at the helm of the carriage, each holding two ropes meant for the two horses leading us.

With their assistance, none of us would need to be out and exposed to the early morning sun, instead shading ourselves in the cool interior. We talked of the return, the bubbling excitement of returning home, but also the terrible realization that the home we were returning to could be completely different than how we left it.

"The world was changing when we left, how far has it changed?" Lucas asked.

"I'll think about it when we get there," Maria said matter-of-factly and then closed her eyes. It was such a succinct and silly way to respond, yet so logical, that no one could refute her words. The discussion died out, and all that remained was a pledge. We'll deal with it as it comes...

With no gnoll army to stop our advance, the journey was smooth. They had lost their leader, and were no doubt in the process of a restructuring. According to Donivan that event would be unbelievably bloody. The strong were respected, and because of that, no gnoll would be found wandering randomly. Their gates were closed, as this was a most vulnerable, but exciting time for them.

The trip in the carriage was a short two hours, and besides the bumpiness of the road, which the luxurious interior of the cart battled for us, was mostly pleasant. We stopped at a crook in the road at the base of a mountain. A simple left turn led upwards towards a slope and wrapped around the northern face out of sight, the path too thin for the carriage to pass. "We go on foot from here," I said.

Lucas and Jessica had already walked to the front, gently patted the horses to keep them calm and removed their reins. They would have to be set free, as no one was coming for them, and we had no plans of returning.

I was expecting something treacherous, or exciting as we ascended the slope, but instead was met with nothing. Really, just nothing. Besides the endless forest around us as we ascended, there was nothing of note to see. The entire mountain was plain and boring, containing no caves or interesting features or encounters. It was shaped in a mundane fashion, as if a child had used clay to form it in their hand.

"How did Donivan enjoy exploring this?" Anna asked while wiping a brow. The sun was high above us now, and with no trees for shade, sweltered upon our skin.

"His upbringing wasn't exactly exciting," Glenn offered, "any exploration was probably a godsend for him." It was true, though. Donivan lived with the nobility, his upbringing heavily monitored and tailored to a specific path. There was no room for imagination or anything else, just your lofty duties and the goal your family had for you.

I looked at the map again as we crested the first bend. "The portal is here..." I pointed. "In between these three mountains somewhere." My eyes scanning the map and then our surroundings.

Everyone grouped around and carefully inspected the slopes around us as well. "We should be in the right place," Lucas said. From our viewpoint here we could see the exact depiction of the mountains, and it aligned with the map.

We were on the southernmost mountain, on its north face staring at the towering two in the distance. The portal was somewhere between these three, which meant we needed to descend to the valley below.

Alan grabbed a baseball sized stone and hurled it down a scree. It rushed with tremendous clangor, echoing into the gorge below where it eventually stopped with a thud, slamming against the trunk of a tree. Only the leaves shook, and not even a bird or animal stirred below.

"It's not too steep..." I consoled everyone. We always had the option of returning to the entrance and taking a detour, but that would be at least an hour of backtrack in the scorching sun, and no guarantee we could reach this elevation from that entry point. "I have an idea..." I said with a devious smile.

That didn't seem to inspire any confidence in my teammates, but without asking I already had my skeleton minions around us. "Don't be shy." I said. Spikey Number One and Spikey Number Two both ominously standing behind Maria and Anna.

Their faces went dark. "Mike...what are you planning."

"Just treat it like a slide." I gave one more piece of advice and then my two generals gently bear hugged the two women and walked them towards the edge of the slope of rocks. "They'll keep you safe."

"Are you sure?" Maria was the most frantic of the two. In fact, the general embracing Anna was slowly being covered in a layer of frost, her face not appearing happy.

"I'm positive!" I said gleefully before turning to Thomas in a whisper, "give them each a shield, will you?"

"Hey! I hear—" And before Maria could finish her sentence, the general jumped onto his ass and slid down the mountain slope in a rush of dust and debris, "I'LL KILL YOU MI—" the last part of her words cut off fading as she raced below.

Anna's departure went much smoother, the cool ice on the skeleton general cutting the friction down tremendously. She slid down much more comfortably, but gave me a death stare before turning to face the ride ahead.

My skeletons didn't fear the friction of sliding down the side of a mountain, and so we each found ourselves in their embrace of death, sliding down the scree like it was a water slide. Anna and Maria were the two most unruly in the group, and thus I was forced to make them go first. The rest had no issue using my undead soldiers as skim boards.

# Chapter 41: The Scarlet Portal

"Now how did Donivan find this?" Mark asked, all of us glancing around at this beautifully elevated forest. Its own little paradise in the mountains. My earlier suspicion that it was not accessible from below was proven true. We were on a floating plateau, connected to the base of all three mountains, and up twenty or thirty meters from the actual forest floor.

"It seemed he did do some exploring," I said.

"Or he took a bad fall," Maria scoffed, still wiping off dirt from her face and hair. I would probably be dealing with this fiery mess for a few days. Water off a duck's back…Water off a duck's back…

We walked forward carefully, regardless of the fact Jessica had given us no indication of enemies. The lighting here was bad, not only did the mountains block out a portion of the sun, but the thick vegetation hadn't been cleared in an age, hundreds of years even.

As we did our best to triangulate, nothing out of the ordinary popped out at us. There were trees, and more trees. There were no caves, no dens, or pits, or treacherous falls. Eventually though, something did appear.

Jessica called our attention to an old stone well, one that appeared hundreds of years old. The wooden roof that had covered its mechanical parts had been thoroughly destroyed. Instead, there was a rusted old handle attached to mostly rotted wood. The rope was nowhere to be seen, most likely fallen into the well long ago.

"Is this the portal?" Maria asked. This thought hadn't occurred to me but we had spent the better part of an hour searching this small plot of land, with our speed and insight… we had covered almost all of it and had discovered nothing but this.

"Judging by the position…It must be," I said. "I will check." I turned and looked at Spikey Number One, my zweihander-wielding skeleton general. With a nod, he put the zweihander on his back and leaped into the well without fear. He could be resummoned, after all.

The splash we expected to hear didn't come, instead the silence made me more excited. Was there a portal resting at the bottom? I took a moment to share his experience, and after realizing that he was still falling, wiped a bit of cold sweat from my head. I shouldn't tell them.

Eventually, after four or five long seconds, there was a splash ever so faint. I confirmed it myself, that my general was ok and now in the dark in a deep cavern below. He spotted the portal! A dim glowing portal in a cavity not far from where he landed. My excitement was tempered by one significant observation: it was different from the one we entered, not translucent and reflecting. Instead, it burned red and menacing.

I didn't want to voice my reservation about the nature of the portal. We were going through the portal regardless of where it was, or what it looked like. That was the determination we had as a group, and nothing I told them now would change that.

"The portal is down there, so I'll go first," I offered. Sending Anna and Maria again would probably have me on thin ice for the foreseeable future, better to just get it over with now. Before anyone could offer any logical reason to not jump, I was already on the edge of the well wall. With a slight push, I slid off and disappeared below.

I was mentally prepared already. The growing darkness and the dimming of the stone around me would have had a much bigger effect if I hadn't known what was coming. Even so, I felt like I was jumping into the maw of a great beast.

Suddenly the embrace of the stone well disappeared and the dim lighting along with it. Darkness surrounded me on all sides and even with my special eyes, it was so dark I could only just make out the grey of the cavern walls as I fell. A moment later I hit the water, and it was not as soft a landing as I had hoped.

Instead, it felt like slamming into concrete. The air in my lungs ejected itself immediately, and I desperately scraped for the surface before breaching it, filling my lungs with oxygen. My eyes quickly acclimated to the darkness, and eventually I could see the low hue of the portal in the distance. I swam quickly, doing my best to block out the creepy thoughts of what creatures might lurk in a dark abyss like this.

The next person didn't jump for at least thirty seconds. I could see them falling this time, my eyes fully accustomed to this interior. My vision in pure darkness shifted to something black and white, each dark structure being just a different shade of grey. It gave me depth perception and allowed me to easily pick out structures in the dark.

A red silhouette appeared from the cavern roof, and I immediately recognized Jessica. Her body in my night vision was glowing red with heat, and then it quickly cooled to a low orange. The water temperature must be barely above freezing. "Over here!" I called out to her and she quickly swam to the shore and sat beside me.

"Kind of fun…" she confessed. It seemed she was of the thrill-seeking variety.

"YOU DARE THROW US IN?" I heard Maria's voice echoing as she fell, and then a splash, Anna followed right behind her. These two were rowdy and growing rowdier. I wasn't sure if it was something we needed to address as a group, or it would calm itself down once we returned to Earth.

This dungeon had been somewhat of a getaway from the daily terrors. I hoped once we returned to that level of anxiety and danger, Anna and Maria would naturally lose this learned trait of theirs.

"Over here!" I yelled at them. Eventually, after dozens of chillingly cold minutes, we were all ashore in this massive underground cave. The portal glistened menacingly in front of us, like a fiery abyss ready to devour us.

"What are we waiting for?" Jessica asked, and then walked confidently through the portal, all of us swiftly following behind her.

I was the fourth one to pass through the portal, and despite my first time being relatively uneventful when arriving here, I couldn't say the same thing about this time.

**Your ability has—**

"Aghh, what the hell?" I heard Richard groan as I spawned out of the portal. I was five or six feet in the air and plummeted like a rock on arrival. There wasn't even a chance to put out my arms to cushion my fall as a sickening dizziness assaulted my senses.

I landed hard, and my vision swam as the ground and the sky reversed directions and swirled in front of my face. A mess of green and red and brown in my vision represented the contents of my stomach, the only blessing being that I had managed to expel the contents onto the ground and not all over myself.

The dizziness wouldn't stop, and only after I closed my eyes and sensed my surroundings with my body did it start to dissipate. I could feel the cool earth below, the jagged vine that stabbed uncomfortably into my shoulder blade, the smell of moist earth and a fire somewhere smoldering in the distance. It grounded me, literally.

Jessica was the first to recover, and out of a cracked eye I watched her quickly assess our surroundings and stand up. My undead as well had spread out on instinct and taken up a defensive posture. It took a minute or two before I could open my eyes completely without fear of vomiting. There's nothing left anyway.

"Did everyone make it out?" I looked around at my cohort, now unstably crawling off the ground and finding their bearings. The taste of my last meal and stomach acid unpleasantly masking my breath, and the smell of everyone else's slowly permeated the area.

"I'm he—" Alan started and then caught the vomit in his throat. The sound alone had Glenn and Mark curled over again, and that started a chain reaction that sent Alan over the edge again. I nearly started hurling but quickly closed my eyes and concentrated.

The responses came slow after that, but after a dozen minutes, everyone was sitting up with open eyes. Our bearing was wobbly, and it was Jessica who continued the conversation. "Let's move first." She was pinching her nose as she spoke.

Priority number one was to get out of wherever we were. The stench of our weakness was now strong in the air, and it was anything but fresh. I looked around carefully as Jessica led us in a random direction, taking in whatever I could.

I didn't know where we were currently, but the scenery reminded me of the gnoll forest. I assumed we were spit out of the dungeon where we went in, or at least nearby, considering the dungeon had been inside a massive pit filled with water. Dropping us out there might not have been very convenient.

Tall trees towered into the sky all around us. The canopy they created blotted out the sun and left the entire area dark and dreary. It felt as if an invisible miasma floated along the floor, and the daunting fog didn't help to deter that picture forming in my head.

Even worse was the prickling feeling stinging the back of my neck. Sixth Sense left me feeling uneasy. It was the feeling I got when something bad was going to happen, and imminently at that. I had received a few messages when leaving the dungeon, but this prickling feeling was the reason I hadn't allowed myself a moment of distraction to read over them.

Jessica had a stern look on her face as well. She would have told us if she had detected anything, but over the months of battle and training as a hunter, she had developed somewhat of a sense herself. I could see it in the way she carried herself. The taut muscles of her upper body were ready to explode in a moment. "I feel like I'm being watched," she caught my looking at her, "but there's nothing around."

"I feel it too." I grasped the back of my neck and felt the goose-bumps forming over my skin. In fact, almost everyone had an un-easy feeling, and it wasn't just the brain fog and fading dizziness; yet there was nothing around us.

"Doesn't it look kind of red?" Maria pointed at a distant tree trunk. The sun illuminated the tree through gaps in the canopy. "Like the color of blood?" Her face grimaced.

"That...it's just the sunset, surely," Richard replied. "You've all never seen a red sun?" Even he didn't sound sure of himself.

"Since when does the sun set before noon?" Maria snapped back. It also didn't make sense for the setting sun to be so high in the sky at this time, it would be on the horizon and the red hue of its glow would never reach the trunk it highlighted.

Jessica carefully studied the canopy above while the two bickered. To me, and probably everyone but Jessica, the view of the sky above was too patchy and incongruent. The shadows of the branches and leaves from below meshed into one solid blur that made it hard to tell where the sky started and the shade of the canopy began.

Eventually though, Jessica spoke, "I don't know why…but the sky is crimson." No one knew what that meant, but I guessed based on how I felt right now it wasn't a good thing. "Let's… keep going."

"We need to know what's happened," I said, "form up for a fight." My undead spread into a proper formation as everyone pulled their weapons and assumed their positions in our best formation. We moved at a snail's pace through the forest, and eventually found the break we needed.

We crested a hill and could see the remnants of a battle. In fact, it was the place where we had been surrounded and were forced to brute force our way through with Richard and my summoned undead acting as a battering ram.

Past this point though was where the open field outside the western section of the gnoll realm was. I could see it through the maze of trees just half a mile in the distance, a break in the trees that led to an open field, and I knew that there we would get our view of the sky.

Nothing scary popped out at us as we walked. In fact, it was utterly uneventful and that made me even more uneasy. As we approached the end of the woodlands, the red hue became more ominous, more apparent.

Only when we were at that edge of the forest could we see the divide. Just a few feet out of the forest was a world bathed in crimson. The red hue of the sky stretched far and wide, infecting everything it touched with an ominous lacquer of blood.

# Chapter 42: The Eye in the Portal

The sun I had expected to see was not there high in the sky. Instead, there was a mass of swirling reds and oranges of varying depth and darkness that formed a circular mass in the sky. It constantly undulated outwards, receding and licking the air around it like ocean waves. Each time it did, the air seethed and created mirages from the extreme heat.

The ominous feeling inside me only grew as I looked at the alarming scene in the sky. It took me a second to realize what I was looking at, and before I could open my mouth...

"That looks like the portal we walked through," Jessica said. The portal we had entered though, while red and ominous, didn't have that feeling of heat this one did. In fact, if I closed my eyes now, I could imagine the sun was still there in the sky basking me in its warmth.

"What does it mean?" Alan asked. "What is it?"

I looked away, and then back several times, eventually confirming my prickling was because of that presence in the sky. "I got several notifications when we exited the dungeon," I replied, "let's all check what we've received and see if there are any clues."

**You have leveled up.**
**All skills have leveled up.**

**Your ability has evolved.**
**You are the first to conquer a D rank**
**dungeon. You have received a title.**
**You are being watched.**
**I stopped reading at that moment and**
**quickly opened my stats, hearing a few**
**gasps around me.**

**Name: Mike Reynolds Class: Necromancer**
**Level:** 28 **EXP:** 50%
**HP:** 1580/1580 **MP:** 600/600
**STR:** 5 + 2 **Fear Resistance:** 5
**AGI:** 2 **Shadow Resistance:** 5
**DEX:** 5 + 1 **Disease Resistance:** 30
**VIT:** 29 + 39 **Cold Resistance:** 5
**WIS:** 27 + 48 **Lightning Resistance:** 5
**Available:** 21 **Fire Resistance:** 15

**Skills: [A] Summon Skeleton LV.** 11 **[A] Summon**
**Skeleton Mage LV.** 5 **[A] Decay LV.** 4 **[A]**
**Reanimate Dead LV.** 4 **| [A] Bone Armor LV.** 3 **|**
**[A] Vast Shadows | [A] Temporary Grave LV.** 1
**| [P] Sixth Sense | [P] Bravery LV.** 3 **[P] Mutated**
**| [P] Pain Resistance LV.** 3 **| [P] Skeletal Mastery**
**LV.** 5 **| [P] Intimidate Living LV.** 2 **| [P] Inner Calm**
**LV.** 3 **| [P] Necrotic Vision | [P] Blood Thirsty LV.**
2 **| [P] Cold Hearted LV.** 2 **| [P] Poison Immunity |**
**[P] Branded**

And while I couldn't be one-hundred percent certain, it seemed that every skill had, in fact, gained a level. Even my passives like Blood Thirsty and Cold Hearted had each leveled up. Interesting though, was that skills provided solely from items had not leveled, like Temporary Grave or Intimidate Living. While the system hadn't provided any number, it seemed like I had received a massive amount of EXP and skill experience after exiting the dungeon?

It mentioned evolving abilities, but what had evolved wasn't readily apparent, not without going over my skills, nor did I see the title I had received, but I did see a new passive in my skill list that glowed an ominous red.

Branded: Your existence has been noted. You are being watched.

"Does...everyone have a branded passive?" I asked the group. Somehow, only Mark didn't have the mark, er brand, and he was the only one who hadn't picked a class. It was an interesting distinction, but everyone who had skills and a class was branded.

"What did we miss while we were gone?" Lucas wondered aloud. I had no other information than the unusual condition, and could only go off my own deductions. The post-apocalypse world was trying to kill us though, so this couldn't be anything good.

"Let's return to the road and get our bearings," Jessica suggested, and no one disagreed. The feeling of being watched only grew stronger as we fully left the forest and walked along the open field. The gnoll encampment stood miles in the distance, towering and imposing as it did before, except there was no movement of troops or banging war drums; it seemed even the fearsome gnolls had closed their doors to outsiders.

"I really don't like this," Anna said, and when I thought she was going to say something useful about the change in the gnoll camp, she added, "I really don't look good bathed in this hue. Why couldn't it be purple instead?"

"Can you keep those thoughts to yourself maybe?" Richard jabbed back, which got him a playful gesture as though she were going to blast him. The two were still the best of friends, despite Maria taking the place of a younger sister and the close bond the two girls shared. None of us knew exactly what Richard and Anna had experienced to bond them before they met us, but it couldn't have been pleasant.

The road was waiting for us just where we left it…I think. The crimson hue coating everything made me feel lethargic. It was menacing and yet so dull as to leave me fatigued. Everything was red, so much that when I closed my eyes the shade lingered behind my eyelids.

"We're losing HP slowly," Jessica announced. "It took time for me to notice, but being in this red light is harming us." We were quite resilient now, and with our passive HP regen being inhuman already, it meant that the red light was doing a considerable amount of damage over time.

I checked my own stats and confirmed I had lost 5 HP in that short walk. It didn't sound like much, but that was just a short ten or fifteen-minute walk. That level of damage over time would kill a weaker person in just two or three hours.

While uncertain, the massive earthquakes and restructuring that left almost every manmade building we saw completely destroyed and uninhabitable…the number of places you could go to escape from this red light were…very few. This entire event was by design. They had lured the hiding rats from their dens and were now cooking them alive, watching to see how they would react. Sick and twisted…

Our current problems all seemed to come from the swirling mass of blood in the sky. The hair on the back of my neck rose and I felt familiar chills from Sixth Sense as I looked at it. The crimson flames licked the air like dancing shadows, spawning beautiful mirages with each touch. It was hypnotizing to look at, almost entrancing.

I found myself wanting to look away, but suddenly couldn't. That ephemeral feeling of unease rushed through me with so much intensity it was unbearable. Sharp pain assaulted every sense, as if an icepick had been lodged deep in my skull and then twisted.

And yet, I couldn't close my eyes or look away. I couldn't open my mouth; I couldn't do anything. Instead, a giant eye was staring back at me. Its golden pupils shaped like two crescent moons, lifeless and uncaring: inhuman, as if it was staring at an ant it could crush without effort.

"Mike?" Jessica noticed my abnormality first. "Mike, what's wrong?" I fell to my knees and couldn't look away from the eye. A fog shrouded my thoughts and I grasped my throat as air wouldn't ender my lungs. An invisible pressure pushed down on me from all sides, threatening to bury me in its embrace. A sickening sweetness filled my mouth as I fought with all my might to break free from its harrowing gaze.

My HP started to decline rapidly as my vision was blurring, and yet that golden pupil remained crystal clear in my view. I feared that even passing out wouldn't save me from its gaze. "Thomas, heal him!" The voice was close yet far, and while my HP increased, the familiar warmth I had come to know didn't reach me.

Whether by sheer luck or quick thinking, Richard suddenly rushed in front of me and shrouded me from the red hue, blocking my vision of the demonic eye. A sudden influx of air threatened to burst my lungs as I leaned over and coughed hard.

The others had already spread around me in a battle formation, assuming an enemy attack. It was, but I doubted it was an enemy attack we could have done anything about it. "Thank you, Richard." I forced out the words through battered breaths. I'd have vomited if there was anything left in my stomach.

"What happened?" Lucas had his back to mine, covering a blind spot behind us as he asked.

319

"The portal, there's an eye in the portal." I didn't know how else to explain it. Either the portal itself was an eye, or something looked at me through the portal. The meaning of being watched suddenly felt much more real.

If the group hadn't seen me clawing at my throat, red faces and eyes bulging, they may have not believed me. The spittle of blood on the asphalt was proof enough of my struggle. The force I had to exert to feel like I was not going to be crushed under that gaze was enough for me to bite a nasty gash into my tongue and for my ears to pop. Fortunately, two heals from Thomas had me back in good shape.

"Either the portal is an eye, or something looked through it… but that gaze nearly killed me." In fact, without my companions here I was surely deader than dead. If the gaze had not depleted my HP to zero, passing out in the bloody hue would have finished me off for certain.

"Everyone is to avoid looking at the sky," Lucas issued the instruction immediately. "We must find shelter right away. After that we should go through our abilities and see what's changed. We need a plan." No one disagreed as we hurried north up the road.

It became obvious very quickly though, that just being out of vision, didn't mean the red hue didn't affect us. Behind trees, inside an abandoned car, under the dilapidated and totaled roof of a metal shed: nothing stopped that ticking DoT, even being covered in a layer of darkness didn't change it.

Fortunately for us we had Thomas, and potions if need be. His MP regeneration was fast enough to use an AoE heal that would top us all off regularly. We were okay for a few days at the very least.

The previous danger washed over like a passing wave, and besides the color change, the surroundings were not much different looking than when we had left. Random downed trees still blocked the road, but the leaves had withered and disappeared with the wind, looking somewhat like a tree graveyard.

# Chapter 43: A Haven in a Post-Apocalyptic World

Only now that I understood the source of my unease, and our lack of solution to that problem, could I justify shifting my attention to browsing the new bounties that had been given to me on exiting the dungeon.

**World Traveler**
**All Stats +5. Grants a small benefit to Mental Fortitude.**
**The gaze of the unknown tempers the mind.**
**When the abyss stares, you find the courage to stare back.**
**Bravery [P] has reached LV. 4**

And as if reading the title was like unboxing a present, my Bravery talent immediately gained a level. Mental Fortitude? That wasn't a stat in the character sheet unless it was retroactively added. I opened my stats again to check.

**Name: Mike Reynolds Class: Necromancer**
**Level: 28 EXP: 50%**
**HP: 1578/1655 MP: 625/625**
**STR: 5 + 7 Fear Resistance: 5**
**AGI: 2 + 5 Shadow Resistance: 5**
**DEX: 5 + 6 Disease Resistance: 30**
**VIT: 29 +44 Cold Resistance: 5**
**WIS: 27 +53 Lightning Resistance: 5**
**Available: 21 Fire Resistance: 15**

**Skills:** [A] **Summon Skeleton LV.** 11 | [A] **Summon Skeleton Mage LV.** 5 | [A] **Decay LV.** 4 | [A] **Reanimate Dead LV.** 4 | [A] **Bone Armor LV.** 3 | [A] **Vast Shadows** | [A] **Temporary Grave LV.** 1 | [P] **Sixth Sense** | [P] **Bravery LV.** 4 | [P] **Mutated** | [P] **Pain Resistance LV.** 3 | [P] **Skeletal Mastery LV.** 5 | [P] **Intimidate Living LV.** 2 | [P] **Inner Calm LV.** 3 | [P] **Necrotic Vision** | [P] **Blood Thirsty LV.** 2 | [P] **Cold Hearted LV.** 2 | [P] **Poison Immunity** | [P] **Branded**

Mental Fortitude wasn't anywhere in the menus, nor in my character sheet. The flavor text mentioned courage, and my Bravery also leveled up after receiving the title, too. However, Pain Resistance didn't change, which I expected to also be some sort of fortitude-related trait. "Does anyone have a stat called Mental Fortitude?" I decided to ask.

"Are you asking because of the title?" Anna asked.

"Yeah, it says increased Mental Fortitude but I don't see a stat for it. One of my passives leveled up after receiving it though."

"Mine did too," Lucas said.

"What was the passive? What does it do?" I asked.

"It's called Steadfast, and it increases my courage depending on how many enemies I'm facing."

"Mine as well, Bravery."

And then Jessica called up from the front a moment later, as if she just checked on her title. "Mine also leveled, Hunter's Courage."

"I don't feel any braver," Maria said.

"Is it important though? Or are we just talking semantics?" Lucas asked.

"Well, I don't think this is specifically important," I answered, "but I was under the impression that stats dictated everything. Now we have an invisible stat giving tangible benefits to us. Does that mean at an innate level I am braver than someone else?"

"Like being as strong as someone with five strength points when you only have one?" Richard offered.

"Exactly."

"How many titles do you think we can have?" Glenn asked everyone.

And before anyone else could give any thought to the question Jessica called out, "There's something up ahead on the map."

I looked at my map and could see somewhere further along the road, well into the point where the map was simply greyed out with no features, a glowing green square. There was no notification, no information about it and touching the map did nothing to identify it. A green square in a sea of grey, and because of the map having no features or landmarks, it was difficult to tell exactly how far away it actually was.

"Any thoughts?" I asked before voicing my own opinion.

"We don't have any direction right now anyway." Alan's meaning was clear.

"Treasure." Anna only had one word to say about it.

It became obvious very quickly which way we were leaning as a group, "Red means stop and green means go," I added.

"Then it's settled." Jessica stamped her seal of approval and we continued moving forward. Alan was feeling a bit more excited so he joined Jessica at the front to dispatch the wandering zombies and ghouls that stumbled upon us. At our current level we would need to adventure into some named or dangerous zone to fight enemies that would give us experience. Out here in the middle of nowhere were simply small fry that Jessica could dispatch with a single arrow.

324

This was a rather uneventful way to travel, but once we passed the lumber farm, the landscape morphed around us into open farmland. I stayed in most days, gaming, and never enjoyed the countryside, but I was feeling even more grateful that I lived here instead of a big city or populated area.

While boring, we had clear skies, a clear view, and a solid road under us. Honestly, it beat the hell out of trekking through a swamp, so I couldn't ask for much more. Moving on foot towards the green square, there were hours and hours of walking we needed to do, but we were making good progress.

"Based on what it looks like on the map we'll be there before nightfall." Lucas had been keeping track of the map every half hour, and I was glad for that. I had spent most of my time thinking about my next move.

My gear was now far and above what it was before, and definitely not something that would hold me back anytime soon. I had an open skill slot right now which came from a reward for killing the Fiend, and at Level 30 I'd receive another. I needed two new abilities that fit well with my current build. Probably, that should be related to my undead troops. I had to admit, my summoned warriors were quite versatile.

The other question we all had was what did the system mean when it said our ability had evolved? There was nothing apparent in my skill sheet. None of my skills seemed any different, either. I came back to the thought that maybe something innate about us had changed. Ability was another word for 'skill', but ability could also mean many things not skill related. Were we just… better now, more able? And if so, what did that mean?

A ton of things came to mind, but until we had tangible evidence it would be nothing but hopeful dreaming. The prickling on the back of my neck hadn't gone away, and I needed to find a new skill soon. In hindsight, it was honestly unacceptable to have gone through the dungeon down a skill, as that could have been unbelievably dangerous.

We experienced a lot of fortunate encounters, but I was sure of one thing. If it was similar to our first dungeon experience, someone would have probably died inside. I had been incredibly lucky, truthfully. Not only was I strong individually, I also had reliable teammates with a variety of skills, and we were good at working together.

Even if I only had a single skill, just my Summon Skeletons, I'd probably be stronger than a large chunk of people. But if I wanted the kind of power to that was going to keep my friends alive in this post-apocalyptic world, 'just enough' wasn't going to cut it.

"I think that's it up ahead," Jessica said. Maybe a mile up was a white building standing two or three stories tall off the road.

It wasn't spectacular in any way, just a plain white cube with a door and dark windows and absolutely no other character at all. Even more interesting were the miles of empty space behind it, as if it flattened the earth around it before appearing. But the most interesting thing of all, "Why is that building standing?" I asked. Every building we'd seen since the quaking had been toppled and destroyed, and we knew now that was by design.

"I don't know, but let's go!" Maria yelled excitedly. "A place to sleep, woo!" And no one could complain with her logic, we could always take a closer look and make a judgment once we were there.

Soon we found ourselves standing in front of the cube, admiring the blood red hue the sky painted it.

"What's it supposed to be?" Anna asked.

"A creepy hotel…" Maria groaned.

"What do you think?" I looked at Jessica.

"There's nothing inside," she answered.

I was confident in her, so I walked forward first and grabbed the door knob, and received a system message.

**Congratulations! You have discovered a resting zone!**

Huh?

**As the first person to discover this zone, you have become its owner.**

That was all the system said. "Hey, what're you waiting for? Open the door." Maria pushed from behind.

"I got a message," I replied, "it's some sort of rest zone." And then I opened the door revealing a fully-furnished, beautiful interior. The darkness I expected wasn't there, even, and that was the most shocking thing. There was electricity inside, lights illuminated everything as if we had gone back in time.

It was dead silent behind me, and when I looked back, I could see my friends all with the same face of confusion and surprise.

"Could...could there be running water?" It was Jessica who asked, and to be honest I expected Anna or Maria to be the first, but they were still too stunned to speak.

"Dibs on a window room!" Richard snapped out of it and ran forward, going inside, with the others following after him. Lucas and Glenn took their time browsing the first floor, while Anna, Maria, Alan and Richard raced up the stairs bickering like children. Thomas went to find a bathroom and Jessica and I found a seat on the first floor and sat down.

It felt like a weight had been lifted off my shoulders as I sank into the couch cushion, "Is this a trap?" Although I wanted to believe in this place, I had to ask, "Maybe it's an illusion?" I waved my hand in front of Jessica's face

She flicked my forehead which caused me to wince in pain, "Seems like you're awake." She grinned.

"You know you're stronger than you think." There was now a red pulse right in the middle of my head, mostly from her flick but a bit of my own rubbing. It really did hurt...

"What is this place?"

I delved into my character sheet and eventually found it. There was an entire section listed here, and the building we were in was there as a skill.

### Humble Abode LV. 1: A small but sturdy home, it should protect you from the elements.

There was more there to read, but something clicked after reading it. "The portal..." I said.

"Wait, you're right," Jessica realized it at the same time, "Branded isn't there."

The debuff wasn't there in my skill sheet, either. Which meant this system-built home protected us from the eye's vision, from its rapid degeneration. It made sense, but not from my understanding of how depraved this world was. I started reading through descriptions and then it became clear—the reason why humble abode was a skill.

It confused me at first, because I didn't understand how a home could be leveled, but then I saw what came next.

### Waves of Demons slain: 0

I should have known the system wouldn't give us anything for free...so we needed to survive waves of demon attacks, and then what? I looked further, and realized there were so many levels to the skill, and that eventually... maybe...

I looked at Jessica. "I think we're going to be really busy," I said. "Huh? With what?"

I wrapped my arms around her and pulled her closer, "Create a bastion for human civilization, save the world, that sort of thing...probably."

Jeremy Chambless was born in Deerfield Beach, Florida and studied Psychology at Florida Atlantic University. Gaming has always been a part of his household: as far back as he can remember, he was holding a NES controller. His own gaming passion has been focused on MMOs and RPGs. Jeremy is an avid LitRPG reader turned writer. A love for RPGs sparked his desire to create *The MMRPG Apocalypse*.

If you have enjoyed Jeremy's MMRPG Apocalypse series you'll be glad to know he's completed an earlier LitRPG series: *The RPG Apocalypse*. And you can follow his progress with book 3 of this current series on Royal Road.

Level Up publishing specializes in LitRPG and GameLit books. You might be interested in our other titles, which can be found at www.levelup.pub/books

To join our mailing list for news about forthcoming books and opportunities to be an ARC reader, just fill in the form on that page.

You can also find us on:
Facebook @LUPublishing
Twitter @LevelUpPub
...and by searching for Level Up WhatsApp group